D0251159

THE

SWEET

GOODBYE

THE

SWEET

GOODBYE

RON CORBETT

BERKLEY
NEW YORK

BERKLEY
An imprint of Penguin Random House LLC
penguinrandomhouse.com

Library of Congress Cataloging-in-Publication Data

Names: Corbett, Ron, 1959- author.
Title: The sweet goodbye / Ron Corbett.
Description: New York: Berkley, [2022] | Series: A Danny Barrett novel; 1
Identifiers: LCCN 2021044396 (print) | LCCN 2021044397 (ebook) |
ISBN 9780593440353 (hardcover) | ISBN 9780593440360 (ebook)
Subjects: LCGFT: Detective and mystery fiction. |
Thrillers (Fiction) |Novels.
Classification: LCC PR9199.4.C6677 S94 2022 (print) |
LCC PR9199.4.C6677 (ebook) | DDC 813/.6—dc23/eng/20211014
LC record available at https://lccn.loc.gov/2021044396
LC ebook record available at https://lccn.loc.gov/2021044397

Printed in the United States of America
1   3   5   7   9   10   8   6   4   2

Book design by Alison Cnockaert

To Julie Oliver

THE

SWEET

GOODBYE

PROLOGUE

THE FIRST TIME I worked undercover, I arrested my brother. We were both beat cops in Detroit, and I didn't feel bad about what happened to him.

An undercover ATF agent told me once that if you believe the Bible, betrayal is the second thing people ever did. He was a good agent, a good man, and it was his way of telling me not to feel bad about what I've come to do for a living. He was a man of faith as well, so he probably believed he was offering me the gift of forgiveness. I didn't tell him that I never have worried about it.

The people I befriend, betray and send to prison are people you never want to meet, that the planet is better off without. They live and wreak havoc in a near-alternate universe of depravity and wealth, violence and deceit, monsters that have taken human shape.

I believe that. There are monsters out there. My kid brother is one of them.

It took all of forty-five minutes for my first field commander to convince me to work undercover, that my brother had crossed a line that should never be crossed. It was what any good cop would want. Today I look back on that conversation and can't remember why any of it surprised me. My kid brother had crossed a line.

I see lines crossed all the time now. No one around me drives straight. No one is what you would ever call honest. I've been working undercover twelve years.

Maybe that's why I'm having trouble shaking my last case. Too many lines got crossed. Too many crooked rides. I'm not doubting my actions. I don't think that's it. I'm just not understanding why I've been left feeling guilty about them.

I've been trying to figure it out. Starting with the night I met Travis Lee, because that's when I think that case started, the true date, the first time something seemed different about that investigation. That's what I've been looking for—things that were different. I haven't found much. Only thing so far is I think what happened in Maine last spring might have been a love story.

More than anything else, it might have been that.

I'm not sure if I'm right about this, not sure it's all that important even if I am right, so why bother mentioning it at all? I don't have those answers. All I know is it strikes me as the one thing that was unusual about that case. And maybe the one thing we all missed.

1

TRAVIS LEE LEFT the Starlight Club and stumbled toward the cab pulling up to the curb. He bounced off the rear panel, bounced off it again, then found the door latch and steadied himself. He turned to the woman beside him and yelled, "Ta-da!"

After that, he opened the door and fell inside.

The woman didn't move. She was a tall woman dressed in a full-length mink coat that shimmered beneath the neon lights outside the nightclub, made the fur look like a gasoline spill rippling upon dark water. In a few seconds the cabbie got out to see what was happening. He looked at the woman, then at the open door, then leaned in the car and gave Lee a shake. When he stood up, the woman asked, "Is he passed out?"

"I don't think so, ma'am. He's not snoring or anything."

"Trav, darling," she yelled into the cab, "you need to put your legs inside the car. The man can't wait here all night."

But there was no answer. "I'll give him another shake," said the cabbie. "What's his name?"

"Travis Lee."

"Really?"

"No, I'm just having fun with you. Can't you see I'm having fun?"

The cabbie looked startled; then he blushed and put his head back inside the cab. "Mr. Lee, your wife can't get in. You need to sit up, sir. . . . Sir, do you hear me?"

The woman pursed her lips and waited; in anger or anticipation, it was difficult to tell. She had lips that might always leave you guessing about something like that. Eventually she bent her head and whispered something in the cabbie's ear.

His body twitched as she was talking, but when she was finished, he nodded, grabbed Lee's legs and started pulling him from the cab. When he was halfway out, the woman grabbed one of the legs and helped finish the job. They slowed a bit when Lee's head was coming out, but not enough to stop it from bouncing off the curb. It was a low curb. They slowed. There was still a bounce.

When he was laid out on the sidewalk, the woman stepped over him and got into the cab. The cabbie looked around a second—embarrassed, it was easy enough to tell—but when his eyes stopped darting around, he ran to his door, got in and drove away. Through the rear window, Amanda Lee could be seen shaking snow off the collar of her coat.

———

DAMN, THAT WAS cold.

I looked at the departing cab. Back at Travis Lee. Almost a Muddy Waters song. March in Northern Maine? It was still cold enough to kill someone if they were left passed out on a sidewalk for the night.

I looked around but saw that the cabbie had been right. No one else was outside the nightclub. Last call in twenty minutes and not a car in the parking lot except mine, parked twenty feet from the front entrance. Good chance it was going to stay that way.

I reached inside my jacket pocket for my phone, about to make an anonymous 911 call. If that could have happened—that simple act of placing a phone call—a lot of things would have played out different in Birmingham. I'm not saying some people would still be alive, or that failure would have become success—nothing as grand as that—but it would have been different, what happened, and probably not as bad.

What *did* happen that night was three men suddenly came running down Delco Street. It looked like they were trying to make last call at the Starlight. They were dressed in dark green factory pants, heavy work boots and plaid jackets. They ran past Lee—lying there in his blue suit and camelhair overcoat, shiny black shoes pointing toes up like garden spikes—looked at him but kept going.

I watched them make the front door of the Starlight but not go through. Watched them stare over their shoulders, talk among themselves, laugh and, just like I knew they would, watched them come walking back.

Damn. This really is a Muddy Waters song.

═══

THEY HAD SURROUNDED Lee by the time I got there. Two of the men were staring at him. One of them was a fat man with a belly so large, it had the contours of a baby seal. The other was whippet thin, with dark cratered skin and sunken cheeks, restless eyes that darted around like mercury droplets. A bad meth addict. The third was a boy: a teenager poking Lee with the toe of his work boot, chuckling and waiting to see what might happen.

"Evening, boys. Want a hand getting him back in a cab?" I asked.

The boy put his boot down and looked at me. His face was covered in zits, half of them popped, so there were blood trickles on his cheeks. His skin was pale, and with the red lines on his face, he had the coloring of a clown.

"Look like a four-man job to you?" he said.

"You never know. He looks like a big enough lad."

"Thanks, pal. We got it covered."

"Are you sure? I figure a workingman can always use an extra hand. Know what I mean?"

The boy looked at me with an expression so curious and uncomprehending, I felt a pang of sadness. This was a kid who needed things simple and linear, no curves, nothing unexpected. We stared at each other a few seconds but it was the fat man who eventually said, "You're too late, asshole. Bugger off."

"Bugger off? What are you talking about? I'm just here offering to help."

"Help yourself to his pockets, I'm bettin'. It ain't happenin' for you, buddy."

"What the— Are you accusing me of being a thief?"

"I ain't *accusing* you of nothin', asshole. What I'm *telling* you is that if you don't fuck off right now, I'm gonna stomp your head till you're stupid. You missed your chance. Come back trollin' another night."

His friends laughed when he said this and the fat man broke into a broad smile. Their laughter continued for several seconds until they noticed I wasn't leaving.

"Are you fuckin' thick?" said the fat man, taking a step toward me. But the whippet didn't move. He licked his lips and turned to stare at the front door of the Starlight. The clown boy did the same.

It would just be the fat man.

When the swing came, it was a haymaker and that's what I'd been expecting, had already placed my bet on by the way I was leaning, so that when it came I could step under it easily, be in a crouching position when I brought my fist up at a perfect sixty-degree arc, at double the normal traveling distance for an uppercut. Landing it right where a man would never want a punch like that to land.

The fat man grabbed his groin and tottered several seconds before he fell. When he did fall, it was sideways, and slowly, like a felled tree might fall if it got tangled up in the branches of another tree.

Several seconds passed after that before he screamed. When it came it was like the screaming of late-stage childbirth. He was still screaming like that, his friends dragging him into the shadows surrounding the nightclub, when I heard a man's voice say, "Well, that was rather fun to watch. Why in the world did you bother?"

I looked down at Travis Lee. He was sitting now, rubbing his head and looking at me. I thought of the best way to answer his question. Decided to go with a partial truth.

"I work for you, Mr. Lee."

2

A LIGHT SNOW had started falling and Lee looked up and down Delco Street. Looking for his cab, looking for his wife, looking for more men approaching—I wasn't sure. He didn't seem in a hurry. Didn't seem surprised that he had just awoken on a sidewalk outside a nightclub either. "You work for me?"

"Only been with you a little while, Mr. Lee. I'm a tree marker. Working your Algoma Limits right now."

I could see now that Travis Lee looked like his surveillance photos. Sometimes there's a discrepancy and you wonder about that later—the things a camera can't seem to catch—but with Lee there were no surprises. He looked like the photos—fifty-five years old, a prosperous middle-aged ex-jock, still with a full head of blond hair, more girth around the middle than when he'd played college football for Harvard, but still handsome in a middle-aged-jock way.

If you had to guess his occupation, you might have said lawyer and you would have been right with your first guess. Although being born in Birmingham, Maine, meant Travis Lee was also part of the family business—Lee Forestry Products, one of the oldest lumber companies on the Northeastern Seaboard.

"Do you need another cab?" I asked. "I think the first one has gone."

"Appears my wife has gone as well. What's your name, pal?"

"Danny Barrett."

"Give me a hand up, will you? Seems I owe you a drink. Let's go inside and I'll settle my account."

===

WE WALKED TO the back of the Starlight and sat on stools. The nightclub I found out later was built in the '40s and looked it: a large club laid out for big bands and jitterbug dancing, with the floor in front, a stage beyond that, circular tables fanning out from the dance floor all the way to the back of the room, where the bar was. There were chandeliers, a fading mural of a starry night and red leather booths big enough to seat six people easy.

A gilt-edged mirror hung behind the bar, with tall shelves of liquor bottles spaced about every six feet. The club even had two wooden phone booths, the ones with the accordion doors and inside seats. The phones still worked. The phone books were from 2002.

We sat at the bar and Lee ordered a McCallum's neat with Pabst chaser. I told the bartender I'd have the same. "The Algoma Limits," Lee said when our drinks arrived. "That must mean you're working out of the Sleigh Bay mill. I haven't been to that mill in months. How come you know me?"

"Birmingham isn't that big a city, Mr. Lee. Anyone in town richer than you?"

"My brother. My wife one day, maybe."

"Well, I know you, Mr. Lee. I suspect everyone in Birmingham knows you. That was your wife who left in the cab?"

"Tall, good-looking woman in a ridiculous fur coat?"

"Don't know about the fur coat part, but the rest of it sounds right."

"Yes, that would have been the lovely Amanda. Appears she has jumped ship on us, Mr. Barrett. We shall have to continue the voyage without her."

He laughed when he said that, and then he took a swallow of his Scotch. His face winced when the liquid hit the back of his throat, his body shivered for a second, but then his jaw went slack, his eyes closed and, when they reopened, he looked happy. "You're not from around here, are you?"

"That obvious? No, I'm from Detroit."

"That's an odd place for a tree marker to come from."

"My uncle owned a lumber company in the Upper Peninsula, near Escanaba. Spent my summers working there when I was a boy. He taught me how to do it. He told me once that a man who can work a timber limit and mark only the best pine, the best cedar, the man that could do that was worth more to him than a busload of Harvard business graduates."

"My father would have agreed with him," said Lee. "He sent my brother into the camps, to learn stuff like that, but Tuck never took to it. With me, he didn't even bother. Sent me straight to Harvard."

"Oh, shit, I'm sorry, Mr. Lee," I said. I knew Lee had gone to Harvard. I didn't mind looking clumsy right then.

"Don't sweat it. I've heard plenty of Harvard jokes," he said, and motioned to the bartender for another round. "So what was it like growing up in Detroit?"

"Great. Say Detroit today and people feel sorry for you, but I remember when there wasn't a boarded-up store anywhere. The clubs were booming. I walked into a club once and Ben E. King was playing. He had a full horn section. Thursday night. Wasn't even a cover."

"You're making that up."

"Want to know what song he was singing when I walked in?"

"Now I *know* you're making it up."

"'Stand by Me.' Heard it for the first time in the Copper Penny Club. Yeah, Detroit was great. What about Birmingham?"

"Same thing, I suppose. Town was printing money back then. Not just the mills. We had a fishing industry once. Lot of the boats worked under sail, looked like a field of kites out on the St. John some summers. It was beautiful. I'll never forget that."

"Town's doing OK though, isn't it? Don't scare me, Mr. Lee. I just got here."

"We're surviving, Danny, like every mill town in Maine is surviving. You came here looking for work, so you must know a thing or two about surviving. Have you taken to it?"

"I think it's better than the alternative."

"The wise man's answer. I should buy you a drink for that."

"I've had enough for tonight. Thanks, Mr. Lee."

"Said I *should* buy you a drink. Didn't say I *would*. I don't pay for clichés. The Ben E. King story was worth a drink. Better than the alternative—that doesn't get you much around here."

"Well, I'm still calling it a night. Would you like me to get you a cab before I go?"

Lee seemed to consider it a minute before saying, "That won't be necessary." Then he took a phone from his pocket, and using the careful gestures of a truly plastered man with experience at being truly plastered, he sent a text. He was careful and slow about it. I doubt if there would have been a single typo.

"I have a ride coming," he said, and put his phone away. We walked outside and stood under the awning. It was snowing heavier now, the flakes falling through the arc of the streetlights and making the street darker than it would have been normally.

"Thank you for the drinks," I said, and Lee waved me off, an actual reverse swat of the hand. Coming from him the gesture didn't seem dismissive or patronizing, didn't anger me the way it might have coming from someone else. We talked about the snow and whether it might be the start of a storm, Lee saying it didn't look like it.

We hadn't been doing that more than a minute when a Honda Civic pulled up to the curb. The car had Bondo spots on the hood and rust around every tire well. A woman was driving.

Her head was turned and I never saw Pearl Lafontaine that night. Just saw her yellow dress, so simple it looked like plainsong to me, the zipper in back slipped down an inch. When she leaned over to unlock the passenger door, she kept her head turned and all I saw was that dress and a flash of red curls, a long, lithe body twisting in the interior darkness of the car.

"Good luck out on the Algoma," said Lee, shaking my hand one last time before he got in the passenger seat.

I watched the Honda pull away from the curb, its tailpipe exhaust mixing with the falling snow so that the tires were hard to see, made the car look like a parade float drifting down the street. I remember that. Their car seemed to drift away.

3

THE NEXT MORNING I pulled open the curtains in my motel room and saw that it had kept snowing. It had capped the roof peaks and church spire around the Three Pines Motel, powdered the streets, dusted the fences; it made the world look clean and innocent for a change, as though the world got up that morning and decided to dress for a wedding. I looked at the snow and decided to walk to my meeting with FBI special agent Paul Linton.

Linton was angry, so I wasn't in a hurry. He'd phoned last night to make sure I knew he was angry, calling as soon as I'd lost sight of that Honda drifting down Delco Street. Linton was in his mid-thirties, in good shape, looked like a former athlete at some Ivy League school, although he could swear like a drill sergeant. I didn't mind the swearing. It was the greased-back hair and yellow ties I might find unforgivable before the investigation was finished. He had been monitoring me from a surveillance van parked blocks away, by way of a camera hidden in a streetlight across from the Starlight.

"What the fuck did you just do?" he asked when I'd answered his call.

"Had a couple of drinks in a nightclub. Not a bad place, really."

"You were *not* fuckin' authorized to make contact with Travis Lee. You were just supposed to keep eyes on him."

"You'd rather I let him get mugged? It was a field decision. I'll stand by it."

"Damn fuckin' right you will. Debrief tomorrow, nine a.m."

I showered and got dressed, ate a bowl of cold cereal, then another. There was no hot plate in the room. Just a small fridge. I wondered what it would take to be trusted with a hot plate at the Three Pines Motel. I put on my work boots and parka, and by eight fifteen, I was walking down the service road behind the motel.

I had been in Maine for nearly two months, but hadn't seen much of the city. I had spent most of my time in the North Maine Woods, where Lee Forestry had lumber camps and timber rights.

The service road ended at Dickinson Street, a main east-west thoroughfare into downtown Birmingham, and I was soon walking past redbrick duplexes with exterior stairwells and small wooden porches, fenced gardens the size of compact cars. The air was cold and my breath came out in small clouds that spun a few seconds before fading away.

A few blocks from the river, I walked past the remains of the Davidson-Struthers Footwear factory. It took up two city blocks, all red brick and busted windows. I found out later that Davidson-Struthers used to be one of the largest shoe factories in New England—had a near monopoly on white spats for a while—and was one of the first large factories to close in Maine, before the textile mills even. That morning the factory reminded me of some beast the city had slain but forgotten to drag away.

I tend to work in places past their best-before dates—mill towns that no longer have a mill; fishing ports where the fish are remembered like mythical beasts; towns and cities where the workforce is unemployed, working recall hours or gone. People having their financial security threatened are what a lot of crime depends upon. From what I've seen, they might even be the straw that stirs the drink.

The Portland FBI field office seconded me just before Christmas. I stand six foot one, weigh around two hundred pounds most days. I like undercover assignments where I can grow my hair long and I was having no trouble passing as a forestry worker in Birmingham, Maine.

It was the Boston field office that had first noticed the money—a wire transfer of a hundred thousand dollars going from an ecstasy dealer in Rothwell Heights into one of the corporate accounts of Lee Forestry Products. It was sloppy and something had probably gone wrong with the transfer, but it got the Feds looking into Lee Forestry for the first time.

The company was family owned, fifth generation, all assets and equity split between two brothers, Tucker and Travis Lee. In the fourteen months since that wire transfer, the FBI had located $251 million in the company's bank accounts that lacked "provenance." That's the word the forensic accountants like to use to mean no legal or plausible reason to exist. It's a polite word. Allows the accountants to avoid words like "crooked" or "dirty."

That one of the oldest lumber companies in Maine could be a tier-one money launderer was odd right from the start. What made the case odder was that no one knew where the money was coming from.

A lot came in wire transfers that couldn't be traced back to an original source, but just as much came in cash deposits that went right from cube vans into the vaults of the Birmingham branch of North Maine Savings and Loan. Lumber used to be a cash business, and there were still old timber boys with backwoods mill yards who operated that way—but a quarter-billion dollars?

Six months ago an FBI agent had gone undercover at a Lee bush camp in the North Maine Woods to try to figure it out. He was a good agent, one who had worked many years in Brownsville, Texas, going about as deep underground there as it was possible to go. Some in the bureau had considered him a rising star.

His body was found three months after he went into the Woods, bobbing under the ice of Baron Lake, about a mile from the bush camp. There had been no indication the agent was under suspicion. No warning signs. No one knew if the drowning had been an accident or murder.

I got the call two months after that. About normal, I would say, for a high-level racketeering investigation, the time needed for senior law enforcement officers to accurately assess just how badly their case had exploded.

THE SURVEILLANCE VAN was parked on Dechamps Street, four blocks from the boarded-up remains of the Davidson-Struthers Footwear factory. I knocked twice on the back door, and it slid open. There were three men in the van. When I entered, two of them took off their headphones and left. The man who stayed behind sat on a bench at the far end of the van.

Paul Linton was wearing a dark blue suit with a yellow tie that morning, the tie knotted so tightly, it looked like a suspended kernel of corn glowing in the semidarkness of the van. "I was told you knew how to do this sort of work," he said when I sat. "After what I saw last night, I'm beginning to wonder if I was fed a ton of horseshit."

It was a line he had clearly rehearsed, so I let him enjoy it a few seconds before speaking. "I don't know what you've been fed," I said. "I do know I didn't have much choice about last night."

"Really? What about letting shit happen? I thought nonintervention was a credo for you deep-undercover boys. Like fuckin' *Star Trek* or something."

"You think we're on a spaceship?"

"Don't be fuckin' cute, Pet—"

"Barrett."

"What?"

"The name I'm using is Barrett. Never use another name. That's the protocol. You should know that."

Linton leaned back and gave me a nasty look. "You were not authorized to make contact with Travis Lee. You were only there to help us keep surveillance on him for one night. Do you have any fuckin' idea how much your little stunt might have cost this investigation, *Barrett*?"

"Probably jack," I said, flashing him a smile. "Nothing Lee said in that nightclub was going to end up in court. There's nothing there you can use. And what do you think it would have cost the investigation if I'd sat on my ass and let him get his head kicked in?"

"Pretty dramatic. Those men could have rolled him and taken off. No harm, no foul. That's probably how it would have played out."

"That fat fuck was going to kick Lee in the head. No way he was walking away without doing that. Do you need me to file a report on last night?"

Linton glared at me and I knew what he was thinking. He was wondering if I knew what I was doing by asking a question like that, getting angrier and angrier when he kept coming up with the right answer. As soon as a report gets written, it gets filed and then it becomes discoverable evidence that needs to be turned over to defense lawyers when charges are laid.

But if nothing Travis Lee said in the Starlight was going to be part of the investigation, then Linton could skip the report and maybe even feel clean about what he was doing. He wasn't burying evidence. Just not doing his job.

"So nothing at all from your barroom chat with one of the main suspects in this investigation?" he asked.

"He misses the old cod boats. The ones with the colored sails. If you can do something about bringing those back, he'd appreciate it."

"A comedian. Somebody should have warned me. Hold off on the report."

Linton rapped on the side panel of the van and the two other agents returned. They gave me only a cursory nod of their heads before slipping on their headphones. I stood and let one agent, the shorter of the two, take back his rolling desk stool. They were more wiretap and rolling-surveillance operatives than field agents, but they both carried weapons and I figured they both wanted to shoot Linton by now. They had been working with him for six months.

The van was set up with the bench on the passenger side of the vehicle and a bank of four video monitors suspended above a desk on the driver's side. Three of the monitors were turned on and I bent to look at them. Two of them showed the street outside the surveillance van, front and back. The third showed an office, three men sitting around a desk. One of the men was Travis Lee.

"Want to see a bit of the show?" asked Linton.

"Sure."

4

THE FBI'S PLAN was simple. A quarter-billion dollars in mystery money should have set off all sorts of warning bells at North Maine Savings and Loan. Not a single chime had rung.

The bank manager had to be part of the money-laundering scheme. His name was Robert Powell and he was a high school friend of Tucker Lee. I hadn't seen any surveillance photos of him and leaned in to take a look—balding, wire-rimmed glasses, mid-fifties, a paunch that was present even though I couldn't see it. Robert Powell was what central casting would have sent me if I'd asked for a small-town banker.

Linton had made his play three weeks ago and the banker caved in the first meeting, started crying and saying he had been forced into it, back in '08, when it seemed like the sky was falling—the sky or capitalism, it had seemed the same thing back then. He'd only done it to keep the mills open. He kept crying and saying that until Linton showed him the ownership papers for a forty-four-foot Sea Ray that he moored at Bahia Mar Marina in Fort Lauderdale and the deed for a Bahamian country home in his wife's name. Then Robert Powell stopped crying and asked what it would take for full immunity.

Quite a bit, as it turned out, but Powell agreed to all of it. He would wear a wire. His phones could be tapped, home and office; a camera could be put in his office.

Most important, he agreed to kick the Lee money loose.

That was the play. The banker was going to tell the Lee brothers they needed to get their money out of his bank. They were going to be given less than a week to do it. Linton was going to sit back and see where they ran.

TRAVIS LEE DIDN'T look as bad as I would have expected. The suit looked freshly pressed. His hands weren't shaking. Compared to his brother, you might even say he looked healthy.

Tucker Lee wasn't that tall but he must have weighed close to two hundred fifty pounds, maybe more. The bank chairs were wooden and he kept crossing and recrossing his legs. The chairs were probably a tip of the hat to the forestry industry and what it meant to Birmingham. Tucker Lee looked like a man who could have done without the homage.

"Are these Henderson chairs, Bobby?" he asked the banker.

"They are, Tuck. Might have been your family's wood that made them, back in the fifties."

"I'm sure it was. We had that contract. It was Hendersons that were on the *Charlie Rose Show*. Till he got canned. These look like the same chairs."

"Any idea how much a chair like that would be worth today, Tucker?"

"Don't tell me, Bobby. It'll just piss me off."

The two men laughed. Travis Lee smiled but didn't laugh. The office they sat in was nondescript in every way except for the wooden chairs and the black-and-white drawings on the walls, drawings depicting log runs from the nineteenth century. The old squared-timber runs. They had the same runs in the Upper Michigan Peninsula. Men would have died on every one of those runs, signing on in the spring and never knowing if they were coming home that summer. No different from combat. No different from heading out to sea.

They died after they were drowned or got crushed between the booms, or murdered by one of the criminal gangs that had sailed the St. John back then—the Shiners, the Travelers, the Pat Lowry Gang. There were a lot of ways to die on those squared-timber log runs.

It was squared timber—the wood once used to build naval ships—that made the Lee fortune. Andrew Lee arrived in Portland in 1845 from Aberdeen, a young forward-steerage merchant who quickly saw that the only serious money being made in Maine was by men who sold squared timber. In 1847 he bid on timber rights so high up the St. John River the land was nearly touching the Canadian border. No one had ever bothered bidding on those rights and Lee got them for a pittance.

The river was wild up there, with class III rapids, waterfalls and eddy pools. The cost of building dams and chutes to get timber to market was considered prohibitive. No one understood why Lee had purchased the rights, and as he had not been in Maine long, the more experienced lumbermen in Portland snickered at him. Wondered if the lad had bothered to look at a map.

Andrew Lee surprised everyone by not bothering to build chutes or dams. He just ran the rafts down the river and sold whatever wood made it through. It was so dangerous, it was a wonder anyone took the work, but that was another thing Andrew Lee figured out early: there were always desperate people in this world, and if you had left Europe, the comfort and predictable routine of Europe, for a cabin in the Maine woods, you were one of them.

Every spring men would come crawling out of the forest like bears from hibernation, eager to sign up for the Lee log runs, men with gaunt faces walking beside women with night-terror eyes holding the hands of children so malnourished you could almost hear their bones creak whenever a stiff wind passed over them. All that history had been alchemized into black-and-white etchings of men piloting Huck Finn rafts down calm rivers.

"Well, shall we get started, Bobby?" said Tucker Lee, repositioning himself in the chair one more time. "Travis and I are just dying to know why you needed to see us this morning."

"Yes, thanks again for coming in so early. I'm afraid there are a few things we need to discuss."

Powell looked nervous when he said that and Tucker Lee stared at him before saying, "What sort of things are we talking about, Bobby?"

"The sort of things you're probably thinking about, Tuck. Our sideline business."

"What about it?"

"I can't do it anymore."

Tucker stared at his brother, then back at the banker. "I don't think you can just *quit*, Bobby. *I* can't just quit. This is something that needs to be discussed. What is the problem exactly?"

"No problem. I just don't want to do it anymore. We need to shut the accounts."

"You can't be serious. For what reason?"

"The reason doesn't matter, Tucker. Those accounts were a service I offered you a long time ago, thinking it was going to be a short-term thing. I no longer want to offer the service. I don't have to give you a reason."

"Reasons are always good, Bobby," said Travis Lee, speaking for the first time. "Reasons, excuses, I don't like to leave home without one or two in my back pocket. Do you *have* one of those?"

"I just told you I didn't need one, Travis. A reason *or* an excuse. It's my call. Always has been."

"Don't be stupid, Bobby," said Tucker Lee. "It's not like Lee Forestry has a fuckin' *savings account* with you. Do you know what you're asking us to do?"

"Yes, I know what I'm asking you to do. I've given it a lot of thought, Tucker, Travis, and this is the decision I'm making."

"Why so much thought, Bobby? It's not much work for you. You prosper from it. Why walk away from a good thing?"

"Tucker, please—"

"I'm fuckin' *asking* you!"

Powell leaned back in his chair and let out a long sigh. When he spoke again, it was with a voice both tired and resigned, a voice that had made up its mind about a bad thing, deciding it needed to be done, this bad thing, whatever the consequences might be—it was a good acting job, although he was a banker and I told myself I shouldn't be overly impressed.

"I'm getting out, boys," Powell said. "This can get nasty. I'm half expecting it. But this is happening and I'm not going to give you boys a chance to stall or try to talk me out of it."

"What does that mean, Bobby?"

"Means you're contacting whoever the fuck owns this money, Tuck, and you're telling them they have to move it out of my bank by Friday. And I'm going to watch you make that call. If I don't watch you place that call, as soon as you leave my office I'm phoning the state banking inspectors and telling them there're multiple problems with your accounts."

"You cocksuckin' little fuckin'—"

"Save it, Tucker. This is happening. You're not bullying your way into a different ending."

"You're an idiot. You'd be just as fucked as us if you called in the banking inspectors."

"Yeah, but I'll be first man off ship. I'm going to float better than you boys."

"You'd cut a deal?"

"In a heartbeat," said Powell, and again I was impressed with his acting skills. Not even the glimmer of a knowing smile. "You've got to move the money, Tucker."

"I don't have a way of contacting our partner right now."

"Then you're fucked."

Powell leaned back in his chair and allowed himself a cocky smile. He might have been in a tough spot, but the two men sitting on the other side of his desk were in a tougher spot and that was normally enough to make any banker happy. Tucker Lee looked like he was going to explode, but I noticed there was a questioning look on his younger brother's face. The play had been moving at train-wreck speed and Tucker Lee had been swept along in the draft, but there was something in Travis Lee's eyes that made me wonder if he was questioning the story. Not the brother I would have expected.

The stalemate lasted about a minute and a half. No one talking. No one moving. No one staring anyplace in particular. Finally Tucker Lee sighed, reached into a jacket pocket, pulled out a cell phone and punched a number.

In the surveillance van, the silence was so absolute, I heard the beating of another man's heart. The murmur of shallow breaths sounded like waves crashing on a beach. There was a sharp inhale of breath from all of us when Tucker Lee cleared his throat and said, "Beau, I'm at the bank. We may have a problem."

5

THE FBI HADN'T been able to get a court warrant to tap the Lees' cell phones, so we never heard that first conversation, just Tucker Lee's end, which was nothing more than those first two sentences. He waited a few seconds after saying them, then clicked off the phone and told Powell the owner of the money would call him back. Best he could do right then.

But it was enough.

"He called another lumber company," one of the tech boys yelled, his hand up in the air, his other hand pounding on his keyboard. "Five Star Forestry. Wait. . . . Wait. . . . Private company. Incorporated in Portland twenty-three years ago. . . . CEO is Beau Lafontaine."

The only thing missing was the sound of champagne corks popping.

By ten a.m. Linton had all the corporate filings for Five Star Forestry and had begun working on warrants for the company's bank accounts. Five Star seemed to conduct all its business in Northern Maine, most of its timber rights in the North Maine Woods.

By noon it was confirmed Beau Lafontaine had no criminal record in the United States. He also didn't have a Social Security number, a date of birth, or any digital footprint other than his name appearing on the incorporation papers for Five Star Forestry.

Linton phoned the Portland field office and asked for an agent to be assigned to the case to start doing computer work and find out how that was possible.

Around two in the afternoon there was a punching-fists-in-the-air moment when it was learned Lafontaine might not have a criminal record in the United States, but he had an arrest record. In Canada. Where he had been picked up twice by the Sûreté du Quebec and charged with smuggling.

The charges were nearly forty years old and they had never gone to court, but it gave us two photos of Lafontaine on the Sûreté database, along with fingerprints and a date of birth that would have made him fifty-eight. The photos showed a long-haired teenager with sullen eyes and bad scars on both cheeks. His permanent address was listed as a bush camp in the North Maine Woods. Another thing that didn't seem possible.

Linton got a Sûreté staff sergeant in Sherbrooke on the phone and asked him to take a look at Lafontaine's physical file—if there was one—to see if there was anything more. After being put on hold for ten minutes, the sergeant came back and said yes, Beau Lafontaine had a physical file.

"It's a thick one," he added.

"Are there criminal convictions missing in your database?" asked Linton.

"No, he has just the two arrests. No convictions. He's mentioned in some reports. I can fax you what I have."

"Fax?" said Linton, his voice thick with derision. "Do you have an electronic version of the file you can send me?"

"No, I'm afraid not."

"I don't even know where I'd get a fax in this hotel. We have the correct dates for those arrests—1983, 1984?"

"That's correct."

"Courier the file to me. Here's the address for the hotel."

A couple hours later, the Portland agent assigned to the investigation that morning phoned to say he had been going through the case reports and was there a family connection between Beau Lafontaine and Travis Lee's girlfriend? Did anyone know?

Linton started banging his desk and hooting like his basketball team had just made a buzzer-beating shot to win a tournament.

MOST PEOPLE WILL tell you things turned bad in Birmingham the next day. I'm not one of those people.

I think it turned bad right then, with that phone call from Portland. That call was the real thing that led to the next thing. That was the moment a diner waitress walked onto the stage and took over the play.

There were no warning signs though, so that day must have seemed golden to Special Agent Paul Linton. Shortly after the Portland phone call, the warrants arrived for the bank accounts to Five Star Forestry and he started preparing a list of the banks he would need to contact.

By the end of his workday, Linton knew where the Lee mystery money was coming from. Knew the connection between the Lee brothers and Beau Lafontaine, a mysterious figure that was being dragged from the shadows of the North Maine Woods. He was already looking at topographical maps of bush camps run by Five Star Forestry in the Woods, already had the narrative for an eventual court case taking shape in his mind.

Linton got good and hammered that night at the bar in the Alexander Hotel. Phoned his wife when he was back in his room, slurring his words and telling her he might be back in Portland within a week.

At one p.m. the next day, Robert Powell was shot dead in front of the North Maine Savings and Loan.

THE SWEET GOODBYE

PEARL LAFONTAINE HAD *finished her shift at the Red Bird Diner and was cashing out at a service table near the washrooms, one hidden from the customers behind a folding Japanese screen. Two other waitresses were also cashing out. They were much younger than Pearl and from time to time they would look out the windows of the diner, giggle and look back at Pearl. She paid them no mind. Kept her head turned to the cash running through her fingers, keeping a running tally in her head.*

The killing of the banker was all anyone had talked about in the diner that morning, which wasn't surprising, although it meant Pearl was more tired than normal by the end of her shift. People expected a diner waitress to know something about stuff like that: murders three blocks away, private details of a scandalous divorce, anything lurid and worth a whisper.

It was awkward conversation the first few hours of her shift before Pearl thought to say, "The crime scene tape is still up around the bank. I hear that don't happen too often. Why would the cops need two days?" Then she'd walk away and people seemed happier after that. Facts and speculation are the same thing to a lot of people.

When she finished her cash-out, she put the money and credit card slips in an envelope and licked it closed, finally allowing herself a look out the window of the diner. The Mercedes was parked where she expected it to be, in the southeast corner of the lot, in the shade of a large beech, the white SUV with the ten-thousand-dollar sound system and windows tinted darker than the law allowed, but what police officer in Birmingham would ever call a Lee on something like that?

She took the envelope and gave it to Gwen Snyder, the owner of the Red Bird, standing behind the lunch counter holding menus and looking as vigilant and vaguely threatening as a Wells Fargo guard. Some of the other waitresses changed into their street clothes when they left the diner but Pearl was still wearing her yellow uniform with the white piping.

"Back at five today, are you, Pearl?"

"That's right."

"Got some curlers in tonight from the bonspiel. You won't wanna be late."

"I won't, Mrs. Snyder."

The women nodded at each other and Pearl stepped outside. Sometimes Mrs. Snyder gave her a conspiratorial smile or a poorly executed wink when the Mercedes was parked outside, but today there was nothing. Like most people in Birmingham, Gwen Snyder seemed distracted that day. Pearl walked past her Honda and opened the passenger door of the Mercedes.

"Go for a ride, girl?" asked Travis Lee.

"Just got in, didn't I?"

═══════

SHE WOULD HAVE been sixteen the first time she said that. He would have been twenty-two, his senior year at Harvard and back for Christmas. They met at the Tudor, a roadhouse in the unincorporated township north of the St. John River.

She knew who he was. Everyone in Birmingham knew who he was. The Lees were the largest employer in the city, old man Thomas and his two sons, Tucker and Travis. She had even attended high school with him for one year, senior year for him, freshman for her, which had happened only because she'd skipped two grades at Bustard County Elementary, her report cards at the time saying she liked to read, which set her apart from most of the other children in the school and got her bumped ahead.

Bustard County was rural and poor and might as well have been the dark side of the moon for people like Travis Lee, who grew up on the Lee estate ten miles upriver from Birmingham. Her dad hated the Lees, but then most people in Bustard County felt the same way about the family, or any other family that was rich, happy and successful for reasons that did not seem right to them.

Her dad had cursed him only two weeks earlier while watching a college football game on television, Harvard versus Navy, her dad watching just to see Harvard get pummeled, which most people were expecting. But Navy had trouble scoring, and late in the fourth quarter, Travis Lee threw a pass on a fake-punt play that went for a touchdown and won the game. A television commentator said it might have been the first trick play Harvard had called in 108 years.

Her dad threw his beer at the television set. "Can you believe how fuckin' lucky that asshole is? I could have made that fuckin' pass."

It might have been true. It was a pretty easy pass. But it won the game and people around Birmingham were calling it the Christmas Miracle Play by the time he returned for the holidays. She saw him sitting on the other side of the Tudor, throwing back shots of tequila, and she knew that was what he was celebrating. Or maybe he had something else to celebrate every day. That seemed possible for a Lee.

She sat at a large table crowded with people from Bustard County, which was about an hour drive from the Tudor. One of her brother's friends had asked her along, to help split the cost of gas, he'd said, although maybe it was more than that. He sat beside her most of the night. Was protective of his seat. At sixteen she was starting to attract boys, and men, who wanted to sit beside her.

Lee looked at her several times before approaching the table. She must have been looking too; otherwise how would she have known that? "Hi, folks. How y'all doin'?" he said when he got there, wobbling on his feet, smiling in the oblivious way of rich drunks. No one at the table bothered to answer him.

"I'm celebrating with some friends tonight. Want to join us?"

Another dumb smile. Someone at the table snickered. The boy who had asked her along said, "We're good, pal."

"Aw, come on. I'm buying."

"So fuckin' what?"

"So fuckin' what? You kiddin' me? Means you don't have to pay, pal. That's so fuckin' what. Come on, let me get a round for the table. I recognize some of you from high school."

The boy sitting beside her started to rise from his chair, his fingers already bunched into a fist, his mouth set firm. It didn't look like he was planning on saying anything else.

"I'll have a Pabst," she said quickly. "Billy will have the same. What about everybody else?"

With her asking the question, the table quickly placed a drink order. He turned it into a comedy routine trying to remember it all—most of the people at the table had decided to go with cocktails—and he had people laughing before he walked off to the bar. The boy sitting beside her looked angry and she knew there would be trouble when the drinks came. She leaned over and whispered, "Come on, Billy, let's run a bar tab on the schmuck." Then she added, "I'm really looking forward to the drive home."

That was enough. Lee bought three more rounds for the table and ended up sitting beside her. He even got Billy to laugh a couple times and she didn't think she'd seen Billy Clayton laugh more than once or twice the whole time she'd known him. Then, at closing time, Lee did something she'd never seen anyone do before.

While talking to Billy, he whispered to her. Like he was talking double, having two conversations at once, never an interruption in the other conversation, but she heard him say, "Out back, ten minutes."

She was a little drunk by then and thought she might have been hearing things. But when he got up to get the next round, he looked right at her and winked.

That wasn't her imagination.

She headed to the washroom. When she went through the back door, he was parked there, waiting for her, behind the wheel of a car model she had never seen before, something long and black and shaped like a missile. The passenger door opened with a pneumatic hiss.

"Go for a ride, girl?"

———

THIRTY-FOUR YEARS? SHE *looked out the window and wondered if it had really been that long ago. It had snowed earlier in the week and there was still powder on the branches of the cedars by the river. On some of the trees, it looked like a chalk outline. She wondered if there had been a chalk outline on the sidewalk for the banker. Did they still do that? Why did they do that?*

"How was your shift?" he asked.

"You came down to find out how my shift was, hon?"

"No."

"Might as well ask me, then."

"Did you know Beau was going to do that?"

"Don't know that he did, hon."

"You're kidding, right?"

"Don't know that I am. Where was Tucker when that banker got shot?"

"That's almost funny. Are you making a joke?"

She didn't answer. They had driven out of the city and were on Highway 7 now, heading up the shoreline of the St. John River. The trees were hardwood now, still without their leaves, and the snow did not cling to the branches.

"Fuck, Pearl, what just happened?"

"Banker got shot."

She said it so quickly, he laughed. "Banker got shot. Yeah, that's the short-story version."

They drove a few more miles in silence. When he spoke next, he asked, "You on a split today?"

"Yeah. First off tonight, so I got to be back by five."

"That still gives you a couple hours."

"Yeah, it does."

───────

HE TURNED INTO *the parking lot of the St. John Motel, paid for a room in the courtyard and parked the SUV behind a large maple. She waited for him outside the vehicle while he took a pint of Ballantine's from the glove compartment.*

He mixed drinks in juice glasses she found atop a small fridge. The glasses had paper lid protectors, crinkled like doilies. He ran the tap water until it was as cold as he could get it for her drink. Made his neat, then put the drinks on the side table next to the bed.

They were in no hurry and he refreshed their drinks once before they were finished. She had a beautiful body. Not much had changed. What was once taut was now firm; the beautiful blue eyes now had laugh lines framing them. He didn't think there was much more change than that. Afterward, he turned on the television while she went to a chair in front of a desk-type vanity and began brushing her hair. She had put her sweater back on but was still in her panties. The room was warm. An electric radiator hummed in the corner.

"Do you know how long we been doing this?" she asked.

"Having sex in motels in the middle of the day?"

"Yeah."

"Long time."

"Twenty-five years."

"You're not counting Boston?"

"No."

"What made you think of that?"

"Justin Long came in the diner today. He lives down in Portland now. Made me think of high school."

"Yeah? You ever date him?"

"Wouldn't you like to know?"

She laughed and he went back to watching television. It was a game show that had a car spinning on a pedestal, and a woman jumping up and down. The woman eventually stopped jumping and sat in the twirling car. "Do you remember what I used to say about us having a week together?" he asked.

"Course I do."

"Tell me."

"You don't think I remember?"

"Do you?"

"Want me to say it the way you used to say it?"

"Sure."

"Pearl Lafontaine"—and she put on an exaggerated Southern accent— "if we had a week together, why, they'd be writing folk songs about us forever."

"You do remember. I don't know why I asked you to say it. I knew you hadn't forgotten."

"You asked because you like to hear it. And because you still believe it. Maybe."

"I do. Do you ever think we should have tried for more than a week?"

"No. We've gone about it the right way."

"Why do you say that?"

"'Cause it's true. We see the world different, hon. I was raised believing the toughest days are always ahead, and you were raised believing they don't even exist. That would have been a problem."

A few seconds later, a chime came from inside her purse and she stopped brushing her hair. She took out a jewel-encrusted cell phone. Baubles and bright, shiny things, he thought. She'd always been that way.

When she put away the phone, her mood had changed though. She bit her lower lip for a few seconds before saying, "You should probably take me back to the diner, hon. You have things to do."

"Who was that?"

"Beau. He wants to see you tonight. You and Tucker."

"Tonight? Where?"

"The Grill Room at the Alexander. Eight o'clock."

"Beau lives in the North Maine Woods. How the hell can he get here to-night?"

"Ah, hon." And she went to sit beside him, ran her fingers through his hair, probably as blond and full as the day she met him. He had led a charmed life. The Prince in the Tower. She had often looked at him that way. "Beau owns a plane," she whispered in his ear. "Did you forget, hon?"

6

THE SÛRETÉ DU Quebec file on Beau Lafontaine was delivered to Linton's hotel room the day after Robert Powell was murdered. I was in the room when the courier came. My assignment had been changed and we were looking at a topographical map of Paradise Lake, the lake in the North Maine Woods where Beau Lafontaine had his main lumber camp. That's where I would be heading when I got off the Lee shuttle bus the following day. The map had it as forty-seven miles away.

Linton opened the package and began to read the file, passing me the pages one by one when he'd finished with them. For a man with no criminal convictions, it was a lengthy file. More than fifty pages, although only three photographs. The Sûreté sergeant had missed one. Two of the photos were the booking shots from the smuggling charges when Lafontaine was a teenager. The third was more current, an attachment at the end of one of the reports, an FBI surveillance photo taken eight years ago. It showed a middle-aged man walking out of a strip club in lower Manhattan owned by the Hells Angels. It still had the original notation from the agent who took the photograph—*"unknown long-haired countryman."*

Beau Lafontaine had black hair that fell past his shoulders. He was dressed in denim—pants, shirt and jacket—with a belt buckle as large as brass knuckles. He wore snakeskin cowboy boots with silver tips. He had a half beard and what looked like bad knife scars on his cheeks; he was smoking a cigarette and smiling at the camera, as though he knew it was there. He didn't look to be a big man, but on a crowded Manhattan street, you would have been careful not to bump into him.

Unknown long-haired countryman. That was pretty good.

The file consisted of the two arrest bookings and two lengthy case-assessment reports, the ones that get written at the end of covert operations. The first report was for an operation code-named Baton, a joint Royal Canadian Mounted Police and Sûreté investigation into smuggling in the North Maine Woods. Because the Woods ran right to the Canadian border and were uninhabited, smuggling had always been common. It was an accepted way for poorly paid lumbermen to supplement their incomes. It had escalated though, according to the executive summary of the report; at the same time, it had gotten deadlier and better organized.

Beau Lafontaine was identified as a high-ranking member of the Malee, the oldest of the smuggling gangs in the North Maine Woods. The Malee were descendants of Acadian refugees and French voyageurs and they had worked the bush camps for centuries, gaining an almost mythical status among other lumbermen. Lafontaine's mother had come to the Woods from Birmingham as a young girl, and soon married Guillaume Lafontaine, a Malee leader who ran the Little Creek bush camp.

That's where Beau Lafontaine was born and that's where he lived for three years, before his parents moved to another bush camp. Then another. And another. Lafontaine was raised in the North Maine Woods. The report said he might be the only person in the United States who could claim that. There were no permanent roads or settlements in the

North Maine Woods. The population—according to every census that had included the counties of the North Maine Woods—was zero.

It was 3.5 million acres—a swath of land in the contiguous United States the size of four Rhode Islands—and no one lived there.

The North Maine Woods were America's last true frontier, a place where you could fall off the grid, not fake doing that—with general delivery mailing addresses and Gore-Tex tents—but *really* do that. Operation Baton concluded smuggling in the Woods *had* increased dramatically, while also becoming more dangerous, the contraband no longer Canadian whiskey or American lobsters but methamphetamine, automatic weapons and Asian women who were moved like chattel between strip clubs in Boston and Montreal.

It attributed the change solely to the Malee, which the report said had become "a ruthless and deadly cultlike criminal organization." Its leaders were seen as seers or prophets and the report estimated the gang now had effective control of nearly one hundred miles of an international border. It defined effective control as "the ability to smuggle contraband across the border at total, or near-total, control of timing and location."

The joint-task-force investigation wrapped up after two years with arrests in the Eastern Townships of Quebec of several associate-patch bikers affiliated with the Hells Angels and some shady nightclub owners in Montreal and Boston. Not a single Malee was arrested. The cops had been unable to infiltrate the lumber camps of the North Maine Woods.

The second report was more recent, written four years ago, a postmortem on another joint-task-force investigation between the RCMP and the Sûreté, this one called Broken Wings, into the activities of the Hells Angels chapter in Sherbrooke, Quebec. Lafontaine had his own chapter in this report.

He was identified now as the leader of the Malee. Some heavily redacted wiretap transcripts let you know the Mounties had finally been able to get an informant inside a Malee lumber camp. A good informant it looked like, a go-between for the Malee and the Angels.

During the joint-task-force investigation, the cops became aware of a dispute between the Angels and the Malee over transportation costs through the Woods. Threats were made. The Malee held on to a shipment of meth headed for the Angels' clubhouse in Sherbrooke. There were more threats. A wiretap picked up Yves Tremblay, president of the Sherbrooke Hells Angels, threatening Lafontaine, promising to "burn those fuckin' woods down" if his shipment wasn't delivered within the week.

The go-between set up a meeting between the two men. You could tell from reading the case notes that the Canadian cops were over the moon about what was happening. The informant would wear a wire to the meeting and that audio recording might become the linchpin for a criminal case against the Hells Angels. Maybe, finally, a criminal case against the Malee of the North Maine Woods as well.

Tremblay took three of his most trusted men to the meeting at Paradise Lake. The go-between led the way. Five days later the informant was found hanging from a tree beside a logging road near Sherbrooke. His recording equipment was shoved in his mouth. As for the bikers— they were never seen again.

Poof. Four Angels gone. That was quite a trick.

Now there was a banker dead in Birmingham, killed twenty-eight hours after we first heard the name Beau Lafontaine, and that was looking like quite a trick too.

"Might have been a good report to have seen yesterday," I said when I put down the last page. But Linton didn't answer me. His breathing had turned shallow and ragged, and in a few seconds, he stood up and went to the bathroom. I heard water running almost immediately.

I was still in Linton's room a few minutes later, rolling up the topographical map, when there was another knock on the door. This time, one of the other FBI agents staying in the room next door. He had sheets of paper in his hand.

"We just got a lucky break," he said. Linton gave him a blank look. Probably wasn't the day to be talking to him about lucky breaks. "We got the warrant for the Lee brothers' phones this morning," he continued. "Here's a transcript of a conversation they had fifteen minutes ago."

Linton reached for the paper. He read it and then asked, "Travis Lee placed the call?"

"Correct. We think the original message must have come from the girlfriend."

"Get downstairs and see if we can set something up." He turned and looked at me. "Looks like we can use you for one more night, Barrett. Beau Lafontaine is on his way to Birmingham."

7

THE LEAR LANDED at the Birmingham Regional Airport at seven thirteen p.m., looking as sleek and shiny as a star sliding down to earth. It was the sort of plane you don't see often in Northern Maine. A Cadillac SUV from a local car service was waiting on the tarmac to greet it. A young driver in a gray uniform was standing beside an open rear-passenger door.

I sat in my rental car on the other side of the fence surrounding the commercial hangars. I had a pair of Bushnell 10x42 binoculars and good sight lines on the Lear. I watched the rollaway stairs get wheeled to the plane, the door open and Beau Lafontaine step outside. He stood on the top step a second, stretching his back, and I took a good look at him. I would have guessed his height at five seven, maybe eight, not a tall man, but he looked lean and fit, with skin so weathered and burnished, it resembled the underside of tanned leather.

He walked slowly down the steps after he'd stretched, and when he was on the tarmac, I saw that he walked bowlegged. He had long black hair, and just like in that FBI photo from New York, he was dressed completely in denim—pants, shirt and jacket—with a large silver belt buckle that twinkled in the predusk shadows. A second man followed Lafontaine off the plane and looked much the same. Only bigger. With more hair.

The young driver watched them come down the stairs and started shifting his weight from leg to leg. He was almost hopping by the time the two men reached him. *The boy's nervous,* I thought, and suspected he had spent the last several seconds debating the wisdom of shaking these men's hands.

He made the right call and didn't try. I watched him usher the men into the backseat of the Cadillac, never open his mouth, never take his hand off the door handle.

I FOLLOWED THE Cadillac into downtown Birmingham, thinking about the men I used to see in my uncle's bush camps. The good ones all looked a bit like Beau Lafontaine, had the same stature and build. The towering, hulking lumberjack—the Paul Bunyan of children's stories—that was a myth. At least I never saw one in the camps on the Upper Peninsula.

Big men couldn't run fast in the woods when a man needed to run fast. Big men were no good in canoes and pointer boats, the only boats used during a log run. Big men tired easily. Big men ate too much food. No, the men who did best in the bush camps were men who looked just like Beau Lafontaine.

When we arrived at the Alexander, the Cadillac pulled into the valet-parking lane and I kept going, turning around in two blocks and coming back, parking across the street from the hotel. The surveillance van was four vehicles ahead of me. I'd been sitting only a few seconds when my phone vibrated. It was Paul Linton.

"What time did he land?"

"Seven thirteen."

"What kind of plane was it?"

"Some sort of Lear. Looks like the sixty series."

"Sweet ride."

"I have the tail numbers. The wives are inside?"

"Yeah, Tucker's idea. He told younger brother it would make the meeting look more casual, like they weren't worried about seeing Lafontaine. Travis didn't think his wife would come and it would be a nonstarter, but he asked and she agreed and here we are. They're just finishing dinner. We're expecting the wives to leave when they get started."

"You have someone in the restaurant?"

"Got them both inside. So it doesn't look suspicious, one of them eating by himself."

"So I stay here until they leave? Follow the Cadillac after that?"

"You got it. You can stand down."

Stand down? Did he just say that?

———

THE FRONT OF the Alexander was floor-to-ceiling windows. I pulled out my binoculars and watched Lafontaine enter the hotel. He and the other man cut through the lobby and entered the Grill Room. There was a wide entrance for the restaurant, with a maître d' table, and I watched them walk toward the Lee table. Watched the other diners keep their heads down while they passed, wait three seconds, then lift their heads and turn to stare.

Every diner. Every table. As I watched the heads bob up and down, I wondered how many knew that the boots on Lafontaine's feet looked to be Tony Lamas or that he had just flown into Birmingham on a Learjet registered in his name.

The maître d' seemed to know. He ran hurrying ahead of Lafontaine, snapping his fingers for more chairs to be brought to the Lee table. Before he got there though, the brothers were rising from their chairs, throwing their napkins on the table. Travis Lee was dressed in what looked like the same blue suit and white shirt he had been wearing when I saw him at the Starlight. Amanda Lee was wearing a low-cut dress that didn't seem right for the season. The other woman was wearing a high-collared gray dress, and sitting on the other side of the table from Amanda Lee, she might as well have been a shadow.

When the maître d' reached the table, Tucker Lee whispered into his ear. The man nodded his head furiously and then began scurrying toward the rear of the restaurant. Lafontaine and the Lees followed. The two women stayed at the table, eating desserts and not talking to each other.

━━━

IT WAS MY turn to phone Linton. He picked up on the first ring.

"The wives didn't leave."

"I see that, Barrett."

"They're going to a meeting room."

"Probably."

"Will one of your guys reposition?"

"Too risky. We weren't going to get much from the restaurant, anyway. You know how well OmniMics work in restaurants."

"So what are we doing here?"

"Waiting. Follow that Caddy when it leaves. You can continue to stand down."

Yeah, he really said that.

━━━

I'VE ALWAYS TAKEN chances. When I was a teenager in Detroit, I lived three blocks from the main rail yard. Had forty-three lines coming in and out of that yard, but it was a shortcut to the bars in Greektown, so I cut through that yard just about every night. I had to judge distance and speed. Often had to cut between moving trains. Cutting through that rail yard saved me about ten minutes.

A few years back there was a newspaper story about a Wayne State coed who was hit and killed in that yard. I knew exactly what she'd been doing. Another risk-taker. I was sad to see her go.

I sat there looking at the Alexander Hotel, doing nothing as best I could. While the man we were after, who had just become the focus of this investigation, was on the other side of that courtyard, just past that water fountain, the one that wasn't spouting water because it was still cold enough to freeze pipes at night and water fountains in Northern Maine were wishful thinking at the best of times. Just past that fountain, inside that hotel, talking to the Lee brothers, the man who could do magicians' tricks with Hells Angels. *Right there. Right now.*

I opened my car door and headed toward the hotel.

8

I WALKED TO the end of the valet-parking lane, patting the pockets of my jacket. When I reached the edge of the hotel, I bent my head and cupped my left hand around my mouth. One more step and I was around the corner.

Look like a smoker and you can go anywhere these days.

Behind the Alexander was what must have been a lawn in the summer, running right down to the St. John River, although tonight it was an ugly field of mud and melting snow, cardboard coffee cups and old newspapers, broken plastic toys, hockey pucks, some busted Christmas ornaments. The early days of spring are never pretty.

I started to walk behind the building, calculating where the Grill Room would be, and then the direction the men went when they left the restaurant. They might have gone to a room on an upper floor—in which case I was wasting my time—but I suspected the small meeting rooms were on the main floor.

The St. John River was no more than forty feet away. A ribbon of moonlight fell upon the water so wide and lustrous, it looked like a brushstroke of oil paint on canvass, some bold, beautiful brushstroke. You'd leave a curtain open to catch a sight like that, wouldn't you?

There were three wings to the Alexander, but I figured they were heading toward the west wing when they left the restaurant. I approached the lit rooms of that wing with caution, dropping to my knees and inching forward until I could peer over the windowsill. At my third window I glanced inside to see a sitting room of some sort, with floor-to-ceiling bookshelves and dim lighting—the Reading Room I found out later it was called. I was still peering inside, noticing there was a fire burning and the window was open a crack, when I heard a man's angry voice.

I ducked and held my breath. Ten seconds. Twenty. Held until I heard the man continue talking: "Never mention that fuckin' banker to me again. You got that, Tucker?"

"Beau. I am so sorry. It's just that Bobby said he was going to—"

"Shut the fuck up."

I was right beneath the window and wanted to reposition to the side but didn't think I could. Men who had spent their lives in the bush were good at spotting shadows moving in the night. And Beau Lafontaine sounded close. I stared out at the river, trying to keep my muscles taut, my body rigid. The ribbon of shimmering light on the dark water seemed more lustrous than before. Ablaze. Like a break line running beside a wildfire.

"Have the cops been to see you, Tucker?" I heard Lafontaine say, and I let my breath out slowly. I turned my neck, which was starting to kink. When I did that, I noticed Lafontaine's reflection could be seen on one of the panes of the bay window. He was rubbing his chin and staring at the line of fire out on the St. John River.

"No," said Tucker Lee.

"What 'bout you, Travis?"

"No cops. Been asked about it by everyone *but* cops. Town's not talking about much else."

"Maybe that be a good sign. That story the banker tell you—'bout him becomin' a pussy—maybe it's true."

"What other story could it be?" asked Tucker.

"That he be a rat-fink bastard squeezing you boys for the cops."

"He seemed pretty genuine to me."

"Well, bad luck, then."

More silence. Now that I was staring at his reflection, I could see that the scars on Lafontaine's cheeks could not have come from a knife fight. There were far too many of them. I had seen scars like that before, in the lumber camps of Michigan, on the faces of bushmen who had been working in the camps since they were children, the scars left behind by bramble bushes and scrub pine after they'd been sent to work in brush too thick for grown men.

"Maybe we should do what he said, then, Beau. Get your money to a safe place."

"That be a good plan, Tucker? Hear that, Francois? Tucker likes the banker's plan."

"I hear that," said a man whose voice I had not heard yet. "Maybe he don't like your money anymore, Beau."

"That's not it at all," Tucker Lee almost screamed. "We're happy with the arrangement. Travis and I, we're *very* happy with it, Beau. We'd love to continue. But what if Bobby left files behind that the inspectors can find, or the next bank manager—I'm just thinking of the best way to protect you, Beau."

"Protect me? That what you call it? Sound more like you want rid of me, Tucker."

"No, no, that's not it at all, Beau."

"Yeah? What if I'm workin' in the bush, Tucker, and the man I'm working with tell me to take my tools and go home. Is that man protectin' me or firin' me? What do you think, Travis? Protect me or fire me?"

Travis Lee took his time about answering. "This isn't going away, Beau. I think that's what Tucker is saying. Killing the banker might not have solved anything. In the long term."

"You boys think I kill that pussy fuckin' bastard?" He turned away from the window to face them. "I not come to Birmingham in months. How did I kill that banker? Where the fuck were you boys when that prick got shot?"

I was tempted. Would have done a great many things to see the expressions on the Lee brothers' faces when that question was asked of them. A great many things—except stick my head above that window-sill with Beau Lafontaine standing there.

"Is that a serious question?" I heard Tucker Lee say.

"When I not be serious, Tucker? Where the fuck were you?"

"I . . . I was at home. Working."

"And you, Travis?"

"Same. But not working."

"You drunk?"

"Yes. Don't remember much about that day. Bad timing, I'm beginning to think."

"Yeah, story of your life."

"We're getting sidetracked here," said Tucker Lee. "We need to be talking about the best way to—"

"Shut up."

It was funny the way Lafontaine said it. Quick and about an octave lower than how he'd been speaking, something sudden and menacing to the words, like a whiplash coming out of the darkness. The man who had come with Lafontaine laughed heartily.

"My money ain't going anywhere," Lafontaine continued. "That's what I came here to tell you boys. I not give a rat fuck about that banker and I not give a rat fuck about his inspectors. You boys ride this out."

"Beau, the chances of your money not being found if there is a . . . Fuck, Travis and I will be sitting ducks."

"You touch my money, you're dead."

Another whiplash. I could hear Tucker Lee sucking in his breath.

"Both of you dead. You sober enough to understand that, Travis?"

There was a short silence, so Travis Lee must have been quick about nodding. "Your banker friend," Lafontaine continued, "he's a fuckin' hound dog. You know that? You know that, eh, Travis? Cops going to have plenty of suspects."

"Is that true?" said Tucker Lee, an almost springtime lilt suddenly to his voice.

"World always passes you by, eh, Tucker?"

"I knew nothing about—"

"Let the cops solve this murder. New bank manager come in and he be like the old bank manager. Leave it to me. You understand?"

There was a long silence this time. After two minutes had passed, I began to wonder if I had missed the sound of a door opening, the men leaving the room, but there would have been the scraping of chairs on the hardwood floors, the final tinkling of ice in highball glasses. No, the Lee brothers were being stared down like back-alley dogs. Right to their bellies.

"All right, let's go have some drinks with the ladies," I finally heard Lafontaine say. "Hey, Travis, what with that dress your wife wearing. She think it August?"

―――

I STAYED BENEATH the window for another five minutes, giving them time to leave the room and get back to the restaurant. Clouds had moved in and the light on the river was broken now, not as lustrous, ragged patches of light gleaming far out in the darkness. The wind had picked up and there were waves.

When I moved I stayed close to the wall of the hotel. As I rounded the corner, I made sure to keep my head down while rubbing the toe of one boot into the pavement. I pulled up my coat collar at the same time. I probably could have broken into a run and gotten away with that too. All smokers look guilty nowadays. You can behave like a stalker, a nervous terrorist—you name it—but as soon as people see a cigarette, or *think* they see a cigarette, they go, "Ahhhh," and forget about you.

I was still going through all the benefits of pretending to be a smoker when I stepped off the curb in front of the Alexander, looked up, and standing there at the end of the valet-parking lane smoking a cigarette was Travis Lee.

"Tree marker," he yelled in surprise, "what the fuck are you doing here?"

I take chances. Every once in a while, even to me, they seem like stupid chances.

9

TRAVIS LEE WAS doing the introductions, making me sound like a long-lost friend.

"Amanda, this is Danny Barrett," he said, looking at his wife. "The tree marker I told you about, the one outside the Starlight who punched someone out for me? Remember? Lad probably saved my life that night."

Amanda Lee looked at me, and a flicker of interest passed across her eyes. She smiled at her husband and said, "That was the night I had to leave early, wasn't it, darling?"

"Yes, that night."

Amanda Lee's interest grew into a smile. I looked at her and remembered how she had dragged her husband out of the cab that night, stepped over him to get inside, how she had talked the cabbie into going along with it, smiling the whole time. I smiled back.

"Come on, Barrett, join us for a drink," said Lee. "God, I owe you that much at least."

"Don't mind if I do," I said, not bothering to remind him that the debt had already been paid. The maître d' motioned for another chair.

I looked around the table and waited, smiled at the Lee brothers, their wives, Beau Lafontaine and the man who looked a little like him, only bigger.

This was going to need a report.

=====

AFTER I WAS seated, it was Tucker Lee who spoke first, rolling his eyes a few times before saying, "What do you mean, he saved your life, Trav?"

"Some guys were trying to mug me outside the Starlight and Barrett here chased them off. Gave one of them a right-lovely punch to the crown jewels."

"Mug you? In Birmingham? Impossible."

"You go outside much at night anymore, Tuck?"

"Not to the Starlight. Why would I?" And he flashed me a self-satisfied smile. He didn't frequent the same drinking establishments his brother did—probably didn't do much of anything his younger brother did—and he was damn proud of that. I continued to be amazed at the physical shape of the man. Tucker Lee looked to be about as wide as he was tall, looked like he could roll down the aisle of the Grill Room like a beach ball if he gave his chin a tuck and pushed off with his legs at the right angle.

"You work for us?" he continued. "Marking trees, is that what I heard?"

"Yes."

"Where do we have you working?"

"Your Algoma Limits. Up near the border."

"Finding much?"

"You've got old-growth stands up there. Yeah, I'm finding lots."

Tucker Lee smiled. The waiter arrived right then to take another drink order for the table and I ordered a McCallum's neat with Pabst chaser. The waiter crinkled his nose. Travis Lee laughed and slapped me on the back.

"Yeah, you're a tree marker all right. Want to blow this joint off and head to the Starlight?"

"Trav, honey, he *just* ordered a drink," said Amanda Lee, placing her hand atop mine. "At least wait until it arrives."

"Right, right." And Travis Lee looked around the Grill Room. He was half in the bag and getting restless.

"What brings you to the Alexander, Danny?" asked Amanda Lee.

"I was told you could get a good meal here. I'm heading back into the bush tomorrow and I wanted a good supper before I left."

"Well, you've come to the right place."

"Not sure about that. A bit fancier than I was expecting. I may just stay for the drink."

"Stay for several. We've finished supper and are in no hurry. My husband had some dreary business meeting that, thankfully, is finished. Shall I do the introductions?"

"Please."

"You already know Travis. The man who's been grilling you is his brother, Tucker. This is his lovely wife, Velma. And these are my husband's business associates Beau Lafontaine and— I'm sorry. I don't know your name."

The man glared at her, then looked at Lafontaine, as though unsure he should answer the question. Lafontaine gave an almost imperceptible nod of his head and the man said, "Francois Duval."

"There you go. Beau owns Five Star Forestry."

"Mr. Lafontaine, I've heard of you," I said. "You have rights near the Algoma, don't you?" I stood and reached my hand across the table. *Come on, touch my hand. I want to feel your pulse. Feel the blood running through your veins.*

Lafontaine looked at my hand but didn't move. I left it there. I didn't mind making things awkward. Eventually he half stood and grabbed my hand, squeezing it tightly. "Yeah, we have timber rights near the Algoma. Got a bush camp at Paradise Lake. How far that be from where you markin'?"

"Paradise Lake is about a mile from the northern tip of the Algoma. So not far. Your rights run right up to the border, don't they?"

He didn't answer. Let go of my hand slowly and took his time about sitting down. He never took his eyes off me.

"They *do* go all the way to the border," said Tucker Lee, filling in the sudden silence. "Same as our rights go all the way to the border. I don't think the Canadians are hauling much of anything out of those woods these days. They should let us do it."

Tucker Lee laughed and gave his belly a happy pat. It was hard not to stare at him. Usually when people say someone is as wide as they are tall, it's an exaggeration, figurative speech, but with Tucker Lee, it looked damn near true.

Our drinks came and Tucker Lee continued talking, asking me questions about the Algoma, what the company might expect for wastage when it started hauling out the trees, whether it was all old growth or had anyone worked it before? The answers seemed to please him and he had two more Scotches before giving his belly a happy pat and then he said, "Well, it's been a long day. Would you mind getting the truck from the valet, Velma? I think I may have had one too many cocktails."

The small, nervous woman in the high-neck gray dress put down her napkin and rose. She awkwardly said it was nice to have met me, although we hadn't said one word to each other.

"Trav, honey, should we be going as well?"

Amanda Lee smiled at her husband, who almost jumped from his chair when she asked the question. *A place to go.* "Velma, wait up. I'll go with you."

He stumbled away from the table, forgetting to say goodbye to me. Like with all drunks, time was fluid for Travis Lee. The tree marker he had been so effusive about thirty minutes earlier—the one who had probably saved his life—was now a blurred face sitting at a crowded table, no different from any of the blurred faces and crowded tables he had stumbled away from before.

I watched him make his way out of the restaurant, slapping some hands raised to him by other diners, stopping at one table and saying something that made the couple throw back their heads and laugh. Velma waited patiently a few steps ahead of him each time he stopped.

"Francois, you can go outside and wait with them."

The man who had come with Lafontaine nodded and left the table without speaking. I watched him leave. When I turned back, Amanda Lee, Tucker Lee and Beau Lafontaine were staring at me like I was a dinner entrée that had arrived at the wrong table. They seemed to me at that moment like feral beasts, people dressed up and pretending to be something they were not, like those paintings of dogs playing poker or monkeys typing in an office. One day the world needed to invent a machine that would display a person's true nature as easily as other machines displayed bones, an X-ray machine for venality and meanness that would have lit these three up like Day-Glo skeletons swinging from Halloween trees.

"I guess I should be leaving as well," I said. No one objected.

I took my time about getting up and walking past Beau Lafontaine, noticing for the first time that there was an odor to him, something moldy and pungent, which made no sense to me, how something could be stale and strong at the same time. I knew then that Beau Lafontaine was a man who traveled in the company of things you never saw—the odors of a Maine lumber camp, a fourth-generation grudge, a waistband-tucked handgun, a quarter-billion dollars in the North Maine Savings and Loan. It would always be something like that.

10

IT WASN'T UNTIL the next day that Linton finally got to see the crime scene. The FBI investigation into Lee Forestry was a secret to everyone on the Birmingham police force except the chief and two others. An FBI special agent showing up the day of the killing would have exposed the investigation. So the Birmingham police chief kept the crime scene tape up an extra day.

I was on the shuttle bus back to the North Maine Woods when Linton had his walk-through. He had sent me a text after I left the Alexander, demanding to see me the moment I came back from my eight-day rotation. He sent it while I was following Lafontaine's Caddy back to the Birmingham Airport, where his Lear took off at eleven thirty-seven p.m. I drove back to the Three Pines Motel and got five hours' sleep.

It was the chief who gave Linton the walk-through. His name was Hugh Kowalski and he had been the chief for more than fifteen years. I'm sure he still is. It was Kowalski who told me later what happened that day.

"The shooter would have been in that parking garage, third level," he told Linton, pointing to a parking garage directly across the street from the bank. "Through-and-through head shot. People heard only one shot and we found only one fragment. We've sent it to your forensics lab in Boston, but I'll tell you right now it was a .260 caliber Remington."

"Pretty common hunting round."

"Maybe the most common in America."

"The distance?"

"Forty yards."

"Sight lines?"

"Elevated position, no obstructions of any kind, it would have been a perfect sight line. It's where you would have built a deer stand."

Linton stared down the street. He was surprised no one had objected to it being shut for two days. "I bet half the men in Birmingham own what could be your murder weapon, and all of them could make that shot," he said, and Kowalski nodded. The chief figured it would have been more than half. Not just the men.

"What about the cameras?" asked Linton.

"No cameras."

He turned on the chief in surprise. "What do you mean, *no cameras*? How the fuck can you not have cameras on a street with a parking garage *and* a fuckin' bank?"

"Billy Granger—he owns the garage—Billy says he's never had a problem and he doesn't spend money on things that aren't a problem. Bank has plenty of cameras inside, but only one outside. It's focused on the front door and Mr. Powell was shot twenty yards to the left of that door. Camera caught a bunch of people running by after the shooting. That's it."

"Nothing has turned up on your canvass?"

"Nothing yet. Shooter had a darn good position. That half wall in the garage is four feet, so it would have been easy to hunker down behind until it was time to make the shot. There were no cars parked on the third floor when we got there. It's possible no one ever saw the shooter."

"How thorough was your canvass?"

"Thorough," said Kowalski. He sounded annoyed but he didn't mind sounding annoyed. He didn't like secret investigations being run out of his police detachment and he didn't like Paul Linton. "If this murder has something to do with your investigation, I should be told about it, Special Agent."

"All in due course, Chief."

"Don't know if that's a good answer."

"Excuse me?"

"If I'm going to be assigning men to work this case, I need to know what's going on. I'm not going to waste my detectives' time."

"You can treat this as a normal murder investigation, Chief," snapped Linton. "When the FBI has information relevant to your investigation, you'll be informed, although it looks to me like your men can't even protect a crime scene. Who the fuck is that guy?"

Kowalski looked to where Linton was pointing. A man in a rumpled mauve suit and two-tone shoes was staring at the dried blood pool in front of the bank. He had bedraggled hair and bluish facial stubble, and he looked like he had slept in his clothes after getting drunk the night before at a party that encouraged the wearing of mauve suits and two-tone shoes.

"Where the fuck would a dandy like that come from?" snorted Linton. "You got some queer joints in Birmingham I don't know about?"

"I've never seen him before."

"Well, are you going to get rid of him?"

Kowalski opened his mouth to say something but then thought better of it. He approached the man, who was far enough away that Linton couldn't hear them speak. Just see the man in the rumpled suit ignore the chief for a few seconds, then look up from the dried blood, take out his wallet and hand Kowalski a business card.

They talked for a few minutes and then Kowalski came walking back. "He wants to see you," he said to Linton, handing him the card. It was an FBI card. "He's checked into the Alexander Hotel," Kowalski continued. "You can ask for him by name. He wants you to bring along anyone who's reporting to you."

"That fuckin' guy wants . . ." And then Linton read the name on the card and stopped talking. To Kowalski it looked like his hand started shaking at the same time.

"I've heard of Jim Flanagan," the chief said pleasantly. "Is he your boss?"

"When does he want to see me?"

"I believe 'right fuckin' now' were the words he used." It was too much for Kowalski. He finally laughed.

11

THE MAINE SKY was turning black to cobalt. It would be another
hour before dawn came and the sun cleared the trees. Most of the men
on the shuttle bus were trying to sleep. There were snores and grunts,
and every once in a while a swear word, English or French, after someone had been elbowed or kicked. There was never enough room on the
shuttle buses. Many, like this one, were converted school buses.

Because the Three Pines Motel was the first stop on the driver's
route, I had the back bench. I probably could have had that, anyway, as
tree markers are treated like goalies on a hockey team or prima balle-
rinas in a touring company—talented, temperamental and absolutely
essential to the success of the venture. Tree markers tend to get what
they want.

They're hard to find too, which was why it was easy for me to get
hired, the woman in the Lee human resources office holding my fake
résumé two days after one of their tree markers had been arrested for
cocaine possession, telling me it was a miracle, me walking through her
door that morning, *that very morning*—a miracle.

I stretched out and looked at the predawn sky. That's the problem with miracles. I don't believe there are any. You just don't know the backstory.

There was a backstory to the murder of Robert Powell. I just needed to find it. Beau Lafontaine was the obvious suspect for the killing, but there were problems with that. According to those Canadian police reports, it was rare for Lafontaine to leave the North Maine Woods, which was the reason those Hells Angels came to him. But if he had killed the banker, that meant he came to Birmingham not once, but twice, on back-to-back nights.

Or he hired someone. But there was nothing in those police reports about the Malee contracting out to anyone, and Lafontaine didn't strike me as the sort of man who would object to doing his own work. More likely, he would insist upon it. I watched the sky, waiting for the thin red line that would soon appear above the trees on the east shore of the St. John River, signifying the day had begun.

The land got rockier the farther north we traveled. By midmorning we were crossing onto the Cambrian shield, with its glacier-dug valleys and its stunted hills, the needles of the white pine glistening in the sun like shards of light. There was snow showing on top of the hills, and there would be more, deep in the bush, where the sun couldn't get through easily. Everywhere else the snow had turned to mud.

We passed the last town shortly before noon, a place called Evange-line, which had about a dozen houses and a gas station where the bus refueled. The houses were split rail or cedar shake, the cedar showing its age, a sickly smoker's-lung yellow, trails of smoke coming from tin-pipe chimneys. After that, we were in the North Maine Woods. Evan-geline was more than an hour behind us by then, so crossing into the Woods didn't register as anything significant or even noticeable; but as soon as we crossed over, we had entered the largest unsettled swath of land remaining in the contiguous United States.

The North Maine Woods were all timber rights: land leased by for-estry companies to harvest trees. It was unsettled land fought over by the Americans and the Canadians for decades in a nasty little border skirmish called the Aroostook War, which no one outside Maine, New Brunswick or Quebec ever knew about. The Americans finally won the dispute in 1842 when the international border was set slightly to the north, awarding the Americans more trees and an uninhabited island in the St. John River. An absurd secret war that seemed appropriate for the North Maine Woods.

For the last twenty miles of the journey, the shuttle bus veered away from the St. John River, driving through a dense forest until it reached the Lee bush camp at Petersen's Gorge. It was shortly past three and I had my kit and ATV checked out within the hour.

"You're not staying for supper? It's less'n an hour," said the shipping clerk as I was signing the paperwork.

"I want to get back into the Woods as fast as I can. Been in the city too long."

"You've been there four days."

"Exactly."

The clerk chuckled and shook his head. Tree markers. He hadn't met one of them that made any sense.

I left camp and made my way up the shoreline of the St. Croix River, a tributary of the St. John. I didn't stop for four hours, other than to switch around some gas cans. I made camp in an old-growth forest on the banks of the river, about two miles from Paradise Lake.

I looked at the sky as I unrolled my sleeping bag. It had a thick bed of clouds and what was left of the day's sun shone behind them intermittently, like sheet lightning in the Caribbean, some distant opaque light. I ate a supper of dry rations and prepared my kit. *It's a perfect night.*

———

SHORTLY BEFORE MIDNIGHT I forded the river and started a half jog, running past moss-covered boulders the size of small cars and trees so wide and tall, they looked like unlit buildings. I wore a black balaclava and a black tracksuit, carried a black day pack. Anyone in the forest that night would have seen me as a shadow moving between boulder and pine.

The Maine Department of Natural Resources had a satellite-photo archive on the North Maine Woods, but it had revealed almost nothing about Paradise Lake. The photos showed one logging road leading into the camp, the road dead-ending at the shoreline of the lake. There were some buildings along the road that could have been anything. A fenced perimeter that would have been unusual for a lumber camp. Nothing else.

I had a bearing on the northeast corner of the fence, and when I reached it, I stopped to catch my breath, told myself I wasn't being as big a fool as I thought I was—about to enter a secure camp with not so much as five minutes of recognizance on the perimeter. I didn't know if there were patrols. Didn't know if there were trip wires.

What I was about to do was crazy, stupid. About as crazy, stupid as shooting bankers on the streets of Birmingham, Maine, I told myself, which was the problem with my job some days. You had no choice but to be as stupid and reckless as the people you were chasing.

I took a riflescope from my pack and glassed the fence. It wasn't electrified. That was good luck. The barbed wire on top was only one strand high, so that was a bit more. I was still scanning the barbed wire when lucky break number three came walking toward me.

The patrol came from the direction of the logging road: two men carrying automatic rifles, walking beside the fence, and it wasn't long before I could hear them speaking French and having an argument. I don't speak much French, but when I heard the word "Canadiens" a few times, I knew it was a hockey argument.

I watched the men pass beneath a pool of light cast by some halcyon flood lamps mounted atop the fence. The first circle of light was fifty feet to the east of my position. They passed through that and then in a minute another circle fifty feet farther on, smaller now, their voices distant. I was up and over the fence before they strolled through the third circle of light.

12

I MADE MY way toward a campfire, slithering on the ground the way a fisher had done it a few minutes earlier: fast and low, passing me before I knew it was even there. I found a tall white pine just outside the arc of the campfire's light and stopped there.

When I peered around the tree I saw there was a picnic table near the fire, with men sitting and playing a game. It was a knife-throwing game, using what looked like homemade knives with bone handles and blades that must have been a foot long. There was a tree they used for the game and they'd bet on it, men slapping money down on the picnic table, then chanting and roaring when a knife was thrown. They played with dice as well, increasing the bet somehow.

As I watched the game, three men came walking down the logging road. They walked to the picnic table but didn't sit down. One started rubbing his back against a tree. The other two paced around the table, never stopped talking, their faces so white, they glowed like kerosene lanterns. *Bad meth heads. Buzzing like fireflies.*

I watched as a man sitting at the table stood up, grabbed one of the meth heads by his shirt collar and walked him to the tree. The meth head was laughing. He carried a can of beer. He was shoved against the tree and stayed there. There was a big roar from the table when that happened and money came out. A bearded man about as wide as the grill of a Mack truck got up from the table, stumbled to where the line must have been for the game—because the knives had all been thrown from that spot—leaned one big arm behind him, metal glinting in the darkness, and threw a knife toward the tree.

It landed chest high, about four inches to the left of the meth head. There was another roar from the table and the big man held up both hands, as though in victory. It didn't look like the meth head ever knew what happened. When he stumbled away from the tree, he dropped his beer can and then he fell to his knees, frantically searching for it. There was another round of laughter from the table.

How could you play a game like that without killing a man every once in a while? I wondered. A few seconds later, the answer came to me. *You couldn't.*

<hr>

I SPENT THE next four hours moving through the Paradise Lake bush camp, looking for Beau Lafontaine. It didn't take long to figure out where his money was coming from. The Malee had moved into the contraband end of the smuggling game, no longer handling just the transportation and logistics. I counted three meth labs, the pungent chemical smell of baked ephedrine impossible to hide, even in the middle of nowhere. There was another tin shed that was a different kind of lab; it had a different scent, ecstasy maybe, or fentanyl. Maybe knock-off Oxy.

And that logging road? It was *busy* from midnight to five a.m. I counted fourteen trucks, coming in and leaving an hour or so later.

It was nearing dawn when I made the shore of Paradise Lake. I had vowed to stay until I'd found Beau Lafontaine's hidey-hole, but I hadn't found it and I didn't want to be running through the forest on the wrong side of the Maurice River when the sun came up. I had time to inspect one last building.

It was an odd-shaped building in front of me. It wasn't a warehouse, wasn't a lab, wasn't a maintenance garage or a cookhouse, wasn't a bunkhouse either, as I had found those on the north end of the camp, three of them: the two-floor wooden bunkhouses you found in all lumber camps.

This was a large one-floor building, about twenty feet wide and more than a hundred feet in length, looked like a half dozen double-wide trailers shoved end to end, with camouflage netting draped over the roof. There looked to be only two entrances, at either end of the building.

I was lying by the shore, looking at the south-facing door, the pre-dawn light strengthening and becoming firm color around me, no longer diffused shadows. I reached for the riflescope inside my pack and wondered if I had time for even this one last inspection when the door flew open and Beau Lafontaine strode outside.

━━━

I STOPPED REACHING for my riflescope. Stopped breathing at the same time. Lafontaine stood no more than twenty feet away, smoking a cigarette. He stared at the rising mist and swirling shadows atop the water, then flicked away his cigarette and walked toward the lake. When he did that, three other men came out of the building.

Two of the men had a third man pinned by the arms and they were frog-marching him to the lake, the man's feet barely touching the ground. He kept his feet moving, as though he might be able to gain traction and break free, but it never happened. His legs flailed and spun like the pedals of a bike after a crash.

He was taken to the shoreline of the lake, to a large flat rock that had water lapping over the edge, the kind of rock you would look for when you had a lot of fish to clean. When the men were on the rock, Lafontaine went and joined them.

"You remind me of a man who used to work here," he said when he was standing next to the man, his voice carrying easily over the open water. "He was a retired army colonel. It was a mistake to have hired him, to have trusted him. Like you, Rene."

"Beau, you have to listen to me," said the man with his arms pinned. "You *have to* listen. This is getting way out of—"

"Why must I listen to you, Rene?"

The man looked at Lafontaine in surprise. "You . . . have to listen. . . . I didn't fuckin' do this. I swear to fuckin' God, Beau. . . ."

"That's why I must listen, Rene? Because you are swearing to God?"

"I . . . don't understand."

"You stand like this before me, yet you think *I* must listen to *you*? That is your problem, Rene. You have never understood power. Only craved it."

"Beau, for fuck's sake, what is going *on here*?"

"I'm trying to tell you a story of a man who reminds me of you. Do you wish to hear the story?"

"Beau, for God's sake . . . *for God's sake.*"

"I'll tell you the story. I think you need to hear it. I believe there are ancient creatures in these woods, Rene, spirits that have been around longer than the Malee, longer than any of us. They are the creatures Champlain wrote about. I brought this colonel to Paradise Lake because I was made to believe he could teach me the ancient ways, teach me how to summon these creatures and have them fight beside me. So the colonel came and he taught me about old generals like Sun Tzu. How I should keep my friends close but my enemies closer. That if I sit by a river long enough, I will see the bodies of my enemies floating by.

"After three months I told the colonel I did not want any more lessons, but as I had hired him for a year and given him a great deal of money, I thought it best if he spent the winter working in one of my bush camps. To settle our account. The colonel objected but I told him I would feel cheated if this did not happen.

"So he went to the camp, where he died a few months later in the spring runoff, trying to gaff a log that had already passed him. He was a poor bushman, as he had been a poor teacher. His greatest skill was making stupid things sound smart. Keep your enemies *close*? Why the fuck should I *ever* do that? I don't want my enemies on the *same fuckin' planet*."

"Beau . . . come here. . . . Please, *please* come back here. . . ."

But Beau Lafontaine had left the rock and gone back inside the building. He was gone less than a minute, and when he reappeared, he was holding something in his right hand, something long and heavy, but it was still too dark for me to make out what it was. Even so my stomach muscles tightened as I watched him step back onto the rock.

"I could sit by the banks of a river and wait for you to drift by, Rene, but who the fuck has time for that, eh?"

Lafontaine jerked his left hand and an engine started. I watched as the man who had been pleading for his life was forced to his knees, moaning and sobbing now, trying to talk but language had left him. He had nothing left but moans, disconnected syllables and some pitiful, animal-like beseeching sounds. Lafontaine raised the chain saw and I told myself to keep my eyes open.

You need to see this.

The man's scream was a guttural sound that came from deep inside him, a scream pulled from some nascent hiding place. He screamed once and never made another sound. Unconscious almost from the start. *A small mercy,* I thought as I watched Lafontaine raise and lower the chain saw, the other two men on the rock throwing body parts into the lake. A small mercy indeed.

THE SWEET GOODBYE

SHE THOUGHT OF the times she had seen him like this before. They had been together many years and this was not the first time she had seen him scared, uncertain, trying to get rid of the fear and doubt in a time-honored way—around Birmingham, anyway, time-honored. Lot of people didn't know any other way.

The carpeting at her feet was wet and the smell of alcohol was so strong, she had to open a window when she got in his car. There was a pint of Scotch in the glove compartment and he had tried to pour a drink while driving. She didn't need to open the glove compartment. Didn't need to see the bottle.

"You going into work much these days?" she asked.

"No."

"Shouldn't you? Keep up appearances and all that?"

Ten days had passed since the killing of Robert Powell. She had not seen him since their afternoon at the St. John Motel.

"It'd be more surprising if I showed up," he said. "I thought you knew that."

"I never heard back from Beau. Your meeting went all right?"

"I suppose."

"What did he want to tell you?"

"Stay the course. I believe that was the core message."

He laughed after he said that and she was glad to hear it. The murder of Robert Powell was not a laughing matter, no way you could call it that, but it showed he wasn't a deer in headlights, hadn't frozen, was capable of more than fear and panic. Maybe.

Other times when she'd seen him like this, he hadn't been capable of much more than deer imitations. That time he came to see her at the Red Bird, seven years after she'd talked to him last, after he'd gone and married Amanda Singer—he was like that. Same for '08, when he came with Tucker and asked for a meeting with Beau, telling her Lee Forestry was about to go bankrupt and thousands of men were about to lose their jobs.

"We're going to lose it all," he'd said, the amazement in his voice no different from a small child learning the truth about Santa Claus.

And then there was Boston. The first time she'd seen him free-falling. A rat-fuck story that maybe was still being played out. Sitting in his car in the parking lot of the Red Bird, talking about the death of Robert Powell, thinking about next steps, she wondered if this was all just a continuation of Boston.

———

WHEN HE GRADUATED from Harvard and returned to Birmingham, he came looking for her. Just the way he said he would when he'd dropped her off at the end of her laneway that first night. She saw him as soon as he walked into the diner, standing just inside the door, flashing her a shy smile and mouthing the words, Where's your section?

She blushed and tilted her head to where he needed to go. As she went to take his order, the other waitresses gave her a puzzled look.

"How you been?" he asked.

"Been good. Didn't think I'd be seeing you again."

"I told you I'd come."

"Yeah, well, people say a lot of things."

"Ain't that the truth? What time do you get off?"

"Five."

"Want to go somewhere tonight?"

"Sure. Would you like to know what the specials are first?"

"No."

He got up and left the diner. She stood there with the menu in her hand, watching him through the front windows of the diner as he walked toward his car.

That was for me?

———

WHEN HE PICKED *her up that afternoon, he had a suitcase in the back-seat, next to a case of Pabst and two liquor-store brown bags.*

"Go for a ride, girl?"

"Just got in, didn't I?"

"Thought we'd go on a road trip. Ever been to Boston?"

"That's where you want to go tonight? I was thinking the Tudor or something."

"No, Boston. Want to go?"

"Fuck yeah."

She didn't need to check in with anyone. Her father was gone; her brothers were gone; she'd never known her mother. She was thinking of asking a girlfriend to come and live with her to share the expenses, but there wasn't that much in the way of expenses, and the farmhouse was in Bustard County, convenient to nothing, so she hadn't asked anyone yet.

As they set out that evening, she couldn't remember if he knew that. Couldn't remember much of what was said that one night they'd spent together. Crazy to say yes to a road trip after one drunken night, but he said he'd come back and here he was. Crazy to say yes, but saying no struck her as a kind of meanness.

He was in a reckless mood. She knew that from the start, and she en-

couraged it. On the way to Bangor, he got two speeding tickets, which he tore up as soon as the state cops were in his rearview mirror. They had sex in his car, and at a public washroom, and in Bangor on a campground picnic table while a family roasted marshmallows at the site next to them.

The risks became greater and more addictive. At a Texaco station near Portland, just before they were going to go on the coastal highway for the final run into Boston, she asked if she could pay for the gas. Give her the money and she'd go pay.

"Why?"

"Just 'cause. You got a twenty?"

"Sure."

"Give it to me. Stay in the car. I'll be right back."

It was a trick her older brother had shown her, the year before he went to Portland and tried to rob an armored car. That trick left her brother dead in front of a Target store. He should have stayed with the twenties.

She was in the gas station about five minutes, and when she got back in the car, she handed him his change. He counted it.

"There's twenty-nine dollars here."

"I know."

"How in the world . . . ?"

"Hon, you should probably be driving right now."

They pulled into a rest stop ten miles down the road, parked between two RVs, and she crawled on top of him while hiking up her dress. He was harder than a piston. When they were finished, she looked out the rear window and two teenage boys were staring at them, their mouths agape. He honked his horn at the boys as they drove away.

She explained to him how the twenties grift worked, how it helped if you were a good-looking girl, but it wasn't necessary. She had a male cousin, a bad meth head, who practically survived on the twenties grift.

"You just got to talk quick and keep the bills moving. Have some coins in your pocket. That always helps. Nobody understands math anymore."

They crossed the Charles River and entered Boston, should have gotten a room at the Four Seasons right away—that had been the plan—but it was *nine o'clock on a Saturday night and checking into a hotel room didn't seem like as much fun as finding a nightclub.*

Plus, the grift was working and the night was young. Hard to stop a grift when it's working. Ask any grifter.

THE BAR WAS *a few blocks from Boston Common, an Irish joint with shamrocks on the window and a house band that sounded like Thin Lizzy. All bar bands in Boston sounded like Thin Lizzy back then.*

He tipped the bartender heavily when their first drink came, then ran a tab. The bar was busy and loud and they were having fun, but they didn't want to stay too long. She had told him a place like this, on a Saturday night, was perfect for running the twenties grift. They were going to see how much money they could raise by hitting a few places and what sort of midnight dinner that was going to get them.

She watched the bartender while he worked, a big man with a full-sleeve tattoo, one of the first she'd seen; watched how he mixed drinks and gave out change, almost no credit cards in that bar, cash-and-carry, a busy bar and he had the till open more often than he had it closed.

"So what do you think, girl, time for us to split?"

"I'd say so." She leaned across his barstool and gave him a good, long kiss before whispering in his ear, "Want to try something new?"

A stupid question. Of course he wanted to try something new.

He went to pay the bar tab and she slid up beside him, the bartender looking at her from head to toe, making no secret of it, then a lecherous smile that might have gotten him a punch in the face from someone who didn't look like a Harvard graduate. The bartender had worked in Boston a long time and knew what sort of smiles he could get away with.

"Ten fifty," he said, finally taking his eyes off her. The bartender took the twenty-dollar bill Travis offered him and opened the till, counted out nine fifty, was placing it on the bar when Travis said, "There they are. I thought I had some smaller bills. Hey, buddy, give me back the twenty. I'll pay you with this. Did you say ten fifty?"

Some coins and small bills were slid across the bar. The bartender gave back the twenty. Some other bills were put on the bar, then some coins; it went back and forth like that, the till open. She made her move when the bartender's back was turned, about to hand over a second twenty, wondering for a second if that was right, holding the fifty cents, which meant ten dollars change. Yeah, that's right.

"You should give him five as a tip, hon. He was a good bartender." She was standing beside him again, smiling at the bartender in a way that she hoped would have him thinking about that smile and what it meant. For a minute or two, anyway. That's all they needed.

The bartender beamed and took the five. That was a good tip back then. In that bar, it probably still was. The bartender waved at them as they turned and headed toward the door.

She thought it had been a good smile. Thought she'd been quick enough. No way of knowing what went wrong. Almost at the door when they heard: "Hey, you two, get the fuck back here!"

They ran. Out the bar and down a side alley, a doorman chasing them, a middle-aged guy in a black T-shirt, built like a weight lifter.

"You try to steal from us, you frat-fuckin' shitheads. Get back here!" he roared as he chased them down the alley.

They knocked over garbage cans and banana crates to try to slow him, but it didn't work. He was already gaining on them when the alley ended in a wooden fence. Travis cradled his hands and boosted her over. She fell into a pile of busted glass, cutting her hands so badly, blood flew around when she waved them at him. "Come on, hon, up and over!"

But he didn't make it. He was straddling the fence, one leg over but the other in the arms of the doorman, whose head was just visible above the fence.

"Kick him, kick him!" she yelled, but it already looked too late. The doorman was starting to climb the fence, reaching a hand up to grab his chest, about to pull him down and stomp him in that alley. No cops were ever going to be called. She started screaming.

And then the strangest thing. It seemed to happen in slow motion right in front of her, as though she had the best seat in a theater. His leg, the one that had been pinned, came free when the doorman tried to grab his shirt. He kicked him as hard as he could.

The sole of his shoe landed square in the doorman's face. The man's head snapped back and then he fell. He didn't make a sound when he landed. No curse. No scream. A thud that wasn't even as loud as it should have been.

Travis stared at the doorman before jumping off the fence. At the way the arms and legs were splayed, at the dark liquid pooling around the head, nothing about the scene looking right or natural.

"Hon, you gotta jump now!"

He jumped and they ran, both of them badly cut now, blood splattering against the redbrick buildings in the alley. They got to his car and he fish-tailed down Charles Street, Pearl hitting him on the arm, telling him to slow down. They were only a few blocks from the interstate.

They never made it to the Four Seasons. They drove all night, stopping at truck stops to rip out every paper towel in the washrooms, wrapping it around their hands to stanch the bleeding. Bought iodine and peroxide at a Walgreens in Portland. She made a joke when he was cleaning his hands, said maybe he should put peroxide in his hair as well.

He didn't laugh. Didn't talk or do much of anything during the drive back to Birmingham. The car seemed stifling from the heat and weight of unfamiliar emotions, both of them looking at the world a little differently now and not caring for it much.

"Do you think I killed him?" he said near the end of the trip.

"I don't know, hon. Fence wasn't that big. Fall from a fence like that shouldn't kill a man."

"He fell funny. And I kicked him good before he fell. I saw his head snap back."

"It was a good kick."

He looked at her strangely and she wished she hadn't said that. They crossed Frenchman Bay as the sun was coming up, their brains racing, their stomachs turning, feeling about as bad as either of them had felt before, her first dry hangover, and when he dropped her off at her farmhouse, he didn't ask when he could see her next.

Two days later she read a story in the Boston Herald about a doorman recovering at the hospital and an ongoing police search for "two lowlifes that robbed O'Casey's Tavern on Saturday night." The composite sketches of them looked ridiculous. She put down the newspaper and started breathing normally again.

A month later he proposed to Amanda Singer.

—————

NOT SINCE THAT ride back from Boston had she seen him look this scared. It needed to be different this time. She reached both her hands out, grabbed him on each cheek and pulled his head toward her.

"Hon, listen to me for a minute. There's stuff I should have told you when we were driving back from Boston, stuff that would have helped you, and I've regretted for a long time not telling you that stuff. So listen to me—you didn't kill Bobby Powell."

A few beats went by and she squeezed his face tighter. "You also got to know that Bobby Powell was no friend of yours. Just like that doorman was no friend. That guy was going to stomp you stupid in that alley, hon. I could have lost you right then. That banker, I don't see him any different from that doorman. He was going to rat you out, hon. Bobby Powell being gone—that's not a bad thing. You gotta see that."

They stayed posed like that a long time, staring into each other's eyes until it felt awkward and then she took her hands away. His mood had changed though. "Ahhh, you're right," he said. "Feel like going to the Alexander for the night?"

"I got to be back at the Red Bird for five in the morning, hon."

"What if I kept you up all night? Would that solve the problem?"

"I've got no clothes with me."

"What if I took you shopping?"

"What if I was hungrier than I've been in a month?"

"What if we ordered room service?"

"Hon?"

"Yeah?"

"Why are we still in this parking lot?"

13

I STARED AT the man sitting behind the hotel room desk. He wore a short-sleeved shirt with wide brown and white stripes, the sort of shirt a doorman working a nightclub in South Boston might wear, except the man in front of me was half the size of any decent doorman. And he was older. You could tell that by the backs of his hands, although his hair was jet-black and he moved around in his chair like a fidgety child.

Linton had phoned me when I got off the shuttle bus and told me to go to the Alexander Hotel, room 1403. He hung up right afterward. Made no mention of my unauthorized contact with the Lees and Beau Lafontaine before I had left for the North Maine Woods eight days ago.

I suspected what had happened before the man behind the desk had answered the knock on the door. He waved me into the room, motioned for me to sit and didn't say a word. The silence lasted so long, I began to think it was a test, although I didn't know what was being tested and what the right response would have been.

Eventually the man said, "I'm Supervisory Special Agent Jim Flanagan with the Boston field office of the FBI. The investigation you have been seconded to crosses my desk. Since you've been away, I have replaced Special Agent Linton as operational commander."

"He just phoned me."

"He's still part of this investigation. Play nice."

"He didn't protect the banker."

"No comment. You report to me from now on. Now tell me about this shithole you just came back from."

"Paradise Lake?"

"You been to more than one shithole?" And Flanagan swiveled his chair to look out the window of his hotel room. He could see the remains of the Davidson-Struthers Footwear factory. "Maybe you're counting this shithole? You're from Detroit, right? What do you think of this place?"

"It's a place."

"That's a right ringin' endorsement. I hate all these shitholes. I was an FBI field agent in Boston for fifteen years and never went farther than twenty miles from the Charles River. Not once. Not till the fuckin' trolls got so much cocaine money, they couldn't keep it all in Boston, couldn't keep it all in New York City. Had to disperse it all over the fuckin' country. You know where I went, the first money-laundering case I worked that took me out of Boston? Sugar Hill, fuckin' New Hampshire. First time I was ever on a gravel road. You believe that?"

"No."

"You're right. But it's more true than you think. You know what brought me to New Hampshire, where the trolls were cleaning their money? A drive-in fuckin' movie theater. Man, I feel old when I tell this story. When I arrested the woman who owned the theater, I asked her why she did it. She told me the theater was going to go under when a guy with some investment money showed up, a guy who knew a thing or two about movie projectors. God works in mysterious ways. She actually said that."

A look of disgust passed across his face. "It's amazing how blind people can make themselves when they're offered troll money. Five years before I arrested this dame, she was in the news because she wouldn't show *Dirty Dancing* at her drive-in. She called it pornography. That dame was fucked up in too many ways to count."

He was laughing and slapping his knee now, looked like he was just getting warmed up. I wondered how far Jim Flanagan could spin a story when he had a few highballs in him. I figured it would be dizzying. Like watching the Flying Wallendas.

I'd heard of Jim Flanagan. I'd been told he had had the record for most racketeering indictments by an agent in the Boston FBI office. He'd brought down Nickie D'Pitrio, and a few years after that, he'd arrested Paddy Busby, the man many said was the real reason Whitey Bulger hightailed it out of Boston. Flanagan worked as special consultant to a film director who made an Oscar-nominated movie about the Busby case, and he married an actress he met on the set. I'd read about that in the *National Enquirer*.

I'd also been told Flanagan probably had more reprimands in his file than any other agent in the Boston field office. He'd once been charged by the New York City Police Department with felony public endangerment after one of his investigations blew up in a spectacular and bloody way on the streets of Manhattan. When he was promoted to supervisor, the Senior Officers Association of the FBI filed a grievance, arguing Flanagan was a poster boy for everything the bureau wanted to change about its in-house culture. When he was given a chance to respond in writing to the grievance, Flanagan handed the association lawyer a piece of paper with two words on it—*Blow me.*

That's what I'd heard, anyway.

———

"SO TELL ME about this Paradise Lake lumber camp."

I gave Flanagan my report. Starting with the reconnaissance of the camp. "They're manufacturing a lot of meth—ecstasy, it looks like too—and they're growing pot. I don't know how much but there must be fields up there." I told him about the truck traffic and the three bunkhouses and the knife-throwing game, told him about Beau Lafontaine with a chain saw in his hand, standing by the shore of Paradise Lake on a big flat rock that would have been a good place for cleaning fish.

"Fuck," Flanagan said when I had finished my report. "It sounds like the old Five Points in New York City. Two hundred fuckin' years ago."

"Sounds about right."

"The Malee. You ever hear of these fuckin' trolls before?"

"No, but the Upper Peninsula in Michigan had people just like them. They're family clans more than anything."

"And you saw Beau Lafontaine kill someone? In his camp?"

"Yes."

"That might be enough to get us in. What's it going to be like dragging that bastard out of there?"

"It won't be easy. It's wild country up there, so I think you're looking at an air incursion. Only one road into the camp, and you need to be driving a logging truck or a tank to get down it. Every river I've seen would have class three rapids or better. It's old glacier country, boulders all over the place, these crazy gorges and chutes. There's no flatland, no farms, no towns, no place for a staging area."

"Sounds like the dark side of the moon."

"Close. Northern Maine."

"The fishing must be good."

"Fishing is good."

"I hate fuckin' fishing. Got anything else?"

"I'd like to bring a camera in with me next time. I'll need authorization for that."

"You're not going to get it. Your testimony goes into the court record these days as no different from an expert witness. Did you know that? According to your file, defense counsel in your last three trials hasn't even tried to get you excluded. What you've seen and heard will be enough. You don't need to risk a camera."

"I disagree."

Flanagan jumped in his chair. A real jump. Like he'd sat on a nail. "What the fuck do you mean, you disagree? I just said you don't need a camera. A camera would kill you if the wrong people found it."

"The people who will be planning the raid on Paradise Lake—I think it's important they see what's waiting for them. Not a description of it. Actually see it."

"You don't think they've seen shit like this before?"

"I don't."

Flanagan stopped talking. Gave me a long look. "Well, look at you—a right fuckin' cowboy, aren't you? Nice to meet you, son."

"Does that mean I get a camera?"

"I'll get you a camera."

"Thank you. Is there anything else you need? I'll be filing my report tomorrow." I smiled after I said it.

Flanagan looked at me a few seconds before smiling back. "A *smart* fuckin' cowboy. You think I could get all this information from your report?"

"If you wanted to read it, yes."

"All right, want to talk about why you're here?"

"Anytime you're ready."

14

FLANAGAN GOT UP from the desk and headed to the minibar. "Want a drink?"

"I'll have a Coke."

"I'm having a beer."

"I'll have a Pabst, then, if you have it."

"Had Miller. Already gone. Just foreign shit now."

"Whatever you got."

"Mind if I ask you a question before we get started, nothing to do with this case. I read your file last night and I was wondering . . ."

"I said it."

Flanagan handed me a Corona. "You've been asked about it before. Shouldn't surprise me. Stone-cold beautiful police work, Barrett."

It was my third undercover assignment. The one that kicked me into the big leagues. I was helping the DEA with a Bandidos clubhouse outside Flagstaff, the chapter president a homicidal beast who thought Blackbeard was being soft when he randomly killed members of his pirate crew a few times a year to keep the others loyal and alert.

Vladine Guerrera preferred once a month for that sort of team-building exercise. I not only infiltrated the clubhouse but became Guerrera's friend, was standing beside him when the raid went down and, just as the biker was expecting me to draw my weapon and fight beside him, I put the muzzle to his head and said, "We've never been properly introduced."

In every case I've worked since, someone has asked me about it. I can tell not everyone believes it. But that's what I said and it was in a court transcript somewhere for the hard-core disbelievers.

"This is the abridged version of the situational report I'll be filing later today," said Flanagan. "The most current assessment of where this investigation stands, using all relevant intel, known facts and working theories—we're fucked."

"Death of the banker causing a few problems?"

"Yeah, a few fucking problems," said Flanagan. "That cat was so stupid, he was buying boats with money that he hadn't even cleaned proper, that he'd skimmed right off the top. All Linton had to do was sit him down, tell him how the people who owned that money would feel about initiative projects like that, and we had him. We'll never find another banker that stupid."

"What did you have before he was killed?"

"We have the Lee brothers on all sorts of financial irregularities that could add up to mail fraud. It's a debate between lawyers whether we have them for racketeering or criminal conspiracy. We don't have Beau Lafontaine on anything right now, but the investigation into him has just started. Your report is going to have a lot of lawyers debating if it's enough to charge him with murder."

"We don't know who was killed."

"Which is why the lawyers arguing for Lafontaine's arrest will lose the debate. We're close to having something here, Barrett, something big with some serious pen time for some serious fuckin' trolls. Could end up being one of the biggest racketeering cases in New England, outside of Boston."

"What about the murder of the banker?"

"It had to be Lafontaine, right? Day after the banker makes his threat, he gets killed. But the timing doesn't sit right with me."

"Lafontaine coming to Birmingham on back-to-back nights?"

"You see it too. Why not do it all in one night?"

"Maybe he hired someone to do the killing? Or sent someone?"

"You've read his file, right? The one the Sûreté sent us? Was there a single note in there about Beau Lafontaine hiring anyone to do anything? That cat is as old-school as the trunk of a '59 Caddy. He would do his own work."

"You think the Lees could have done it?"

"Why not? They have the same motivation as Lafontaine. And both brothers were in Birmingham the day of the murder. The facts don't rule them out."

"Have you interviewed them?"

"No. This investigation is still a secret, remember? How do we ask the Lees questions about Lafontaine, or their bank accounts, without tipping our hand?"

I didn't say anything, although I understood finally why I had been summoned to meet Jim Flanagan, why he couldn't wait for my report. Flanagan seemed to sense I had figured it out, was smiling at me when he said, "Those drinks you had with Travis Lee—how well did you get along with the guy?"

———

I WENT TO my motel room and unpacked my duffel bag. Made a pile of dirty clothes, put them in a plastic bag and left them at the door. Had a shower and changed into a new pair of jeans, a Detroit Lions T-shirt with Barry Sanders's number on it, lay in bed and watched an NCAA hockey game, wondering what Flanagan would arrange for my accidental meeting with Travis Lee.

Some operational commanders came up with meet schemes so elaborate, they scared me. So many moving parts, so much precision timing, I'd lose track of how many ways it could go wrong. Others came up with schemes so simple, they relied on little more than absurd coincidence, and I was scared for different reasons. I figured Flanagan for a smash-and-grab coincidence guy, but you never knew. I fell asleep watching the hockey game, still wondering about it.

It took longer than I was expecting. I slept late, went for a run down the service alleys surrounding the Three Pines, exploring the neighborhood, which ended in woods or shoreline if you ran a quarter mile in any direction. It would be fun to own a Jeep in country like this.

I went back to the motel and showered, had a couple bowls of cereal and looked for sports on the television. Couldn't find any. It was Thursday afternoon. I was reading the take-out menus in the drawer of the motel side table when the call came shortly after six p.m.

"Head down to the Starlight," said Flanagan. "You've got a friend sitting at the bar."

15

THE STARLIGHT HAD a DJ on Thursday nights, the only night of the week it had one. The music was loud when I walked in, with too much bass and no one singing. About a dozen college-aged kids were moving around the dance floor; another dozen sat at tables near the DJ booth. The regulars at the Starlight sat on the barstools or at tables farthest from the speakers. Travis Lee sat at the end of the bar nearest the washrooms.

"Mr. Lee?"

He looked up from his Scotch and stared at me a few seconds. Then something clicked. "Tree marker. Shit, are you following me?"

"Not unless you've been up to the Algoma. Just got back into town, Mr. Lee. Came out for a drink. I saw you sitting here."

"You must like this club."

"I do."

"You have good taste. Sit down. Let me buy you a drink."

"You don't have to, Mr. Lee. I just saw you across the room and thought I'd say hi."

"I insist. Sit down and tell me how we're doing out on the Algoma."

I sat and Lee ordered me a drink. He hadn't recognized me right away, but once he had, he remembered what we were drinking the last time we'd been in the Starlight. The Pabst and rocks glass of McCallum's were put in front of me and I looked around the club.

"This place reminds me of some clubs back in Detroit," I said. "The big booths. The stage with the orchestra wings. This bar— I swear I've sat at this bar before."

"It's a good bar."

"Solid oak. No one would make a bar like this today."

"No one sitting here would know the difference, so why bother? I've seen particleboard trying to pass as mahogany these days. Makes you puke."

"You do a lot of business in particleboard, don't you, Mr. Lee?"

"We do. Still makes me puke. Finding much white pine on the Algoma?"

"You have old-growth stands up there."

"Well, let's hope there's a market for it next year. How's your drink?"

"I could have another. Any chance of me buying this round, Mr. Lee?"

"Absolutely not. It would only confuse George. He runs a tab for me that I settle at the end of each month. No sense running two tabs. You'd be making him work too hard."

We sipped our McCallum's. Watched the college kids move around the dance floor. I wondered how old you should be when you look at something like that and think it really isn't dancing.

"What do you think of the music?"

"Hate it," said Lee. "How could you do anything but hate it?"

"They have this all weekend?"

"Just Thursday night."

"Why come here Thursday night?"

"Why come? Why go? Do you spend much time asking yourself questions like that, Danny?"

"I'm from Detroit. What do you think?"

"Good answer. Well, I've spent most of my life asking questions like that. I suspect much of Birmingham has done the same thing. Last few years, anyway. Why come, why go, why stay, why move? Want to hear an expert's opinion on the correct answer to these questions?"

"Sure."

"Why bother?"

He laughed and took a sip of his McCallum's. Pulled his lips back in a wince and shook his head. He did that two more times and then he ordered a beer.

"What do they have here Friday nights?" I asked.

"Happy hour starts at four. And they have Motown Night. That's *right*. They have *Motown Night* on Fridays. Oh, you *have* to come back."

<hr>

THE NEXT NIGHT we sat at the bar playing trivia with the songs. Who sang it? Who wrote it? Who was playing in the band? You couldn't grow up in Detroit without knowing some of that stuff, and I maybe knew more than most because my dad loved Motown and R & B.

Lee bought celebratory shots of whiskey for two men waiting at the bar for their beer—surprised when the drinks were shoved into their hands—after I correctly guessed Fontella Bass as the singer for "Rescue Me."

"Everybody—and I mean, fuckin' *everybody*—says that's Aretha Franklin."

"I know. But Fontella Bass. She's not even Motown."

"I *know*. Don't tell them."

"Chess Records. Her duet with Bobby McClure on 'Don't Mess Up a Good Thing' is one of my favorite Chess songs."

"Damn, that's good. All this music is years before your time."

"It's before your time too. Good music is good music though, don't you think, Mr. Lee?"

"I certainly do."

It wasn't just music Lee liked talking about. He must have taken some science classes when he was getting his law degree because he knew some physics and asked big bang questions every once in a while, and he knew a lot about plants and trees and I wasn't sure if that was from school or from owning a timber company. He quoted people, or lines from a song or a book, but never in a way that seemed pretentious, and not all the time, just once in a while, and it normally sounded right when he said it.

There was a curiosity to him and he kept up on the news. There was a small black-and-white television behind the bar in the Starlight and that might have been how he did it.

He never once talked sports. A former Division I football player and he never talked sports. I tried to get him to talk about it a few times, thinking it should be a natural, but Lee never ran with it, although he did tell me the Christmas Miracle story. He knew that one by rote, and he was asked to tell it so often by other people, I heard different versions of the story. One version was over in under a minute. One ran almost ten.

I found out later that play was the only time Lee touched a football during a regular-season game at Harvard. He was on special teams, running down punts, but in high school he had been the quarterback, and in the Harvard playbook his junior year, there was a fake-punt play a new offensive coach had added.

That was the Christmas Miracle Play, a play that fooled Navy so completely, there was no defender within twenty yards of the receiver who caught Lee's pass. He told me that had been part of the story for a few years, but when he saw how disappointed people were to hear about that, he started leaving it out of the story. The touchdown became more difficult as the years passed.

He never talked much about the law either, another thing that surprised me. I asked him once if he had practiced and he said, "No need. Plenty of work waiting for me here." And that was rather the point of my dad covering the freight at Harvard. That was made quite clear to me. No need to practice. I already had a job.

He didn't sound bitter or sad when he said that, but I never heard Travis Lee sound bitter or sad about anything. Nostalgic plenty of times—maybe that was a form of sadness—but never anything stronger than that. He reminded me of my uncle, the one who lived in Escanaba, if my uncle had been better educated, less driven and a drunk.

When Motown Night was wrapping up, Lee told me Saturday was Prime Rib Night at the Starlight, and insisted I come back.

"Prime Rib Night?" I said doubtfully.

"It's good. Trust me."

"You not getting tired of me yet?"

"The man who knows *two* Fontella Bass songs? No, I'm not getting tired of you yet."

16

THAT SATURDAY WAS the busiest I ever saw the Starlight. Every table was filled most of the night, the waiters running between them, the bartenders dancing in front of the gilt-edged mirror, shaking drinks and opening bottles of wine. We ate at a table not far from the bar, and people would often stop and talk to Lee. The men always held rocks glasses in their hands. The women always wore dresses with zippers running down the backs.

The visitors normally stayed until Lee made them laugh; then they walked away. Lee was so good at doing this, he could make people stay as long or as briefly as he wished, could make people laugh almost at will.

Amanda Lee came in that night with a woman she introduced as a coworker, accompanied by two men who were cousins of the coworker. There wasn't a vacant table near us, and they didn't have reservations, so they were seated in a small, cordoned-off area near the bar that the restaurant kept for people like Amanda Lee.

After being seated Amanda Lee came to give her husband a kiss on the cheek and to say she hoped he didn't mind but the cousins were just there for the night, the coworker was a dear friend and "I can sit with you any old time, can't I, dear?"

She gave me an indifferent stare when Lee introduced me. Said she couldn't recall meeting me before. "Is that right? I've met you? My memory these days, I swear."

When she left an hour later, Amanda Lee didn't bother coming back to our table, but blew her husband a kiss while walking out the door. A couple came up to our table right after that, then another, and a good twenty minutes had passed before Lee said, "You're wondering why I stay with her, aren't you?"

"None of my business."

"Didn't say it was. But you question it. I can *feel* you questioning it. You're going to become rather bad company if I don't answer the question, so I would like to say we all have our burdens to bear, many of them rightfully earned. I also want to inform you that leaving someone presupposes your personal situation will improve. And that is the missing variable, I'm afraid. It has never struck me as an improvement— Amanda with lawyers."

He laughed at his joke, and a few seconds later, a man dressed in a burgundy suit, holding the arm of a woman twenty years younger, came up to the table and asked Lee if he could tell them the Christmas Miracle story. His wife—his third, he told me proudly—had never heard it. Lee asked the wife's name before he began so he could work it into the story a few times. The couple got the full-length director's-cut version. Lee leered at the woman a few times when he was telling the story. Each time he did that, she giggled and slapped him on the arm.

The prime rib wasn't bad, and when we had finished our meal, I asked Lee how long Saturday night had been Prime Rib Night at the Starlight and he said after thinking about it a few seconds that he couldn't remember a time when it *wasn't*. Red meat on a Saturday night, happy drunken people moving between tables, Travis Lee making everyone laugh on their way to the washroom, the waiters and the bartenders counting their tips, a cover band about to come on and do a not-bad version of Jimmy Reed's "Bright Lights, Big City."

The Starlight was like a sanctuary that night, a place for people to come and seek shelter, pretend for one night—Prime Rib Night—that nothing in their lives had ever changed, no one had ever said goodbye, no factory had ever closed and the world outside wasn't really the world outside.

SUNDAY NIGHT WAS the opposite of Saturday. The quietest I ever saw the Starlight. By then we had become weekend barflies and nothing had been discussed. When I walked in the bar, I expected to see Lee and he probably expected to see me. We didn't even speak until my drink was in front of me.

"Quiet night," I said.

"Yeah, it usually is on Sunday."

I was there less than an hour before deciding to leave Lee at the bar. I had spent three nights drinking with a curious man, and I figured I had pushed my luck about as far as it could go. The other nights there had been distractions for Travis Lee. There wouldn't be anything like that tonight. We were the only two sitting at the bar. Only two tables were occupied. One bartender had already been sent home.

"I think I'm going to call it a night, Mr. Lee."

"It's not even eight o'clock," he said, looking at his watch.

"Back at work tomorrow. I should go back to the motel and get some sleep."

"That's right. I forgot. What time are we picking you up?"

"Six a.m. I'll be sleeping outside tomorrow night. Up near Baron's Canyon. Ever been there?"

"No. Just seen photos."

"I'm looking forward to seeing it. I want to thank you for your hospitality this weekend, Mr. Lee. I hope you don't think I was ever expecting anything. I've never spent so much time with the man I work for. Hell, I don't even work for you. You own the freakin' joint."

Lee laughed and raised his glass. "If only that were true," he said, and when he said that, I hesitated, because it was the sort of opening you look for when you're working undercover, a chance to turn the conversation in a way that would benefit you and might not be too obvious.

So I hesitated. Ran through my mind what Lee had already told me, or what I had figured out after three nights of undercover surveillance work that doesn't get any closer. After I had done that, I said, "I want to thank you again for everything this weekend, Mr. Lee. It was fun."

17

I WALKED TO the Three Pines. The sky was a light indigo color, the streetlights not turned on yet. At a 7-Eleven I bought a burner cell phone, a six-pack of Pabst, some bread and sliced ham. I phoned Flanagan from the motel room after I had eaten a sandwich.

"So whatta ya think, pal?" he asked.

"He knows all about the money laundering. He knows Beau Lafontaine well. Calls him his little bush buddy. He's a criminal and I think it's eating him up. Or something's eating him up. He's not in great shape."

"He's a lush. What did you expect? What about the banker?"

"I have trouble seeing it. I think he's too wet to do much of anything."

"There're plenty of drunks on death row. Did he ever speak to you about Powell? A direct reference?"

"Once. Someone came up to us at the bar and talked to him about the shooting. After the guy left, I asked Lee about it and he said he knew Powell, but his wife knew him better. He laughed when he said that. Then he got serious and said he shouldn't be laughing. His wife was stressing out over the murder. That's the phrase he used. Stressing out. I asked him why and he said, 'Well, who isn't? The whole town is stressing out about it. A murder on the streets of Birmingham? You didn't see that every day.' I didn't pursue it any further because I thought I'd already taken too many chances."

"Sounds like you had."

"Funny thing was—and I'm normally pretty good at this—I never thought I was going too far with Travis Lee. He's not a suspicious man. I don't think he cares about much in this world, maybe him at the top of that list."

"Not caring too much. That's another good trait for a killer. You really don't like this guy?"

"Can't rule it out, I suppose. Just the way I see it."

I waited to see what Flanagan would do with the out I'd just given him. Most of the people I work for appreciate being given an out. In most cases the undercover agent doesn't know everything that's in play and the person you're talking to, saying, "No way it's *that* guy"—he could have spent the last two years telling *his* boss it *is* that guy. No one plays nice after that. So give an honest assessment, tell them anything is possible and let them decide. The good ones get it right. The bad ones, well, it was always useful to know a thing like that.

Eventually Flanagan let out a sigh. "Well, I suppose we'll keep trying to figure this out while you go off on your vacation. You're back in the North Maine Woods tomorrow?"

"Should be within two miles of Paradise Lake in two nights. Hoping to go in a few times on this rotation."

"Well, good luck, pal. Look in the bottom drawer of your dresser when you get back to the motel. You'll find what you were looking for."

———

FLANAGAN TOLD ME later that Hugh Kowalski came to his hotel room early the following morning. The Birmingham police chief arrived unannounced and got him out of bed.

"Sorry to get you up," he said. "I wanted to see you before the day started. You're running the FBI investigation now. Is that correct?"

"That's correct. We've met before, Chief. In front of the bank."

"I remember."

"Would you like to come in?"

"If you don't mind, yes."

Flanagan stood back and Kowalski entered the room. The chief sat at one of the desk chairs, putting down a manila envelope he had been carrying. He was probably about the same age as Flanagan, but didn't try to hide it, a tall, thin man with sad eyes that seemed to capture the light so you were drawn to them and couldn't help but notice how sad they were.

"So how are you doing, Chief?" asked Flanagan when they were sitting around the desk. "It's been a long time since you've had a murder in Birmingham, hasn't it?"

"Last one was a fight outside the Claude Hotel. That would have been 2012. Half of downtown saw it."

"This one's a little different."

"Yes, this one's a little different. Still hard to believe. Everyone in town knew Bobby Powell. Everyone liked him. Your banker. Maybe you're obligated. Although he helped some people back in '08."

"Got himself into a bit of trouble that year as well."

"That's what I hear. The Lees? There's going to be quite a shock in Birmingham when the story comes out."

Nothing was said for a few seconds. "*Is* it starting to come out?" asked Flanagan.

"No. We're keeping your investigation on a need-to-know basis, just like you want. Officially, that means only three of us in the department. With an unsolved murder though . . . well, I don't know how long you should expect to keep something like that a secret."

"I'm living on borrowed time?"

"I'd say so."

They laughed. A short laugh. Men at work.

"Well, let's hope we can wrap this up quickly. You say it'll be a big shock. Is Lee Forestry your largest employer?"

"No, that'd be the government. Public works, highways, some brush work on the Appalachian Trail. That's what keeps a lot of men busy these days. But for the number of mills that are left, yes, Lee Forestry would be the biggest."

"How well do you know the family?"

"Socially, I don't know the Lees at all. Don't run in those circles. But I know them. Everyone in Birmingham knows them. I see Tucker at chamber of commerce events and curling bonspiels. Travis is a good ol' boy who probably should have been born down south somewhere. My dad knew their father pretty well. Thomas Lee. Don't know if I ever met a colder man. The boys' mother died a long time ago. Tom's been dead a long time too. Fifteen years? Somewhere around that."

"What about their business partner, Beau Lafontaine?"

"Never met him. Have you?" Kowalski laughed after he said it. He knew the answer. "I know the Lafontaine family pretty well, but I don't know much about Beau. Not many people do. Just rumors, folklore stuff almost. He's supposed to be a Malee. Have you heard of them?"

"Not until a week ago."

"French bogeymen that live in the Woods around here. Treat that one for what it's worth. But the rest of the Lafontaines, yeah, I know them. Pearl had two brothers, Rene and Marc. Those boys used to knock heads with bouncers on their way *into* a tavern. Marc was killed during an armored-truck robbery in Portland about ten years ago. Rene is doing life in Danforth. Their dad, Jean, was a bad drunk who ran out on the family a long time ago. I barely remember him. The family used to own a lot of land in Bustard County, but it's all gone now. Pearl's just got the farmhouse and a small field, far as I know."

"What kind of person is she?"

"A good person I'd say. Hard worker. I've seen her at the Red Bird for years and I've never seen her in a bad mood or be snotty to anyone. A gal who looks the way she does, she's had plenty of opportunity to be snotty."

"Did you know she was having an affair with Travis Lee?"

"Not exactly a secret in this city. I think it's been on-and-off for years. Don't know why she'd be happy with an arrangement like that, but what do I know? Will this investigation be bad for her?"

"Too early to tell, Chief."

"That'd be a shame. Well, I didn't come here just to chat. I brought you something."

He opened the manila envelope and took out three sheets of paper. "Witness Statement" was written in bold type atop one page.

Flanagan took the papers from Kowalski and started reading. When he put the papers down five minutes later, he said, "Most expensive car in Birmingham. Is that true?"

"Might be. It's an expensive SUV all right. Kid also claims he knows the car. He works part-time as a waiter at the Grill Room. He came in the station house yesterday and gave the statement."

"Nearly two weeks after the shooting?"

"Kid says he didn't think much about it at the time. But now that it's still an unsolved murder, he got to thinking about it, and then he started wondering why that car would have been parked there when the Lee condo is only a block away."

"I thought Lee lived in some gated community upriver."

"He does. He has a condo in downtown Birmingham too."

"This was five minutes before the shooting?"

"That's what the kid says."

"Are there other SUVs that would look similar?"

"Land Rover has a production model that uses the same color white. Looks a little similar. Lincoln has something."

"You need to confirm his story."

"Already showed him a lineup." And Kowalski smiled when he said it. Good police work. He didn't mind Flanagan knowing about it. "The detective who took the statement went to the kid's home last night with a half dozen photos of white SUVs, production year 2019. He picked the right photo with no problem and laughed at the detective, asked her if she really thought he didn't know what a Mercedes looked like."

Flanagan chuckled. When a few seconds had passed, Kowalski said, "Are you going to ask me the next question?"

"You've done that as well?"

"Thought I should. Nothing personal, but I figure the faster you solve this murder, the faster this town can get back to normal."

"How many are there?"

"Six Mercedes GLEs in all of Maine. Five are in the Portland area. The other one is right here in Birmingham. Most people have seen it often enough. It belongs to Travis Lee."

Flanagan told me later that he spent most of that day questioning my competency; wondering whether my judgment could be trusted; and why, if Travis Lee were an innocent man, he was doing such a wonderful job of looking guilty.

THE SWEET GOODBYE

SHE SAT IN *the bar of the Dawson Hotel in Old Town, a forty-five-minute drive from Birmingham. A good, quiet bar with black walnut paneling and brass fixtures as old as the hotel, which had been built in the heyday of squared timber, when some of the richest men in America felled trees in Maine.*

They had been coming to the Dawson for many years and the bartender knew them, an old man now who always made sure, whenever possible, to give them the booth they preferred. Brought drinks to their table, a service they had never seen him offer another.

She liked the bar as much as he did, and although they had started coming to the Dawson for reasons of stealth and subterfuge, it had turned into something else a long time ago. They always came at the right time of day to be sitting in a good bar: late afternoon with the frenzy of lunch passed, dinner not yet served, the time of day when waiters went for their smokes, the beer coolers were restocked and the sun hit the liquor bottles in ways that made the darkest of the bottles look like black opals. She could not recall a single unpleasant moment sitting in a booth at the bar of the Dawson Hotel.

"How you doing?"

"Better," he answered. *"I'm beginning to think this whole thing could blow over. Just like Boston."*

"Think we can be lucky twice, hon?"

"Why not? Maybe it's already happened. We're sitting here, aren't we?"

"I suppose. Never thought I'd see you again after you married Amanda."

"Thought I was going to be the faithful husband?"

"No, never thought that. Just thought I'd never see you again."

"I don't recall you complaining when I came around."

"I don't recall that either, hon."

———

SHE DIDN'T SEE *him for seven years. Had stopped thinking about him. Stopped feeling a pang of sadness when she saw one of his cars on the streets of Birmingham or his picture in the newspaper. And then one night he was waiting for her when her shift finished. And up it started again.*

She was dating a contractor then, a big, happy-go-lucky man who reminded her of Travis Lee, but turned out to be nothing like Travis Lee. He had already moved in with her when Travis Lee came back into her life.

Her house seemed to cause that contractor pain. "Pearl," he'd say, "nobody has plaster lath walls anymore. You can't get insulation in them. They're dirty as hell. You ever had to knock down one of these walls?"

"Once. In the kitchen. There was a big hole from when my dad fell off his chair one night. I repaired it after he left."

"What was it like, taking the wall down?"

"Dirty as hell."

"There. That's it exactly. Nobody has plaster lath walls anymore."

"But why take them down if that's the problem?"

"What?"

"If it's only dirty as hell when I tear down the walls, why are you telling me to tear down the walls?"

"Pearl," he'd say patiently, "nobody has plaster lath walls anymore."

She thinks she kept the walls just to torment him. Even after he offered to pay for the drywall and do the hanging at a discount rate. Maybe he had a right to be nasty in the end. But she never felt any urge to change her house. Many things in life called improvements were just things that were different. The gardens around her house were the exception to this way of thinking. Those were always changing. Each year she expanded them, added a new plant or tree, cut a new rock path. She liked working outside. Ripping down plaster lath walls seemed an unnecessary misery to inflict upon herself.

She still had forty acres, but kept gardens only around the house. The rest of the land she leased to a neighbor who grew cash crops: corn for two years, hay for two, then a fallow year. He paid for the fallow year, even though Pearl never asked him to.

The farm had started with five hundred acres but it got whittled down after getting every bad break a farm could get, Pearl supposed. The county expropriated fifty acres to build a road. Another fifty was sold to settle lawsuits her grandfather had against him when he died. A hundred went to pay back taxes and bank liens. Her father sold two hundred more in what he thought was a good deal at the time, but the land was flipped the next year, and flipped two more times before a developer from Portland started building tract housing.

There hadn't been a house sold yet—in forty years of building on that land—that went for less than what her father got for the whole parcel.

What can you do? Pearl planted rock gardens around her house and forgot her family ever owned five hundred acres. Travis Lee thought it was a good plan. The plaster-lath-hating contractor thought she should find somebody to sue about the forty-year land-flip scam. One reason right there why Travis Lee was still in her life, while the contractor who looked a bit like him had left town years ago after she got a restraining order.

———

THEY ALREADY HAD a room upstairs. It was five in the afternoon and they normally were in the room no later than seven, so he could sleep a few hours before heading home. They could have spent the night. They could have spent days in the Dawson. He didn't do much work anymore. Tucker had started using outside counsel years ago. His wife didn't care if he came home. Strange as it seemed, it was the diner waitress who needed to return to the real world.

She wondered if it would have been different if people had expected more of him. His father had the elder son in Tucker, a boy who had every loathsome trait the father treasured. Travis was the spare and always knew it. No one had ever expected much from him. A quick joke. A good retelling of the Christmas Miracle story; pick up the bar tab; never much more than that.

It was different after he came back, what she thinks of as the middle years in their affair, that brief time when they believed they might be given new lives. Those were the years of gym clubs, cooking lessons and rehab— three times for him, once for her.

He took rehab seriously his first time—it was court ordered after his second DWI. Even more so the second time, checking into a ninety-day program on his fortieth birthday. Not at all the third time, a flight of fancy he told her later, checking out after a week while in the middle of group therapy, Travis asking the therapist to explain one more time what the problem was if the functioning alcoholic was, you know, functioning.

He never took much of anything serious after that. Except for 2008, the last time she'd seen it, when he decided to care about Lee Forestry Products and the people working for the family business. He and Tucker came to her, asking for a meeting with Beau, Tucker explaining he had heard that Five Star Forestry had cash reserves it might want to invest. That's what he told her. Actually keeping a straight face when he said it.

Tucker kept pretending it was a normal business meeting, showing up at the Reading Room of the Alexander Hotel with graphs and financial statements. It was hard not to laugh at him. Beau arrived looking like he'd walked out of a bush camp, wearing canvas pants and a plaid jacket, long hair and a half-grown beard. He smelled of woodsmoke and fish, Marlboros and whiskey. Yeah, just a regular business meeting, Tucker.

It was Lafontaine who spoke first. "Pearl tells me you boys need some help."

"I wouldn't describe it that way," said Tucker quickly. "These are tough times in the forestry industry, tough everywhere really. I thought there might be ways we could help one another, get some economies of scale working."

"You want scales?" said Lafontaine. "Pearl told me you wanted money."

Travis laughed and Tucker said, "Well, we would hope that would be the end result of any business partnership, Mr. Lafontaine, any joint venture. Yes, we would hope to make a profit . . . if all the paperwork is in order. . . ."

"How much you need?"

"How much . . . I think we're getting ahead of ourselves here. We don't know if—"

"I have twenty million I need to park somewhere. You boys want it?"

Tucker stopped talking. Travis laughed so hard, he spilled his drink. "Here's your chance to negotiate, Tuck. Ask him for forty."

"You need forty?" asked Lafontaine.

She should have stopped it right then. A lot of what was happening in Birmingham, it was on her.

═══

AFTER DINNER THEY took their drinks upstairs and made love with the windows open, a warm evening breeze coming in, one of the first of the year. She could hear finches and a cardinal once. There were more songbirds in Old Town. The river was calmer here.

The rooms in the Dawson had four-poster beds and porcelain water jugs in the bathroom, a brass umbrella stand by the door. They laughed about the umbrella stand each time they saw it. Probably never been used. A man who used an umbrella in Northern Maine was a man willing to be shunned. The Dawson was a place half real and half imagined: like morning dreams, cloud shapes and affairs that had lasted many years.

She never blamed him for marrying Amanda Singer. Never expected him to leave her. She had no right to expect that. No right to judge him. In

Birmingham you learned that early. You never looked down on a person for doing what they did, for having dirty hands, for lining up at a soup kitchen, getting stumbling drunk on a Saturday night or having no job. Everyone in Birmingham knew life had a bad habit of giving you two choices, told you to pick and neither one of them was ever what you would call a good choice.

Don't judge. Most times you never knew what the alternative had been.

Amanda Singer was the best-looking girl in Birmingham when she turned twenty-one, and that would have been one of the reasons for the marriage. She had black hair you almost never saw, dark as onyx, hair that captured the light, gave it hues of amber and gold, always changing, always shimmering. Good way to describe the girl too.

"So you think we can be lucky one more time?" she asked.

Her head was resting upon his chest. It was still firm. He was a handsome man in many ways to this day.

"Sure," he answered sleepily. "Things like that happen all the time. Synchronicity is like that, right? A fancy word for things happening twice. Like that tree marker. Happens so often they needed to invent a silly word for it."

She was almost asleep and had to think about it a minute. "What do you mean, like the tree marker?"

"That tree marker who punched someone out for me in front of the Starlight? You saw him, remember? You pulled up when he was there? I bumped into him at the Starlight again this weekend. Drank with him a couple nights. Good lad."

She lay there and tried not to feel disappointment. It was never good to feel that way. Never productive. And it's not like it was a surprise. Hopes and dreams get turned into jokes all the time, just as easily and with no more thought than God sending down a warm evening breeze.

18

THE SHUTTLE BUS ride to Petersen's Gorge was almost eight hours, when you included the pickups before leaving Birmingham. I tried to read but spent most of my time on that next trip staring out the window at the St. John River. A month ago, the river had had ice floes on it the size of small apartment buildings, tall, misshapen floes that sometimes resembled chess pieces. At some moments it looked like an ancient ghost army drifting down the St. John. Now the floes were gone, the river was rising and there would be flooding soon.

I thought of my conversation with Flanagan the night before. Wondered if he believed me when I reported Travis Lee seemed a poor suspect for the murder of Robert Powell. Lee had motive; anyone who could get to the third floor of that parking garage had opportunity. If you didn't like Beau Lafontaine for the killing, you didn't have much left in the way of suspects. In the way of *known* suspects.

A lot of operational commanders would want to hang on to Travis Lee for a while. Keep him as a suspect, if for no other reason than to *have* a suspect. The more I thought about that, the more restless I became. That's the way it goes for me sometimes, when I'm feeling bad about something I've done, but can't feel too bad about it because it was the right thing to do, or it was so much fun, I figure I should be forgiven. It just hasn't happened yet. So I'm stuck feeling bad with no way out. A restless, angry feeling I don't get very often, but I had it then.

When the shuttle bus reached Petersen's Gorge, I checked out my kit and ATV and was gone within the hour. The sky seemed to press down on me as I drove north, the clouds different shades of gray and black running straight as rails, so it looked like wood grain or plates of shale; I drove beneath a sky that looked like it could fall down on me.

When I lost the sun, I stopped for the night, spreading my sleeping bag on a wide swath of fern moss I found near the river. There was the scent of spruce gum in the air and the river was running fast, a burbling childish sound that was pleasant to hear. It was still too early in the season for blackflies or mosquitoes and I slept well. I was moving again before the sun was up the next morning.

Despite my hurry to get to Paradise Lake, I still needed to play the role of Danny Barrett, tree marker. So, as I drove up the shoreline of the St. Croix River, I worked. I did it in silence, the way my uncle taught me, no whistling or humming, no muttering or under-the-breath curses. I had been taught to hate even the hiss of the aerosol can I had to use to mark the trees.

The task never varied. I would stand in front of a tree and judge its circumference. I could come within two inches of that on all but the biggest trees. Then I examined the bark, touching it, smelling it, breaking off a chunk and having a look at the soft ocher-colored wood on the underside. After that, I judged the tree's height. Always in that order. You needed the right movements, in the right sequence, or you were wasting your time. No different from a Sun Salutation.

My uncle wouldn't have known about the Sun Salutation, but he had explained the importance of the right movements, in the right sequence, with the fervor of a yogic mystic. The tap was always the last and most crucial part of the sequence—judging a tree's heart, he called it. A simple gesture that was almost intimate. You leaned in, put your ear upon the tree, gave a three-knuckled tap and then listened. For what exactly, it was hard to say. Perhaps there wasn't a word for it. There were words for what you *didn't* want to hear—hollow, echo, moist, dry—but the sound of a good tree, I don't know what the right word would be.

If you got everything right but misjudged the heart, you had failed. The company that employed you was going to take down a tree that might be diseased or bug infested, and the only person who ever got the blame for a waste of time like that was the tree marker who had worked the stand.

Get everything wrong but get the heart right? Then you were bringing down a good tree and you still had a job. Or a fighting chance at still having a job. You wouldn't want to get the circumference and height wrong too many times.

I worked the outer boundary of two pine stands, marking about a dozen trees in each stand, leaving the forestry sign for one stand to be marked in full at a later date. By midafternoon I reached the pine stand I had been marking the last time I went into Paradise Lake. I parked in the shade of a large pine on the perimeter of the stand, took some large gulps from my water bottle and got to work.

I had been marking for less than an hour when I saw the ATVs. Three of them coming from the direction of Paradise Lake. Coming fast and not even bothering to slow when they forded the St. Croix River, driving right through and throwing a huge wake to both sides of their vehicles. When the ATVs came ashore, they headed straight toward me.

I put the aerosol can on the ground and watched the vehicles approach. I tried to see something in the scene before me that didn't look threatening. But there was nothing.

19

THE MEN HAD long hair and beards, wore canvas pants and thick plaid jackets. Two stayed on their ATVs while the third, the eldest of them, turned off his engine, stepped off his vehicle and walked toward me. He had light gray strands in his jet-black hair, strands that were almost white, and there were enough of them to make him look odd, like a skunk. He was smoking a clay pipe filled with marijuana, and when he was standing directly in front of me, he said, "What the fuck you doin' in this stand?"

"You can see the gear I'm carrying. What do you think I'm doing?"

"You're markin' trees?"

"For Lee Forestry."

"Never seen Lee workin' this far out."

"I'd say you were right about that. It's old growth. Doesn't look like it's *ever* been worked. Mind me asking who the fuck you guys are?"

The man looked at me a few seconds before he smiled. Then, as casually as though he were pulling out a Zippo lighter, he pulled an old-fashioned Colt .45 from his jacket pocket. He pointed the gun at my chest and said, "This ain't Lee land, asshole. It's Five Star. And that's going to be a fuckin' problem for you."

───────

THE TWO OTHER men searched me but it was little more than a pat down. They never checked my belt, where the camera was hidden. They found my sat phone and gave it to the man with the skunk hair. He asked for the pass code and I gave it to him.

Every call and message on the phone came from Lee Forestry. The ones that had come from Flanagan were routed through a phone number registered under the company's name. No message was anything more than someone telling me to go here, go there. When the man had finished scrolling through the messages, he threw the phone onto the seat of his ATV.

"When was Lee thinkin' 'bout comin' up here?"

"No sense marking trees for next year."

"Before winter."

"That's how you do it."

A smart-ass answer, but I wanted to test the waters. The two other men were holding my arms behind my back, but like the pat down, they weren't doing it well. I could easily break the grip. The man doing the talking wouldn't have time to reach the Colt he had placed on the hood of his ATV. I had the spot visualized—where he would be when I reached the gun. It was a good, workable distance.

"So that's how you do it, eh, asshole? You don't think we've worked the bush before?"

"Just saying. You boys seem a bit unclear on how it works. I'm the tree marker and Lee isn't going to like this much."

"Maybe Five Star isn't going to like Lee marking trees that don't fuckin' belong to them."

"What are you talking about? This is Lee timber rights and I'm standing right where I'm supposed to be standing."

"Lee rights end at the Maurice River, not the St. Croix."

"You're full of shit. Check my maps."

My pack had already been dumped on the ground. After staring at me another second, the man turned and walked to the pile, grabbed a topographical map with the seal of the Maine Land Management Office at the top. It was folded and nearly worn through on the creases. Lots of red pen notations, from the land I had already marked. The man found the square for the land we were standing on and examined the map. After a few seconds, he looked up and said, "This map is fucked. Where did you get it?"

"Where does it look like I got it? The state of Maine. Those are the maps you have to use."

"It's wrong."

"Buddy, is this what we're arguing about? A government fuckin' map? This has gone on long enough, don't you think?"

The man looked at me a second and I could tell he was thinking about it. What else would an innocent tree marker caught in the wrong place because of a faulty map say right then? I went through the possibilities. Most would be annoyed and aggressive, maybe about to ask the obvious question—"Why the fuck do you assholes care so much? Aren't there enough fuckin' trees up here to go around?"

What a mistake that question would have been—for an innocent tree marker. I said nothing. Eventually the man threw the map back on top of the pile and said, "You can fake a fuckin' map. Other things, not so easy, eh, my friend?"

===

THE OTHER MEN stayed behind, sitting on the hoods of their ATVs, their legs swinging lazily as they smoked huge joints of marijuana. They stared at us through billowing smoke while we walked toward the river.

"That tree over there—what is it?"

"White oak."

"The one behind it?"

"Black cherry."

"Looks like ironwood to me."

"Leaves on an ironwood wouldn't be that round. And the tree wouldn't be that big. Ironwoods never get that big."

The man grunted and we kept walking. He smelled of woodsmoke and marijuana, gasoline and fish; he walked with the steady heel-to-toe gait of someone who spent most of his time in the bush. Such men didn't run. Didn't fall. The earth could tremble beneath them and they would walk right over it.

When we reached the river, he pointed with his gun at the trees he wanted me to identify. We were standing by a large bend in the river and willows hung low over the water. In the distance were the foothills of the Appalachians, gray and squat on a sunless day. Somewhere a gray jay was piping and chickadees buzzed around our heads, then flew into the strands of the willows and disappeared.

There were many trees by the river and the man with the skunk hair made me identify each one. Black spruce. Red pine. Hemlock. Poplar. Yellow birch. He asked how many board feet Lee would get from the trees I had marked in the old-growth forest, the average circumference, the expected wastage. When he had done all that, the man took the Colt handgun from his pocket and pushed it against my head.

"All right," he said, "you're a Lee tree marker who came up here with a fucked-up map, and that is bad luck for you, pal. You'd want it to be something more than that. State of fuckin' Maine, eh?"

He wanted to hear my last words. I had already taken him for that kind of a man. "What do you think Lee is going to do when you pull that trigger?" I asked quietly.

"Why the fuck should I care?"

"Because you should. Lee Forestry is expecting me back in Birmingham at the end of the week, with a report on these timber rights filed the next day. They're going to report me missing if that doesn't happen."

"Lots o' people go missin' up here. Maybe you didn't know that."

"Sure, but cops come looking for people like me. Maybe that's something new for you."

The man pushed the gun a little harder against my temple. In a few seconds he began to push so hard, it hurt. He was beginning to see the problem.

A man like this, with two bad options in front of him might go, "What the fuck?" and make the wrong choice. I needed to keep talking.

"Buddy, I don't know what is going on up here, and I don't fuckin' care. I've been a tree marker a long time. I've come across meth labs, shallow graves, double-wide whorehouses—you name it and I've stumbled across it in some woods somewhere. I'm good at keeping secrets. Got a few of my own. It sounds like I fucked up with that map, so I want to forget this day ever happened. Maybe I get on that ATV, I cross this river and I never come back. That's how this can play out for you."

It was a long enough speech I knew he was looking for a way out. If I had felt his arm tighten, or the gun pull back as his finger tightened around the trigger, I would have taken him down. The gun wasn't positioned right. The bullet might not even graze me. Once he was on the ground, he wouldn't have had a chance. But skunk hair wanted to hear me out. Was *anxious* to hear me out. Time to close him.

"How happy will people be with you when the cops get here?"

I felt the pressure on the left side of my head ease, then disappear. He put the gun in his pocket and spit on the ground.

"I was wrong. Looks like you're a man with good luck, not bad."

"We all make mistakes."

"Fuck off and get out of here, pal, 'fore your luck changes again."

———

I MADE CAMP that night on a ridge overlooking a deep gorge, water falling like a curtain into a deep eddy of the Maurice River. The coursing river made a hum in the air that had crazy changes in pitch and volume, like musicians in an orchestra pit rehearsing before a show.

The first time I had seen something profane and evil in the woods was long before Paradise Lake, long before I became a cop. It was on one of my uncle's timber rights, fifty miles north of Escabana, just the two of us marking pine and cedar when we stopped for lunch by the banks of a river with a wide mud shore. In spring the river was much larger. There were small trees near us that had been underwater three months earlier, strange hybrid trees with stunted leaves and bark as slick as oil. It was my uncle who spotted the trailer. On the far shore, covered under cedar boughs.

The river was low enough to be forded and we were thirty feet away when we noticed flies buzzing around the trailer. Fat bottleneck flies with bluish green bodies and iridescent wings. I stood beside my uncle in the slow-moving river, water lapping around our knees, neither of us wanting to go any farther.

We had to cover our mouths with our shirttails when we were twenty feet away. My uncle picked up a cedar bough and started sweeping flies away, telling me to stay where I was, not to come any closer. He had his work gloves on, and he leaned in to open the door of the trailer as carefully and as hesitantly as though the metal latch might have been molten hot. As soon as the latch was unclasped, the door sprang open and a body fell out.

The decomposition was so bad, it was shards of clothing that let you know it was a body. What would have been a summer dress, with a pattern of some sort. Strands of hair that looked like composted hay. Limbs that looked like charred logs. I walked back to the river and threw up in the water.

There were two more bodies inside. Both women. They had been inside that trailer a long time, last autumn, maybe before. This was before the days of sat phones, and although we left the timber limits right away, it wasn't until the next morning that my uncle was able to phone the sheriff's office to report what we had found. There was a logging road near the trailer, and that's what the police used to bring out the bodies. My uncle went with them, as they would never have found the road without him. He told me later that the sheriff stood outside the trailer before entering, stared at the body that had fallen into the mud and said to my uncle, "There's two more inside?"

"Yes."

"All female?"

"Looks that way."

The sheriff gave a sad shake of his head. Looked at the trees beyond the trailer. Turned to look at the river behind him.

"How did you know it was three women?" asked my uncle.

"This is the third trailer we've found. There was a bush camp near here recently, wasn't there?"

"I had one on Maleegne Lake two years ago. We were cutting cedar."

"I'm going to need a list of the foremen you had at the camp," said the sheriff, and with one more sad shake of his head, he walked into the trailer. The sheriff always told my uncle he shouldn't beat himself up about what he'd found; the men who brought those women to the bush camp, who found it easier to get rid of them than pay them, those were not the men who worked for him.

But it had been his bush camp and my uncle always felt complicit—it had been his men who had walked inside that trailer and had sex with those women, his foremen, or someone with sway in that camp, who had arranged it.

The murders were never solved, the identities of the women never known. My uncle never took any trees from those timber limits, telling me the land was cursed and nothing good would ever come from it. The land had been touched by evil, he said, as though by pox, and if he thought he could do it safely, he would burn it down, throw salt upon the ashes, wait the centuries required to cleanse the earth's wounds of pure evil.

Sometimes land is so defamed, so blasphemed, it becomes bad land. It is a feat no beast can manage. No storm, no drought, no ice age. Beau Lafontaine, when he was brought to trial, should answer for that crime as well.

I MADE SUPPER and looked out upon the gorge. Let the mist fall upon my face. If I could have camped upon that rock another week, I might have started to feel clean.

There was another reason I was camped on a high ridge, and when I finished eating, I took out my sat phone and made the call. It was answered on the second ring.

"Flanagan."

"Barrett."

He didn't say anything. I could imagine the surprise showing on his face.

"What the fuck are you doing, Barrett?"

"Beau Lafontaine knows about the investigation."

More silence.

"We're blown. I'm coming back."

20

THE HOTEL ROOM was dark, curtains drawn, no overhead light, just a desk lamp and a ribbon of light coming from underneath the bathroom door. Flanagan sat behind the desk, a vermilion-colored tie loosely knotted around his neck, the sleeves of a black shirt rolled up to his elbows. He was smoking a cigarette, flicking the ashes into a wastebasket. There was a bottle of Jameson on the desk, next to a stack of colored file folders. He motioned for me to sit down.

"Drink?"

"Wouldn't say no."

"Jameson's?"

"I'd chase it with a beer."

"Fridge is over there."

Flanagan reached for the bottle of whiskey and poured a good two inches into a rocks glass. Opened the lid of an ice bucket and grabbed some ice cubes. "You're an idiot if you have this neat. Tastes best when it cools a bit. These neat drinkers, they're all fuckin' showboats."

"I'll have ice."

Flanagan dropped the cubes into the rocks glass. It was early evening and Paul Linton had been in the hotel room when I arrived but he was gone now. Flanagan told him to leave. Not in those exact words, but not making any attempt to give Linton a good reason for leaving. "Paul, fuck off," he said.

Now he handed me the rocks glass and gave it a quick tap with his. "To homecomings."

"Homecomings."

"You OK?"

"I'm OK."

"Any trouble getting back?"

"Bug-out story worked fine."

"You look like shit. You know that? Maybe I'm not telling you anything you don't already know. When did you sleep last?"

"I'm just back from the bush. You're not supposed to be looking or feeling your best."

"Yeah, that must be it. Nothing to do with having a handgun pushed against your head."

"Rough day in the bush, then."

"So you think we're blown?"

"I *know* we're blown. Not sure how much Lafontaine knows, but he knows there's an active police investigation against him, knows it's serious and knows it's getting closer."

"You know all that just from that one patrol finding you?"

"I was two miles away. They were on me in less than an hour, suspicious right from the start. That's high-alert stuff. That wasn't a regular patrol. That's a patrol that gets sent out when you're expecting unwanted visitors."

Flanagan thought about that a minute. Swirled the whiskey in his glass, bent to sniff it, then threw his head back and drained the glass as though it were a shooter. He slammed the rocks glass down hard and said, "Well, that's a fuckup, ain't it? How do you think he made us?"

"Before you showed up, Linton was talking about getting some time on a military drone so he could get photos of Paradise Lake. Did he ever get it?"

"Really? You think it was that fuckin' drone?"

"So he got it. I bet that drone couldn't pick up anything because of the camo netting all over that camp and went in too low. If Lafontaine saw it, he would have known what it meant. There're not a lot of recreational drones flying around the North Maine Woods."

Flanagan reached for the bottle and was laughing when he poured himself another drink. "We almost had to blow people to get two hours on that fuckin' drone. It flies out of Fort Drum. The colonel who debriefed me apologized for the photos. They got shit, Barrett. Bunch of fuckin' trees. Colonel said they sent the drone in as low as it could go. You sure you're OK?"

"I'm OK."

"Fucking army. That's almost friendly fire. I should file a complaint against that poker-assed fuckin' bastard. He might as well have lit you up. He knew we had an undercover asset in the vicinity. Want me to do that? We can go after the prick. Have some fun."

"I don't want you to do that."

"Yeah, you're probably right. Army. Waste of fuckin' time. What was your bug-out story?"

"Told the foreman my little sister was in a car accident. She's at the Marquette Regional Health Center, intensive care. I'm listed as next of kin."

"Little sister has a different last name?"

"Sure does. It's complicated."

"That's good. Hard to check out, all sorts of flexibility, just urgent enough to get you back to Birmingham. That was Linton?"

"Yep."

"Small mercies. All right, we need to have a talk. You know we need to have a talk, right? How's your drink?"

"It's fine."

"I believe you. You gotta know that. If you think we're blown, there's a reason for you to think that way, and I need to respect it. You're good at what you do. But what you have—it's flimsy."

"Doesn't feel that way to me."

"I get that, but we don't have much in the way of reconnaissance on that camp. We don't know how odd it is, having a patrol two miles out. Might just be a coincidence."

I didn't say anything.

"All right, that was stupid. I take it back. But we don't have much to back you up. That's what I'm saying, Barrett, and if we're blown—if Lafontaine knows about our investigation—there's no sign of it down here. No money is being moved around. The Lees aren't acting any different. Fuck, that bowling pin Tucker Lee seems almost piss-cat giddy right now. Shouldn't we be seeing some sign that they're onto us?"

"Like a white flag or something?"

"That's good. Good fuckin' line, Barrett. Ever wonder why you don't have a regular boss?"

"Never."

"I can't shut down this investigation with what you've got, and you know it. Too much work has gone into this one. I need more. Some sort of corroboration that we're blown. Tell me that you *do* fuckin' know this."

Flanagan leaned back in his chair and started playing with his tie, flicking it up and down on his chest, whistling a song I didn't recognize. When he stopped whistling, he said, "Well, life's a ruddy fuckin' pageant, and we're all fuckin' fools, as my aunt Millie used to say. She didn't say it like that. I've cleaned up the language for her. Well, the choice is yours, pal. The investigation is going to continue, but that doesn't mean you have to be part of it. You got a ticket out of here if you want one. Nobody would ever question it. You OK?"

"I'm OK. How many times do I need to say it?"

"That should do it. Due fuckin' diligence completed. So we're going to stick with the game plan, Barrett. Tell that foreman of yours that your sister is doing better. You might not need to go back to Michigan. You're talking to the hospital and you'll know more in a day or two."

I finished my beer and stood up. "You're going to try to get some corroboration, right? You're not going to file a report and forget about it, leave me marooned out at the Three Pines?"

"Looking right now. Doesn't it look like it? Barrett, one thing you got to remember."

"What?"

"Big-man game."

Flanagan was laughing and slapping his knee when I shut the door.

21

THE NEXT DAY the Birmingham cops finally went out to interview Tucker and Travis Lee. Flanagan told Kowalski what was needed—had to be a senior cop doing the interview, someone who wouldn't alert the Lees to the FBI investigation, someone who knew how to conduct an interview.

But it couldn't be a detective, as that might look suspicious. Needed to be a patrol officer doing a routine interview, the death of Robert Powell still an unsolved homicide and the cops getting desperate, now talking to anyone who had ever had a meeting with the banker.

The other cop needed to look as rookie as rookies get. To add to the impression the cops were just trying to stay busy. Shortly before noon Constable Michael Woods—a sergeant until recently asking a major-crimes inspector if idiocy had been a lifelong affliction—knocked on the door of Tucker Lee. Constable Jeremy Dalton, a six-month veteran of the Birmingham Police Department, stood beside him.

Tucker Lee lived on the Lee estate, ten miles upriver from Birmingham, ten miles being the distance Andrew Lee II thought was necessary to be safely sheltered from the stench of his pulp mills. As the elder son, Tucker had inherited the estate his grandfather had built, which covered thirty acres of cleared or cultivated land, the grounds sprinkled with water fountains, birdbaths and stone sculptures that had scared Tucker as a boy.

From the master bedroom of the estate, there was a grand view of the St. John River, and Tucker set his alarm each day to ten minutes before sunrise so he could be sitting in his chair watching it: the sun stretching out down the river, glimpsed as a small light at first, up by the Canadian border, then growing and rolling right into Birmingham, chasing shadows down the river as if they were objects being physically removed. Darkness swept away. It seemed biblical to him.

He wished he could have seen the river in its prime. Could have piloted a timber crib right into Chesapeake Bay, although that would have been going back a long time and maybe his great-grandfather had been the last Lee to do that. He'd have settled for the way things had been thirty years ago. They'd had ten mills back then: three pulp, five saw, one board and a shake mill they should have converted into something decades ago, but lost the chance and now it was a useless relic. They had four mills now. None of them were running two shifts, except the sawmills in the spring, and one of them, the pulp mill, had been on layoff recall for nearly a year.

Tucker had read a trade magazine article about converting pulp mills into adult diaper factories and had someone looking into it.

He told the cops all this in an amiable CEO way before he started answering their questions. Woods was patient and let him talk. "I was working at home the entire day," Tucker Lee eventually told him. "I didn't hear about the murder until someone phoned me midafternoon."

"Who called?"

"Not sure if I recall. Let me think. I took a lot of phone calls that day. And made a lot, of course. Someone from the office? It might have been that."

"Why would someone from your office phone to tell you about the murder of Robert Powell?"

"Because it's gossip. Because you don't get gossip like that in Birmingham all that often. And Bobby was our banker, of course. I knew him well."

"Just from the bank?"

"No, we were in high school. And we curled together. Did that for many years."

"A close friend?"

"No. Someone I had known for a long time. Although his death was a tragedy, just a horrible tragedy."

Tucker hung his head and shook it slowly. There were so many rolls of flesh, it was hard to tell he was doing that, but there were tremors that made you believe that's what he was doing.

"Have you spoken to my brother yet?" he asked when his eyes came back up. "His wife knew Bobby better than I did. The past few years, anyway. She socialized with him. They sat on some boards together."

He let it hang out there a few seconds before adding, "Matter of fact, it may have been my sister-in-law who phoned and told me about Bobby. Yes, it *was* Amanda. She was looking for Travis, to find out if he'd heard the news. She was having trouble finding him."

———

TRAVIS LEE LIVED at Sunshine Lake Estates, five miles downriver from the Lee estate, a community of 113 freehold homes ranging in size from modest Tudor to starter castle. Travis Lee had lived there for twelve years, starting with a large Tudor, then buying one of the starter castles when it came on the market after the crash of '08. Most of the multiwing homes had been for sale back then.

The starter castle had two wings and a main hub, six bedrooms including two masters, five bathrooms, four fireplaces, two dens, a kitchen, a screened-in porch and a gazebo, along with several sheds and outbuildings spread over ten acres. It was a ridiculous amount of space, Travis often told himself, for a couple with no children, but it kept Amanda from wanting something larger and thus saved him much time and energy.

When at home he was usually in his den, a wood-paneled room in the basement with walk-out doors to gardens maintained by a Japanese couple who more or less survived on the money Travis Lee gave them. The old couple had found flowers and trees that bloomed throughout the year, so there was always color in the backyard gardens. It cost Lee six thousand dollars a month to maintain the gardens, but he considered it a fair sum for the miracle of sitting at his desk, looking out a window and seeing cherry blossoms in February.

It was eleven fourteen a.m. and Lee was sitting at his desk in the den reading the *Boston Globe*. An intercom chimed. He reached across the desk and pushed a button.

"Yes?"

"Trav, you have some visitors," his wife said.

"Now?"

"Yes. Would you like me to send them down?"

"Who are they?"

"They're police officers, dear."

═══

ONE OF THE cops looked to be in his late fifties, the other one right out of the police academy. Or high school.

"Good morning, Mr. Lee. I appreciate you taking a few minutes to talk to us," said the older cop when they were in the den.

"No trouble. What's this all about?"

"Robert Powell."

"Ahhh, yes. Well, please, sit down." And Lee waved them toward the leather couch on the other side of his desk. "May I fix you a drink?"

"Thank you, Mr. Lee, but we're not allowed to drink while on duty."

"An ill-thought-out regulation. You're forgiven. I had feared you were going to tell me it was too early in the day."

Lee got up from his desk and went to a nearby credenza, fixed himself a Scotch and water. "How long has it been now since Bobby was killed?"

"Nearly three weeks, Mr. Lee."

"Why are you here now?"

"We're expanding the scope of the investigation. We're pretty much talking to any customer of the bank now, Mr. Lee. Your company could be one of the biggest customers at North Maine Savings and Loan. Is that right?"

"I believe we *are* the biggest."

"How often did you see Mr. Powell?"

"Not that often. Although I saw him the day before he was killed. My brother and I had a meeting at the bank. And I'd seen him two days before that. At the Starlight."

"The day before? What time was your meeting?"

"Early. Seven thirty. There were some renewal forms Tucker and I needed to sign and we wanted to get it out of the way before the day started."

"And the Starlight, what night was that exactly?"

"It was Prime Rib Night, so Saturday night. He was there with his wife."

"Did you talk to him that night?"

"He came to our table and we had a short conversation. Can't really remember what we talked about."

"How did Mr. Powell seem to you when you saw him recently?"

"Seemed fine."

"How well did you know Mr. Powell?"

"Well enough, I suppose. We were in high school a few years. A long time ago I think my wife dated him. Tucker curled with him. He knew him much better than I did."

"Did you ever see him socially?"

"Not often. He's been at the house for a few parties. He had children, so he ran more in that set."

Woods was writing in a steno pad. He stopped to flip back a few pages, then forward. Then he said, "Everyone gets this question, so don't be offended, Mr. Lee. Where were you when Mr. Powell was shot?"

"I have no idea."

The room was silent a few seconds before Woods said, "Sorry?"

"All right, we may as well get this over with. I had a blackout that day, Officer Woods. I know it's turned out to be a rather bad day to have one of those, but I have them regularly and I had one that day. I remember the morning, up until about ten, then nothing until six when I woke up on that couch you're sitting on right now."

"You had a blackout?"

"Yes."

"Any idea what caused it?"

"McCallum's."

The cop stared at Lee a long minute before saying, "You were drunk?"

"Plastered. It was a two-drunk day for me. Once in the morning, once in the evening. Blackout in between."

"You say you've had blackouts before, Mr. Lee?"

"Many times."

"Are you getting any treatment for them?"

"Why? They don't bother me any."

The two cops exchanged looks and then Woods laughed, ran a hand through his hair. "I'd heard you liked the Starlight."

"Love it."

"When did you start drinking that day?"

"Probably had my first one around nine. Hair of the dog. Amanda was there for the first couple. Then she stopped. I've never understood how people can do that."

"So you were passed out on this couch for the day?"

"Never said that. Said I had a blackout."

Woods looked at him but didn't ask a question. The younger cop looked at Lee as though he were speaking Sanskrit.

Lee smiled and said, "I see you two gentlemen have led exemplary lives. Let me explain. I'm a pilot. Did you know that, Officer Woods?"

"No."

"Haven't flown in years, but I used to love it. I had a blackout once that lasted three days. I can function during a blackout—most serious drinkers can—and that particular blackout ended with me waking up in the cockpit of my plane at an airfield outside Memphis, Tennessee. I think I was on my way to see Graceland."

The younger cop burst out laughing. Then he quickly put a hand over his mouth and blushed. Woods looked at Lee a few more seconds before saying, "So if I'm understanding you right, Mr. Lee, you have no idea where you were when Robert Powell was shot, although you could have been anywhere."

"Nice summation," said Lee, and then he asked the cops if they were sure that they didn't want a drink. It seemed rude to him, mixing his second without at least asking.

22

I STAYED IN my motel room for four days, waiting to hear from Flanagan. The foreman at Sleigh Bay texted me the second day, asking how my sister was. I told him she was still in postoperative recovery, but nobody was telling me much. I hadn't left Birmingham yet, as I wanted to talk to a doctor first.

The next day he texted and asked what the doctor had said. I told him I was still waiting to hear from one. Later that day he phoned to tell me he was sorry, but he'd had to hire someone to finish the Algoma Limits.

"You're a good marker, Danny, and it's a shame what's happened here, but I've got to finish that job."

"Don't feel bad," I told him. "I thought you would have let me go as soon as you heard about my sister."

"I wouldn't do that to a man. Wouldn't be fair."

"I appreciate that."

"You weren't with us long enough for recall, Danny. I'm sorry about that. I can pay you until the end of the week. You can stay at the motel

~~till the end of the month, if you need. Anyone asks you about it, tell 'em~~ to call me."

"That's very generous. Thank you."

"You get this cleared away and you get back in touch with me. You understand?"

"Yes, sir. Good luck out on the Algoma. You've got some beautiful stands up there."

It sounded like the foreman was choking up a bit when I clicked off the phone. Good people. It was nice to know they were still out there.

———

IT WAS FULL spring by then but there were few signs of it in Northern Maine. The buds on the hardwood trees had yet to appear. There was still more snow than mud in the fields. On walks or runs, I was still zipping up my coat, blowing hot air into my hands.

The seasons were taking their time about changing. Stuck somewhere the other side of the Appalachians. I wondered how Flanagan was doing shaking the trees. Had the Lees given something away in their police interviews? I was taking a long walk, almost back at the motel, thinking about phoning him, when I heard a car horn honking.

I stopped and turned. Saw Amanda Lee sitting behind the wheel of a white Land Rover, waving at me out an open window.

———

STRANDS OF HER hair were being wisped around, so they looked alive. Animated. If I'd had more time to think about that, I might have come up with the mythological character she was reminding me of right then, but Amanda Lee never gave you much time to think.

"Are you just going to stare, or are you coming over to talk to me?" she yelled.

I walked over. "Slumming today?"

"That's funny. You don't think I know this motel?"

"Don't know what I should say to that. Probably something witty, right?"

"Doesn't have to be. Witty is overrated. Witty is for people who don't want to go all the way."

"What does that mean?"

"Means it's for people who like to snicker but not laugh. Fight but not get hit. Means it's a hand job. I know plenty of witty people."

"Good to know. Why are you here, Mrs. Lee?"

"Just driving around, looking for something to happen. That's from a song. Do you know it?"

"Don't believe I do."

"Travis tells me you know a lot of songs. He's an old rhythm-and-blues guy. Guess you know that."

"Motown too."

"There's a difference?"

"Yes."

"You should teach me one day. Travis doesn't have the time. Or the interest."

I didn't know what to say to that one either. I hadn't known what to say to anything she'd said so far and so I just stood there, looking at her black hair getting whipped around in the wind—hair so black and luxuriant, it looked like onyx-bejeweled tassels spinning over her head, like her body should have been dancing. Gray jays were hollering in the woods behind the motel. I could hear air brakes from a truck out on Highway 7 and kids playing a game of pickup hockey, but I couldn't see the kids or the highway. The only car on the street was Amanda Lee's. It was one of those moments when you feel the world had tilted a little—like when you walk down a busy street and turn a corner, and the next street has not a person on it, a deserted street, and until that deserted street becomes your new normal, for a few seconds, it feels like you've slipped out the city's back door, left the stage and found the wings.

"Are you going anywhere right now?" she asked.

"Not really."

—————

THE KING EDDY Hotel was on the French Line, a former corduroy road by the river. The French Line had shanty cottages that must have been two hundred years old and corner stores that still sold pop in glass bottles. It was a crooked street that became a county road once it was past the city limits, and it had a crooked mix of buildings and businesses: shanty cottages and muffler shops, redbrick homes and one-bay garages. The French Line was industrial, residential, urban, rural; it probably broke every planning code there was in Birmingham, and in the middle of it all stood the King Eddy Hotel.

It wasn't the Alexander. What gets called a "boutique hotel" today: a steerage-forward warehouse from the 1800s, converted into a hotel with a café and coffee shop on the main floor. The café had the original pine floors painted chocolate brown, sandblasted brick walls, tiny windows looking out on the street. A waiter greeted Amanda Lee by name and led us to a table along the back wall.

The Lees seemed to have their own places for their secret lives, I thought as I sat down. Nightclubs in downtown Birmingham for him, cafés on the French Line for her. I wondered if there had been agreement on the matter, although perhaps it was organic. Like puff fish and skunks, the Lees had maybe found a way to decamp and send out a scent that kept the other at bay.

She ordered a bottle of chardonnay and we drank it during lunch. She asked questions about Detroit, said she'd always wanted to live in a big city, was hoping she could live in Boston one day or have a "pied-à-terre" there at least. She blamed her unfortunate circumstances on her husband. "Trav will never leave this place," she said sadly before ordering another bottle of wine.

After our plates were cleared, coffee and snifters of Grand Marnier appeared without an order being given to the waiter. She was sipping her liqueur and looking at the dessert menu when I asked, "Where are you hoping this will go?"

"Haven't thought it through all the way, Danny."

"World of possibilities?"

"I'd say so. Wouldn't you?"

"Not sure that I would. Lots of things happen in this world that leave you feeling afterward like you didn't have much choice about it, leave you feeling like you'd walked into a scene from a play, everything blocked out, people just waiting for you to get there."

"You're describing fate. That's a little grand for a tree marker, isn't it?"

"It would be. But I don't think I'm describing fate. Just scenes waiting to happen."

"Is this a scene?"

"Feels like one. Why should we be sitting here today? Would you have predicted it yesterday? The unforeseen, the unexpected, it happens every day, even though most of us spend our lives trying to avoid it."

Amanda Lee took another sip from her snifter, let the liqueur sit in her mouth a second before swallowing; then she laughed and gave her hair a flip. "Sugar, is that a pickup line? Because if it is—it's *very* fuckin' good. Let me take a guess how the scene ends. We're in one of the rooms above this café fuckin' our brains out, because it was meant to be, one of those unforeseen things that keep happening to us. Yeah, I could see you having great success with a line like that."

She laughed and kept drinking, flipping her hair back and rubbing a foot against my leg. I regretted what I had said. You get used to talking when you're undercover, spinning a story here, a story there—so used to it that sometimes you say things you should have kept private. An old ATF agent told me once that was a common career ender for undercover agents. Forgetting who you were.

Maybe it was the same way for actors, politicians and people like

Amanda Lee, who had been cheating and pretending for so long, any sort of straight game would have shocked her as much as time travel and an alien invasion. I hadn't figured out yet why some things in this world seem preordained, while other things seem a goat's rodeo. Things I haven't figured out yet make me nervous. I should have kept that one to myself.

"I like your husband."

"I like him too. That is Travis's great skill. Being liked. He rather excels at it."

"I also work for him."

"Why are you talking about my husband?"

"So you can understand why this isn't going anywhere."

"Are you serious? I just told you that pickup line of yours was wonderful."

"It wasn't a pickup line."

She stared at me a few seconds before laughing again. "My God, you think Trav would be *hurt*. Danny, I don't know whether to laugh or cry. Travis doesn't care. Do you really think we have a *marriage*?"

"What do you have?"

"Would it be terribly cliché to say we have an *understanding*? It's like being in the military. Don't ask. Don't tell. Do they still have that? I can't remember. But it's like that, Danny."

"Has anyone ever said no to you?"

"Has anyone ever . . . ? You know, you're starting to piss me off. I thought you were interesting, and maybe the best-looking bush pig I've seen in a long time, but pissed off, yeah, that's what you're making me right now."

"Sorry about that. Do you normally feel that way when someone says something kind about your husband?"

That was the parlay that ended the game. I knew it would. She recoiled as though I'd slapped her. She actually *did* slap me. Leaned across the table and gave me a drunken swat on the cheek. A bit more dramatic than I thought was justified, but maybe I'd had it coming.

"I can see I'm drinking with a child," she said, and waved for the waiter to bring the check.

"I'll get it," I said.

"Damn fucking right you will," she answered.

If Amanda Lee had walked out right then, like she could have, I probably would have found myself later that day thinking about my feels-like-walking-into-a-scene riddle and deciding Amanda Lee was an argument against it.

There had been no purpose to it. No change of course. Although it had felt at first like something that needed to happen, it didn't feel that way at the end.

But she didn't walk out. As I was waiting for the check, her phone rang. She looked at the number and a quizzical look came to her face. If we had been going upstairs to one of the rooms, she might have been more circumspect and left the table.

But I was already old news, someone she would never see again, and she spoke as though I wasn't there. I never heard the voice of her caller, just Amanda Lee's end of the conversation.

"Hello. Amanda . . ."

"I'm surprised to hear from you. . . ."

"You're joking, right? . . ."

". . . I *may* be interested. In hearing about it, anyway. Where do you want to meet?"

That was it. A four-line conversation. But I have it memorized. Same way I have her facial expressions memorized—the surprise at the start of the conversation. The doubt midway. The curiosity at the end. I can recall how she nodded and whispered what would have been an address, or a place-name, just before she clicked off. Sounded like "Saint," and then a word that started with an "R" or a "W." I lost it after "Saint."

I have all that memorized because five days later I was repeating it to Jim Flanagan about a dozen times. And lunch with Amanda Lee seemed again like a scene that had been blocked out, just waiting for me to arrive.

23

TRAVIS LEE STAYED parked in front of the building for nearly an hour before walking in. Cameras caught him doing that, but he told me the same thing. He spent the hour staring at the building and wondering what to do. "You never get better at it," he told me. "What was that Hemingway line about going bankrupt? It happens two ways. Gradually, then suddenly. Same thing with a free fall."

He looked at that building and wished it were decades ago, when Birmingham was booming, when that building was being constructed, right after World War II and the city was on the cusp of its next great economic boom—postwar housing construction. Which happened to coincide with the peak circulation years for every newspaper and magazine in America. Pine and cedar for the homes; jack spruce and every garbage tree God ever invented for the newsprint. Welcome to the state of Maine.

Lee was pretty sure that he was under police surveillance and that the car parked half a block behind him was an unmarked police car. He had noticed it a few times that day. A Ford Taurus. And although that might not mean anything, the undercover cars in Birmingham were all Fords. He knew that. A man was driving the car, which might not mean anything either, but would a woman have been driving an unmarked police car?

Stupid question. Or maybe it *wasn't* a stupid question, just one you should *think* was stupid, to be correct about things, not offend anyone, not start any unpleasant conversations. *Could* it be a woman driving a surveillance car?

He kept free-falling. Unsure of his next move, unsure if the smart play would be to march into that brick building and get on with it or drive in the other direction as fast as he could. The free fall had started three days ago. He came home from the Starlight that night, made himself a sandwich and fell asleep on the couch while watching *Law and Order*. In the morning he checked the bedroom, the sitting room and, before leaving for the day, the fridge. But he didn't find a note.

He got home much later the second night, and when he awoke on the same couch, it was nearly noon. He made the same checks as the day before, checked the garage this day as well, where Amanda's Land Rover was parked. On the third night he was home early and checked the backyard as well as the house; then he checked the gardens, the garage, the floor around the fridge where a note might have fallen.

What to do? In a world that still had reference points—open factories, steady work—there wouldn't have been much to think about. Of *course* you marched into that building and reported it.

But Travis Lee's world right then? This town right now? What was the smart play?

You never get better at it. Free-falling is not the sort of thing that practice makes perfect. Lee wondered if he should stay parked and let that be his decision. Don't move. Do nothing until the cops came to ask what the hell he was doing and they could decide his fate. He was tired of the work.

Travis Lee waited five minutes after having that thought before opening the door of his SUV and heading toward the building. Once inside he went to a woman sitting behind a Plexiglas reception window and asked where he needed to go to report his wife missing.

———

TRAVIS LEE WAITED another ninety minutes in the lobby of the Birmingham police station before a detective came to take his statement. It was a long time to wait, although Lee didn't know that. As soon as he gave his name to the receptionist, she had phoned Kowalski, who phoned Flanagan, and after a conference call with the duty sergeant, it was decided to treat Lee's appearance as though it were a regular missing-person case. No talking about Robert Powell. No mention of an FBI investigation.

Flanagan's only request was that the cops hold Lee for an hour before letting him leave.

"Hope you haven't been drinking, pal," he said when he called me. "You've finally got some work to do. I may have that corroboration we've been looking for."

"You believe me now that we've been blown?"

"Pal, I believe everything's about to blow. Travis Lee just walked into the Birmingham police station and reported his wife missing."

———

THE DETECTIVE LOOKED across the table at Travis Lee. The interview room was small, with no windows, and the smell of alcohol was so strong, it could have passed for disinfectant.

"Have you been drinking tonight, Mr. Lee?"

"Certainly."

"That's a strange answer. What do you mean by that?"

"I mean, no is wrong and yes doesn't seem accurate. Not committed enough. So certainly."

"Are you drunk, sir?"

"No."

"You don't seem drunk. You smell like a distillery though. Why is that?"

"No idea."

The detective began writing in the steno pad he had placed on the table in front of him. "How long has your wife been missing, Mr. Lee."

"She hasn't been home in three nights."

"Three nights, and you're just reporting her missing now?"

"We can miss each other quite easily." And he told the detective about coming home and falling asleep on the couch, searching bedrooms and fridge magnets, but no Amanda.

"But you weren't concerned right away?" said the detective.

"I *was*. I just thought it might have been premature."

"What do you mean?"

"Only a couple nights. Might have been premature to report her missing. Might even have seemed comical to some people."

"Are you telling me it's not uncommon for your wife to stay away from home some nights, Mr. Lee?"

"That's what I'm telling you. But Amanda always makes sure I know where she is. There's some sort of message, some sort of sighting. This time, there's been nothing. Not much fun that way."

"Have you tried to contact any of her friends? Any of her family?"

"No. I'm not sure who I would call."

"You have no children. Is that correct?"

"That's correct."

"Does she have family?"

"She has a brother who lives in San Francisco. Her father lives in Birmingham, but they're not close. Walter Singer. He used to own Singer and Sons lumberyard, out on Highway Seven."

"You don't think her father might know where she is?"

"Quite sure he doesn't. Like I said, they're not close."

"Can you think of any possible reason for your wife's disappearance?"

"A reason to disappear? We all have one of those, don't we, Detective? I'm not sure I understand the question."

"Do you have any *theories* on why your wife has not been seen for three days, Mr. Lee?"

"No."

"Do you suspect foul play?"

"Yes. Don't you?"

"I don't, Mr. Lee. Don't know your wife well enough to think that. Why do you think that?"

"Because she hasn't been seen for three days."

"No other reason?"

"No."

"You have a photo of your wife?"

Lee took out his phone and started scrolling through his photo archive. He found a photo of Amanda in a bathing suit, sitting in a chaise longue beside an infinity pool in Cancún. It had a good, clear shot of her face. He tried to find a photo that didn't have her in a bathing suit, but there weren't many without legs or cleavage. He asked the detective for his e-mail address.

"There you go." And he put the phone back in his pocket.

There was a ping from the detective's phone, and he pulled it from his shirt pocket. He looked at the photo a few seconds before Lee said, "I'm assuming you can crop that."

"Yes."

"It was taken last winter. Most recent photo I have."

"If you can't think of anyone we can contact, Mr. Lee, can you think of any place where your wife might have gone? Do you have a country place or a cottage? Does she have a place she likes? A place she might go to if she wanted to get away from the city."

"We have a condo here in Birmingham, but she hasn't been there. We have a time-share in Cancún. Maybe there, but it's not our time. She'd have to arrange something."

"I'll need contact info for the time-share, Mr. Lee. Do you know if her passport is missing?"

"No, I haven't checked. I'm not really sure where I would look."

The detective told Flanagan later that Travis Lee was one of the strangest missing-person interviews he'd ever conducted. There wasn't any anger, which there often was when a husband reported a wife missing, the husband suspecting a sordid tale of infidelity when the wife was found. There wasn't the heartbreaking confusion you saw with other husbands, who didn't have a clue what had happened. Those were the cases where the wife would be found dead at the bottom of a ravine, a steering wheel pushed through her sternum.

Other husbands were helpful to the point of suspicion. They arrived at the station with a long list of people the police should interview, another long list of places they should check. Those husbands organized ground searches of the area where the wife was last seen, talked to the media, contacted the investigating detective every day with a new theory on what might have happened.

Those were the husbands you charged with murder when the body was found. Travis Lee ticked none of the regular boxes. He seemed genuinely concerned by his wife's disappearance, but not panicked about it. He was helpful, but not over-the-top. It was confusing, and whether Travis Lee had something to do with his wife's disappearance— the detective had no idea. First time he ever did a missing-person interview and didn't have a suspicion one way or the other.

"Anything else you can think of, Mr. Lee, that might help us find your wife?" the detective asked near the end of the interview after one hour had passed.

"No, not really."

"One last question for you, sir." And the detective flipped back through his steno pad. "Yes, here it is. You said your wife has gone missing before, but she always finds a way to let you know where she is. That's correct?"

"Yes."

"It's the reason this disappearance seems out of the ordinary to you."

"That's correct."

"You said after that, 'not much fun that way.' What did you mean by that, Mr. Lee?"

"I mean, it's no fun if Amanda takes off and I don't know about it."

The detective gave him a puzzled look. "For her," Lee said when he realized more needed to be said. "No fun for her."

24

I WATCHED TRAVIS Lee walk out of the police station at nine twenty-three p.m. I was on the other side of the street from the station, a block north of Lee's white Mercedes. He looked unsteady when he walked down the steps, but he didn't sway, didn't look drunk. Looked like someone who had just taken a strong body punch.

I followed him to the Starlight Club but he didn't go in. Left his SUV idling in front of the entrance. The club was busy, with people coming in and out, a flash of bright interior light whenever the door opened. I could see men with rocks glasses in their hands walking between tables. Women sitting at the bar with Jennifer Aniston haircuts from the last millennium. The images clicked past me like an old slide show.

After fifteen minutes Lee put his car in drive and left the parking lot. I followed him toward the St. John River and then down Highway 7 all the way to Farrelton. He drove five miles under the speed limit the entire way. Twice a right-turn signal came on accidentally before quickly going off. If I'd been a patrol officer, I would have been pulling over that SUV.

At Farrelton, Lee crossed the bridge and came back on the other side of the river. But he didn't go to Birmingham. Ten miles outside the city, he turned away from the river and took County Road 2 toward the hills. There was less traffic on this road and I increased my distance, pulling over once to let a cargo van pass and then keeping the van between us.

In twenty minutes Lee turned onto Anderson Side Road, a gravel road that ran through old homesteading land, mailboxes marking the eastern edge of the hundred-acre land grants people were once given, the mailboxes perfectly spaced every hundred yards. There was a near-full moon and I was able to travel with my headlights turned off once I lost the cargo van. I followed Lee's taillights until he turned off the road and headed down a long laneway.

The headlights dipped and rose and then shone on a white clapboard farmhouse before being turned off. I pulled to the side of the road, waited five minutes and phoned Flanagan.

"Where is he?"

"Some farmhouse out in Bustard County."

That's Pearl Lafontaine's house."

"I was wondering about that."

"You've been gone two hours."

"He went driving. I followed him to the Starlight but he never went in. Then he went up the river to Farrelton and back. I don't know why he did that. Now he's at this farmhouse. I'm parked on the Anderson Side Road."

Flanagan started laughing. "Do you believe this fuckin' guy? He reports his wife missing. Then he drives over to his girlfriend's house. He must have a pair of brass ones."

"Or he's not thinking clearly. I'm pretty sure he was drinking while he was driving."

"Is that right? You could have had a cop pull him over if you thought he was a danger."

"Wasn't dangerous at all. Hard-core-drunk cautious."

"That's our boy. Do you think he's there for the night?"

"Looks that way."

"I'll have Kowalski send someone out to relieve you. Don't talk to anyone when they get there. Just drive off. How far are you from the house?"

"Quarter mile south. My lights are off. I'm pulled over near a silo."

———

I STARED AT the light coming from the farmhouse. A rectangle of mustard yellow light shining through the blackness, like something foreign, like a light hovering above a great abyss.

Shadows passed through the light from time to time. Pearl Lafontaine's shadow mostly. Travis Lee appeared only occasionally and then just his head, leaning in from the left side of the light. He was leaning across a table. They were probably sitting in a kitchen.

I thought about Amanda Lee and what would have made her run. She didn't seem like the running type, but her life was falling apart, about to make the transition from gradually falling apart to suddenly falling apart, and maybe she decided to run.

Or maybe there was a body waiting to be found in the woods around Birmingham.

I looked at the light framed in the darkness, the shadows of Travis Lee and Pearl Lafontaine stretching and distorting, and before long, I knew—with a conviction that startled me—that the rest of this story was being decided right then inside that farmhouse. It had become their story in a way. The rest of us were just watching. Waiting for our scenes to begin.

THE SWEET GOODBYE

SHE SAT AT the kitchen table, a Formica table from the fifties with the thick chrome edging and steel legs, blue swirling lines atop that resembled a topographical map. The sort of table that used to get blown up in nuclear-safety movies, along with the wooden-cabinet television, the top-entry washing machine and the crash-test dummy wearing the kitchen apron.

Most of the furniture in the house was furniture she had grown up with. Some of the cabinets and hutches were more than a hundred years old, same for some of the dishware, and there was a grandfather clock in the parlor that was probably older than that, one that chimed every fifteen minutes, and every time that happened, he looked surprised.

"Do you like the chimes?"

"You know what? I don't think I do," he answered.

"You never had a grandfather clock in that little ol' mansion you grew up in?"

"Not that I ever heard."

"I thought every mansion had to have a grandfather clock. Like it was a rule or something. I love those old chimes."

She said it quickly, without thinking, and the silence that followed soon became awkward. How could she not know that about him? It seemed fundamental to her for some reason, character defining in some way—do you like grandfather clocks? Yes or no? How could she not know that about the man she'd been sleeping with for thirty years?

"How's your drink, hon? Can I freshen it?"

"Please."

She went to the pantry and took out a bottle of Ballantine's, brought it to the table. "May as well leave it here," she said, and went to the fridge, came back with a red plastic ice tray. She broke cubes into a mixing bowl and slid the bowl across the table. He shook his head no. After she added cubes to her drink, she sat down and he asked if he could have some ice.

"You're not thinking too well, hon. You're missing her, aren't you?"

"I'd be surprised if that were the case. Don't know what I'm feeling."

"It's missing her. Live with anyone long enough and you're going to miss them. Whether they treated you good or bad, you're going to miss them."

He looked at her, not believing that. "Do you know this is the first time I've been inside your house?"

"I do know that."

"You've lived in this house a long time. You never wanted to live anyplace else?"

"Never. This is my home."

"You've owned it since you were how old?"

"Sixteen."

"How in the world did that work? You've never told me."

"Not much to tell. My dad took off and I ended up with the house. Want some more ice."

"Please."

She went to get the ice tray. Took her time. While she was standing there with the fridge door open, the clock chimed.

HER FATHER WAS a bad drunk who never had any time for her until she turned fourteen and then he found himself living with a teenage daughter blossoming in the upstairs bedroom like some exotic forbidden fruit. Just the two of them living in the house by then.

Problem was, her father never forbade himself much. She was far from the only girl in Bustard County who had to deal with a situation like that. She knew some girls in high school who'd changed in a day, become sullen and withdrawn after they'd been the skip-rope kind of girl their whole lives. Suddenly they started losing weight. Showing up at school with bruises on their forearms. It wasn't hard to tell what girls it was happening to.

A girl named Susan Petrie, two grades younger than her, hanged herself one morning in her barn right after doing morning chores. She was one of those girls. Most got through it though, and you'd see them around town from time to time. They looked sad and lost to Pearl, every last one she knew about.

She didn't know what to do about her father, so she went to the police station one day after school and tried to report him. She got in to speak to a detective, who asked her, while leering at her chest most of the time, if she'd had any trouble with her father recently. Had he grounded her for some reason? Not liked one of her boyfriends?

She walked out of the police detachment without filing a complaint. She told Beau about it soon afterward, not sure what he might do, if anything, but knowing he didn't like her father, and at the very least, he would believe her.

Nothing happened for nearly a year and she figured Beau was going to be just like the cops. She was waiting for high school to finish so she could get out of Birmingham, was thinking of moving to Portland, take some community college courses, just hadn't figured out which ones, when one night, just before midnight, she heard a vehicle coming up the gravel laneway.

Her father was drinking in the kitchen and she heard him bump into some chairs before turning on the porch light. The vehicle stopped with its headlights turned on at the front of the house. Her father was probably shield-ing his eyes when he opened the door and screamed, "Who the fuck's there?"

There was no answer. A few seconds after that came the sound of foot-steps on the porch and she knew her father had stepped outside. "Will you turn off the fuckin' lights, whoever the fuck you are!"

"Get away from the house," she heard Beau say. "Come over here, Jean."

She could have gone to her bedroom window and watched, but she didn't. She wondered about that over the years, if she was being cowardly for doing that, but she didn't think so. She had stood wide-eyed and straight in front of things that were almost as bad. She figured she knew what was going to hap-pen as soon as she heard that vehicle coming down the laneway and that's why she didn't look. She didn't need to. Everything after knowing was a detail.

"What the fuck are you doing?" her father screamed as he came down the steps of the front porch. "What the fuck . . . ?"

She heard the punch, so it must have been quite a punch. Then there was another punch. And what sounded like a kick. There was a loud thump and she knew her father had fallen to the ground. Then there was a scraping sort of noise, like rubbing a knife over gristle stuck to a plate, and she knew her father was being dragged away.

"Wake up, girl," he screamed. "There's some shit going on out here and you gotta—" But then came another punch and he didn't say anything after that. Car doors were opened and shut. The headlights backed away from the house. A minute later she was alone, listening to the sound of water running through a pipe somewhere, a wind that had picked up and was hitting the shutters on her bedroom window.

Two days later Beau phoned and told her to go to a lawyer's office in downtown Birmingham the next day at ten a.m. He said they were expecting her. When she got there, she was ushered into a large conference room where a woman wearing a dress Pearl thought you wore only to the Starlight on a Saturday night served her coffee from what looked like a silver pot. When the woman was gone, two men came into the room, carrying thick file folders.

The men shook Pearl's hand, opened their files and, ten minutes later, had covered the "pith and substance" of what they needed to tell her. One lawyer used that phrase all the time. "Pith and substance." He was the lawyer who seemed most in a hurry.

Her father had given her the farm, plus all the machinery and equipment. He had given her his truck and the contents of both his checking and savings accounts, total: $1,241. Pearl was also being named beneficiary for the twenty-thousand-dollar insurance policy that came with the small pension her father received from the Maine-Sherbrooke Railway Company.

The lawyers showed her where she needed to sign, where she needed to initial, and then they put a stack of paper in front of her. Pearl was halfway through the job, flipping through the paper and looking for the plastic tabs, when she asked, "So where is my father?"

"In California," said the pith-and-substance lawyer. "I gather there was an estrangement?"

Funny word. Anytime it's used, a funny word. Could have said "broken," "twisted," "split," but everyone wants to use the word that rolls off the tongue and sounds almost sweet. Estrangement. Sure, let's call it that.

"That's right."

"It appears your father wanted to make amends. As you can see, he cares for you more deeply than you suspect."

"Yes, I see that."

"His nephew made most of the arrangements. I have never actually met your father, but he is a generous man. It's quite a birthday gift."

"I'm sorry?"

"Your birthday. It was two weeks ago, correct? You're sixteen now? You can't legally own property in Maine until you're sixteen. Your father must have known that."

She nodded. Yes, he must have known that.

———

THE GRANDFATHER CLOCK was still bothering her. How could she not have known a thing like that? It made her feel silly. The way the waitresses at the Red Bird made her feel sometimes when they saw Travis waiting for her in the parking lot.

Beau said she was obsessed with him, and maybe she was. Most people said more or less the same thing. Although she thought obsession was only obsession if you didn't know about it. If you knew, it was something else.

What had happened to Amanda? Likely that girl had run. She knew enough men with second homes and pieds-à-terre far from Birmingham, and she'd probably bailed. It's what Amanda would do. Or maybe she'd done something stupid like contacted an old lover, someone who lived deep in the North Maine Woods, to ask him what the hell was going on and how worried she should be. Would Amanda have been that stupid?

It was a waning moon and she could barely see the cedar break behind her farmhouse. There must have been high clouds in the sky as well. She stared out the window a few more minutes before giving him a shake. He didn't move and she gave him another, harder this time.

"What's wrong?" he mumbled.

"I've been thinking, hon. I don't think you should go home today. Might not be safe. I think you should stay here for a little while."

"What do you mean, it might not be safe?"

"It's just a feeling I have. Will you trust me on it?"

"I'm in trouble?"

"Don't you think you're in trouble?"

He didn't answer. She threw off her bedsheets and looked around the floor for her jeans.

"What are you doing?"

"Having a shower, getting dressed and then I'm leaving."

"Where in the world are you going at this hour?"

"Not going to tell you. But, hon, you really gotta stay here. All right?"

=====

SHE PUT HER car in neutral and pushed it down the driveway behind the cedar break and onto the road. She started the engine and drove away, waiting a half mile before turning on the headlights.

She hoped to make it as far as Little Creek Camp and she came within two miles before the Honda couldn't go any farther, the ruts on the logging road now too deep for the undercarriage clearance of her car.

She drove the car off the road and covered it with cedar boughs, marked the spot by notching an X in a tree. At Little Creek Camp, she got some catcalls—"You get tossed out of a plane, darlin'?" "Look at this—a fallen fuckin' angel!"—but it didn't take long for a young driver with sandy hair and a badly pocked face to say he'd run her up to Paradise Lake.

Those were the words he used, "run you up," although he was talking about a hundred-twenty-mile drive through the North Maine Woods, at what would have been an average speed of about twenty miles an hour.

It was late morning when they headed out, the sun sitting just a few feet above the tree line and long shadows cast across the road. The driver's name was Josh Peters and he had been driving a logging truck for a little more than a year, getting trained at a Manpower office in Portland after losing his job at New England Kitchen Cabinets when it had gone bankrupt two years ago.

"Do you get up here much?" he asked when they had been driving a while.

"Haven't been up here in a long time."

"So Beau Lafontaine is your cousin?"

"That's right."

"Shit, you must have stories to tell. He's a Malee, isn't he?"

"He is. And I do have stories. Want to hear any?"

"Fuck no." And the boy laughed. She waited for him to make a pass at her but it never came. Maybe the boy had set out with that as a possibility, then changed his mind. She was too old for him. She was a Lafontaine, and maybe it was wise to keep your distance from anyone with that surname. Maybe he was never planning on doing it at all, just wanted to help someone stranded on the logging road outside Little Creek Camp. The more they talked, the more she thought it was the latter. A good kid who had been brought up to help people whenever he had the chance.

She wished it had been an older driver behind the wheel, someone who *would have made a pass. She was using the boy, and it would feel better if he were trying to use her as well. Given what might be waiting for them at Paradise Lake, it would be better if this boy were tainted.*

———

THEY DROVE DOWN the logging road, lurching up and down on the ruts, the boy shifting his low gears in quick succession, making good time with the bed of the truck empty. For several hours they drove through a mixed forest of oak and maple, spruce and pine, until the hardwood and the scrub trees started to thin and then it was just pine. The giant trunks looked like windowless buildings, no branches for the first twenty feet, a canopy of branches after that so thick you couldn't see the sky.

It was dark inside that forest and the boy had to put on his headlights. Turn up the heater as well. Two miles south of Paradise Lake, he rounded a corner and slammed on his brakes. The air hissed out fast and shrill and someone must have trained the boy well down in Portland because he shifted his gears down fast and hard, in a way that looked like it must have hurt his hands. The truck slid sideways for about fifty feet before it caught a rut and straightened out. When he finally brought the truck to a stop, the boy stared at the sight in front of them.

Parked sideways across the logging road was a truck that looked like his: a forty-foot Peterbilt with welded-in rails and a forty-foot flatbed. But there were no logs on the truck. Just three men sitting there drinking beer and smoking cigarettes, all with long, dark hair and bulky jackets, heavy boots and pants of stiff brown canvas. The men stared at the truck that had careened to a stop in front of them. None of them moved for a few seconds. Then one man pulled a walkie-talkie from the pocket of his coat and spoke into it, while the other two men jumped off the bed of the truck. The boy turned to Lafontaine and said, "Are you sure we're allowed up here?"

———

THE MAN ON the walkie-talkie had a short conversation. Then he too jumped off the truck and caught up with the other two, and they approached the truck at the same time, not walking together but spread out in a semi-circle. The man with the walkie-talkie went to the driver's door and motioned for the window to be rolled down. When it was, he yelled, "This is a private camp. You need to go back. You should have gone left at the fork in Palmer's Junction."

"Turn around? You know what you're asking me to do?" yelled the boy.

"You don't know how to back this rig up?"

"Twenty miles? I need to go forward and find a place to make the turn."

"Not my problem, asshole. You shouldn't have missed the fork."

The other two men laughed. She leaned across the gearshift so she could see out the driver's-side window. The man whistled when he saw her, but before he could speak, she said, "If you don't do anything else that's really stupid, you might be all right, my friend. My name is Pearl Lafontaine. I'm here to see my cousin."

The man bent lower to get a better look at her. "He's not expecting anyone."

"It's a surprise visit. And it's urgent. I'm in a hurry."

"What did you say your name was?"

"Pearl Lafontaine."

"I've never heard him talking about you."

"I'd be surprised if Beau spends time talking to you at all. You're the doorman, right?"

The man looked startled. But it didn't last long. "Do you think I'm just going to wave you through?"

"Want to see ID?"

"Fuck ID, and fuck this noise. If you were his cousin, I'd know you were coming. Last chance to back this truck up before we torch it and you're walking the fuck out of here, princess."

As he was talking, the man pulled out the handgun she knew he had tucked inside his pants' waistband. The other two men drew handguns at the same time and pointed them at the truck. The boy's face blanched white. The sort of instant whitening you might see on green vegetables when they get chucked into boiling water.

She waited a few seconds. Then she opened the passenger door and stepped out. She took her time about it, one long leg after one long leg. The two men who had yet to talk were looking at her and smiling. The leader looked at her as though she were crazy. When she walked around the truck to stand in front of him, he looked confused, unsure where to point his gun.

"Real disappointed in the help my cousin hires these days," she said. "If you shoot this boy before phoning Beau and telling him Pearl Lafontaine is here to see him, you're a dead man. Today. Within the hour. How well do you know my cousin?"

There was fear in his eyes now. Walking out of that truck with three guns aimed at her, saucy as you please—it had caught his attention.

"He's told you never to disturb him, right?" she continued. "Gets angry when it happens? I get it. I've seen it. But trust me, asshole. If you don't make that call, you're a dead man today."

---

*I*T WAS A *strange drive, the last two miles into Paradise Lake. As though the truck had passed a demarcation line after it passed the roadblock and entered another country. She never got used to it, her cousin's bush camp in the North Maine Woods.*

As they drove down the road, they passed tall wooden poles where the hides of deer and bear were hanging to dry and other poles that had the carcasses bleeding out. Root cellars where old men sat atop stone steps leading down, smoking bone pipes, rifles laid across their knees. There were large nets running overhead through the trees, with boughs and cedar shakes thrown atop. There was no sun on that road. There never would be.

Campfires were burning everywhere and the smoke was thick. The boy switched from his headlights to fog lights and they drove past tin sheds with no windows and other sheds with tall stove-top pipes and a chemical smell so strong, her eyes watered. Most of the tin sheds had sheets of burlap stacked nearby, and in front of one large shack, two middle-aged women sat naked, smoking cigarettes and flicking the ashes into a tin can. Pearl knew the women were filling gelatin caps inside that shack and that everyone working inside was naked. Hard to steal anything when you don't have pockets.

There were spur lines that ran off the main logging road and Pearl could see lights down some of the lines, what looked like kerosene lanterns. There was the tart smell of frying pork and the pungent smell of marijuana mixed with cedar and pine. Somewhere a stereo was playing an old Creole reel, with washboards and fiddles. The singer was French. You could hear the vinyl skipping.

They drove past people marching in single file with heavy packs and others who sat in groups, smoking pipes and passing around whiskey jugs. The road dead-ended at a long rectangular house right by the shore of Paradise Lake. A man was waiting for them at the front door.

The boy didn't stay. He started making his turn as soon as she jumped out of the cab, even looked away from her when she tried to lean in his open window and say goodbye.

He was probably right.

The man who had been waiting opened the door and she followed him. The building was partitioned into many rooms, some with doors, some with curtains for doors, some with nothing at all. They passed from room to room. Several young children slept in one room, in sleeping bags spread out on the floor. In another there were wooden crates with Cyrillic writing stacked floor to ceiling. In the one after that, people were having sex, bodies pumping under a fur blanket she could just make out in the darkest corner of the room.

Finally, the man pushed aside a heavy brocade curtain and she stepped into the last room. It looked like an English sitting room. There were brown leather chairs with heavy brass rivets, dark wooden furniture, crystal decanters, oil paintings of foxhunts and Waterloo Bridge hanging from the walls.

Beau Lafontaine sat beneath one of the Waterloo Bridge paintings. He was smoking a cigarette. He looked at her and she could tell he was angry but trying to keep his emotions in check. That's why his cheek was twitching. Why his mouth was puckered inward when he wasn't smoking. Why his eyes seemed on fire.

He smoked and stared at her a long time before saying, "You should not have come here, ma fille. That was a mistake."

25

IT WAS LATE morning before I got out of bed. No one had relieved me on the Anderson Side Road until two a.m., and when I fell into bed after filing my report, there was an early-morning pink in the sky.

It was a knocking on the door that awoke me. I didn't think a knock on the door was all that important and ignored it. Probably a maid or a desk clerk wondering why I hadn't been on a shuttle bus for a week, and would I need the room after the first of the month? Anything important would have come with a vibrating buzz on my phone.

But the knocking didn't go away. After a while I noticed it came in sequence. Three quick taps. A pause of thirty seconds or so. Then two heavy taps. I wondered if there would ever be a variation to the rhythm, and if so, what it might be. I was still wondering when I swung open the door.

Tucker Lee was standing there, wearing a tuque although it wasn't that cold, and breathing hard. It was difficult to believe knocking on a door could wind a man, but that seemed to be what I was seeing.

"Mr. Lee," I said, not trying to hide my surprise, "why are you here?"

"I came to see you. Isn't that obvious?" His breathing was so shallow, his words wheezed out, yet he managed somehow to still sound annoyed and imperious.

"How did you find me?"

"What do you mean, how did I find you? You work for me. Do you not think I know what motel my workers are staying at?"

"I don't work for you anymore, Mr. Lee. Maybe you haven't heard, but my sister has been in a bad car accident. Back in Michigan. I'm waiting to see if I need to go back. Your foreman laid me off a week ago."

A look of confusion passed across his face. "Why are you still at the Three Pines?"

"I'm hoping my sister will be all right and I can go back to work. Your foreman said to call him if I was still available for work. I'll know more in a day or so."

"Why not go to Michigan while you're waiting?"

I waited a beat and looked at my feet. Then I raised my head sadly and said, "I don't own a car, Mr. Lee. Airfare isn't cheap and I don't have a place to stay in Marquette. If Donna is going to be all right, well . . . I'd rather get my job back."

I saw certainty come to Lee's face, replacing the doubt and confusion that had briefly been there. I might not have been an employee, but I was poor and I *wanted* to be an employee, which was almost as good for Tucker Lee. Maybe better.

"Are you going to invite me in?" he demanded.

Because it wasn't really a question, I didn't bother answering. I stood aside and let Tucker Lee waddle into my motel room.

———

I KEPT THE curtains drawn and turned on the vestibule light. I didn't bother with the main light. I like a room that has shadows. Any room that's lit up so bright, there's no longer any hue or depth to the space, just garish lines as stark, clear and final as men lined up in front of a firing squad—I don't stay in rooms like that. Unless I have to. Courtrooms and jail cells are rooms like that.

Tucker Lee sat in the one chair I had to offer him, a desk chair on wheels that he pulled to the center of the room. I sat on the bed.

"I'd offer you something, Mr. Lee, but I don't really have much. There's no hot plate in the room. Just a fridge. Would you like a pop?"

"I don't want anything."

"Why are you here, then, Mr. Lee?"

The way I asked the question surprised him. Maybe questions in general surprised him.

"There's a bit of a story to that, but it ends with me wanting to hire you."

"That would be great, Mr. Lee," I said, trying hard to sound as though that would be great. "I didn't know you had other timber limits that needed marking this year."

"We don't. You wouldn't be working for me as a tree marker."

"What would I be doing?"

"I'll get to that in a minute. Travis tells me your uncle used to own a lumber company but he lost it in 2008. Is that true?"

"Two thousand and nine. Upper Peninsula Pulp and Forestry. It was pulp mostly, although he had one sawmill just outside Marquette. The company shut down after the *Flint Journal* stopped publishing a daily newspaper. Bunch of other newspapers went under on him at the same time. Newspapers were his biggest customers."

"Banks made out all right, I'm betting?"

"Yeah, banks always do. Until they don't, I guess."

"What does that mean?"

"Oh, nothing. I was just thinking about that banker that got killed in Birmingham last month. Bad joke. Sorry. You knew him, right?"

Tucker Lee looked at me with suspicion. I was going too fast.

"I *did* know him. Robert Powell. Good man. I went to high school with him. We curled together."

"There's a sport I've never tried. Looks like fun. You any good?"

"Very good."

"Yeah, you'd have the strength for it. Those rocks look heavy."

He smiled. I sat on the bed and waited. I could have asked a question about Robert Powell, but I asked one about curling. The suspicion that had been on Tucker Lee's face had vanished.

"Are you going to tell me what this job is, Mr. Lee?"

"Of course I am," he snapped. "Did you think I wasn't? Would I be here in the Three Pines fuckin' Motel if I wasn't . . . ?" And then he closed his mouth. Quick. Like he'd swallowed something that got stuck halfway down. His face turned deep red at the same time, like he was about to choke, but nothing happened, other than his voice seemed to have lost all its confidence when he spoke again.

"My sister-in-law is missing. Did you know that?"

"I didn't," I lied.

"Four days now. The police are looking for her."

"Maybe she just ran away, Mr. Lee. Your brother drinks a bit. No disrespect."

"If that was going to drive Amanda away, she would have run during the honeymoon. It's something else, I'm afraid. I want to hire you to be my bodyguard."

I leaned back and gave him a curious look. "What?"

"You heard me. It's a short-term position but it will pay well."

"Mr. Lee, I don't know what to say. I'm not a bodyguard."

"So what? I'll pay you double what you were making as a tree marker."

"To do what?"

"To be with me. Be a bodyguard. What— Do you think this is *complicated*?"

"Why do you need a bodyguard? Because your sister-in-law is missing?"

"What fuckin' difference does that make? Is that a question bodyguards even get to ask? I'll double your salary and you can stay at my place while you're working for me. It'll be a big fuckin' step up from this place, Barrett."

"This is a crazy idea."

"Double not enough for you? Tell me what you want."

"What I want? How about you telling me what's going on here? That would be a good place to start."

"I don't *know* what the fuck is going on anymore, Barrett. Don't you get it? That's why I need a bodyguard."

"Not good enough. Try again."

Lee gave me a nasty look. "I *did* know Robert Powell, not just from high school. He was my banker. Lee Forestry's banker. The police have interviewed me about his murder. They've interviewed Travis too. Now Amanda is missing and the cops are interviewing me about that. I've never spoken to so many cops in my life. I'm in the middle of something here, Barrett, something not good, and I want some protection."

"From what?"

"I *told* you, I don't fuckin' know."

"Not a clue?"

"Do you think I know everything? You think I'm fuckin' omniscient? You think I'm someone who—"

"What I *think* is your story doesn't add up. There's something you're not telling me. So I guess my answer is no to the job offer."

He leaned back in his chair and looked at me. Then he looked around the room, which wasn't big and didn't have much in it, so it didn't take him long. When he'd finished he looked more tired than when he began. "You met my business partner . . . when you had drinks with us at the Alexander."

"Beau Lafontaine?"

"Yes, Beau." And he lowered his head when he said the name.

"You think he has something to do with your sister-in-law's disappearance."

"Maybe."

"And the banker?"

"I know he didn't like Bobby Powell. There was a . . . conflict."

"Why would he murder a banker?"

"Because it's always a good idea?" Lee laughed bitterly after he said it. "How the fuck do I know, Barrett? I don't know his business, just the part he has with us. But Beau . . . Fuck, you've met him. Do you think murder would be beyond him?"

"I don't think murder is beyond anybody, Mr. Lee."

I hammed it up when I said it. Paused before saying his name. Punched it like a drumbeat. But he never caught it. He was in his own world. Hearing only his voice. Living with his private fears and worst-case nightmares. I don't know what all Tucker Lee had done or what all he knew, but I was looking at a criminal nearing the end of his run. I was pretty sure about that.

"Why me, Mr. Lee? Aren't there companies you can hire that specialize in these kinds of things?"

"A specialist in Beau Lafontaine?" he said before laughing bitterly. "That would be quite something. There are some people who believe he's a Malee. Do you know what that is, Mr. Barrett?"

"French forest gnomes."

"Hah. That's good. Although I think you'd have a different answer if you ever met one. My grandfather ran into a clan of them way up on the St. John one spring. They burned his boat and stole his boom of logs. He always told me he should have died that day. Three men that were with him did. The Paradise Lake bush camp, where Beau works? I've seen it once and I never want to see it again."

"Why did you partner up with him?"

"Your uncle didn't make it. We did. You do what you have to, Mr. Barrett. I don't regret the decisions I've made. I still expect this will turn out to be a series of unfortunate coincidences and you'll be in my personal employ for no more than a few weeks. Coming to you is simply the prudent thing to do, an action made due to an abundance of caution."

"But why me? You still haven't told me."

"Why, I thought it would have been obvious. Beau respects you. Or he's worried about you, I don't know what it is, but there's something there. Did you notice he never took his eyes off you when you were with us at the Alexander? I don't think he's looked at Travis for more than ten seconds. Amanda maybe a bit more than that." And he laughed at his joke. "No, you had his full attention, Mr. Barrett. That's not easy to do. Plus, you're a big son of a bitch that can chase mill workers away from the Starlight with one punch. Or that's what I hear. What do you say? Want to make some easy money?"

He looked at me like it was a done deal. People like Tucker Lee thought easy money closed any deal and were surprised on the rare occasions when it didn't. It was why he'd made the deal he had in 2008: the belief that money trumped everything else, every virtue, every human aspiration and desire. To be left without money was to be banished and shunned by civilization, rendered less than human, transformed into some sad nether creature.

"I'm not your man," I said.

"What? I've already said you can name your price."

"That's not it."

"You don't need money? Fuck, you don't have a job and you're living at the Three Pines fuckin' Motel."

"I'm not a bodyguard, Mr. Lee. I'm a tree marker. That's what I'll keep doing, soon as I find out about my sister."

"You can't be serious. That's not even an argument. If I'm willing to pay you, why should you care what you've done in the past or who the fuck you think you are?"

"It's a good argument, Mr. Lee, not a bad one. You get in trouble when you deceive yourself. When you pretend to be something you're not. Doesn't matter how much money is on the table. I guess you're just learning that."

It was a cheap shot and I said it almost without realizing I was saying it. But I didn't stop when I realized it. I'd had my fill of Lees by then, with their problems and their crimes, my fill of trying to figure them out, whether I should feel sorry for any of them, and I'd certainly had my fill of Tucker Lee, who was trying to buy his way out of his problems like the robber baron he had always been.

He reacted the way I figured he would. A preening display of outrage that started with his jowls going tight and his eyes going beady. Then he moved on to an angry shake of his head, finished up with a slow ascent of his body, in pained gravitas, as he pushed himself up from the desk chair like a surfacing whale.

"I see I have wasted my time."

"Sorry I couldn't be more help."

He gave me a cold stare and walked toward the door. Before opening it, he turned to say he couldn't imagine there being any openings for tree markers at Lee Forestry Products in the foreseeable future. Or any future, for that matter. He thought I should know.

26

IT WAS EARLY afternoon by then. I made a coffee and thought about Tucker Lee's visit. He was scared as hell. Not hiding it as well as Amanda Lee had.

I pulled open the curtains in the motel room. Another spiteful spring day in Northern Maine. The sky was a mercury gray and a cold rain was starting to fall. I would need to contact Flanagan. Not just about Tucker Lee's visit, but about Amanda Lee as well. It only gets worse, hanging on to a secret. Secrets always come out. There is some sort of gravitational rule, some sort of chemical-combustion rule to secrets. They fall and get broken. They blow up in your face.

It was time to tell him about Amanda Lee. Or as it would be put in an FBI report—"unauthorized contact with a person of interest to the investigation." It was a biggie.

I'd heard stories about unauthorized contact destroying investigations that had been running for years, all that work shattered in a single morning of courtroom testimony when it was revealed the undercover agent had slept with one of the accused. Or taken money from another.

Or flat out entrapped a third when the agent went off script in a meeting no one had known about before a defense attorney started cross-examination.

"Sometimes you have to watch the agent as closely as you watch the person of interest," a field commander had told me once after I'd found out that he'd had another agent tail me for a week. He shrugged his shoulders when I took offense to it. "It's not personal. If anything, you should be pleased. The good agents are the ones I worry about."

"Why?" I said, not willing to give him an easy closing line.

"You don't know?" And he looked genuinely surprised when he said it. Although he was good at faking genuine, so I can't say for sure. "Come on, you're not that daft," he continued. "Why do you think you're good at this kind of work?"

"Because I have a mistrusting boss?"

"That helps. The other reason is you fit in with these people. A lot of agents never fit in. No matter how smart they are or how badly they want it, there's some sort of rattle and hum that they don't have. And the bad guys notice it. A good agent can work multiple cases with no problem. Someone that doesn't have that rattle and hum, they won't make it through one."

"Still not an answer."

"Sure it is. You just don't want to hear it."

"Try me."

"All right—the difference between a good agent and a high-target felon is not always visible to the human eye. How's that?"

You get used to it. I know it's hard to believe if you're not in this world, but you get used to it. Not a person you can trust, not a person that trusts you; trapped playing games within games, for teams that swap players without telling anyone, on a field rigged with more trip wires, land mines and things that go boom than an acre of uncleared land outside Sarajevo.

In this world there are few agreed-upon rules, only a small number of transgressions that set off blinking red five-bell alarms. Unauthorized contact was one. The frightening possibility that the undercover agent might decide the person being chased deserved to walk away from the whole mess.

Boom.

—————

I PHONED FLANAGAN and told him about my visit from Tucker Lee.

"He's scared."

"Petrified," I answered.

"That's more corroboration for you."

"There's something else. I've seen Amanda Lee."

There was a long pause before Flanagan asked, "When?"

"Four days ago."

"I don't remember reading anything about that."

"I haven't filed a report. It seems bad now, but I wasn't expecting her to go missing."

"What day did you see her?"

"Tuesday."

"That was the day we think she disappeared."

"I know."

"You didn't think to mention this earlier? What exactly do you mean, you saw her?"

"We had lunch."

"You had . . . Fuck, pal, the last sighting we have for her is Tuesday morning. If you had lunch with her that day, you could be the last person to have seen her. Where were you?"

"The King Eddy Hotel."

"A hotel?"

"Yes."

"Like with rooms and beds and all that shit?"

"That's what they tend to have, yes."

"Fuck, fuck, fuck . . . Stay right where you are, Barrett. I'm coming to see you."

―――――

FLANAGAN SHOWED UP with a six-pack of Pabst about forty-five minutes later. He put two on the table and the rest in the dinette fridge. He seemed to know there was a dinette fridge. For the first time I wondered if my room got checked from time to time. Flanagan opened a beer and passed it to me.

"Why haven't you filed a report on Amanda Lee?"

"If I filed a report every time FBI protocol said I should file a report, I'd do nothing but file reports. There was nothing about our meeting that could have been used in court."

"How the fuck did you meet her?"

"She came looking for me. She was in front of the motel when I came back from a walk. She was driving that white Land Rover."

"Then you went with her to the King Eddy Hotel and had lunch?"

"That's right."

"Whose idea was that?"

"Hers."

"Did you fuck her?"

"No. I could have. She wasn't subtle about it. She wasn't too happy with me when it didn't happen."

"Well, that's a wonderful bit of news. Just keeps getting better. The missing woman didn't like you. You were in a restaurant. Did anyone see Amanda Lee not liking you?"

He stared at me as I remembered the waiter who brought me the check. Flanagan hung his head and let out a sad laugh. "Better tell me the whole story, pal, right from the beginning. Leave anything out, and I'll poleax you. You'd better fuckin' believe that."

He smiled and went to get us more beer. I told him the story, from the way her hair looked as it twirled in the wind—black wheat; is there any crop like that?—to the logo on the napkins in the hotel café. He made me repeat her phone conversation several times, taking notes in a steno pad he pulled from his breast pocket the last two times.

When I'd finished, he didn't say anything. Flipped pages back and forth in his steno pad. Got up from the desk chair and went to get our last two beers. He clicked our cans before saying, "Doesn't seem like you tried to get much information from Amanda Lee."

"I didn't."

"Why not?"

"I didn't want to get played. I'm not sure how much Amanda Lee knows about the money laundering, but I suspect not much. I think it's Tucker's show. It didn't seem like an investigative angle worth pursuing."

"An investigative angle worth pursuing? You've been hanging around shitheads like Linton too long. She seemed like trouble to you. Is that right?"

"That's right." And I thought back to the first time I saw her outside the Starlight, stepping over Travis Lee's body to get inside a cab. "A lifetime worth of trouble."

"You tried a bit harder with Tucker Lee."

"He knows things. And he's pretty scared right now. Wouldn't surprise me if you were able to turn him."

Flanagan drained his beer. "I need to make some phone calls. Why don't you go for a quick walk?"

"How much time you need?"

"Twenty minutes."

―――――

I PUT ON my rain slicker and went outside. The rain was heavier now, the sky black with no breaks. There would be no sun this day. I walked to a Chevron station two blocks away to buy some magazines or a good paperback if they had one. I found a James Lee Burke and stood in line behind a man buying gas for his chain saw.

I had watched the man walk up to the station, coming down the street carrying his chain saw. He wore a raincoat but no hood, and his hair was plastered to his forehead. He didn't have a gas can either, but pumped the fuel right into the chain saw.

Then he came inside to pay. For fifteen cents' worth of gas. Put a quarter on the counter and waited for his change.

I thought about that purchase as I walked back to the motel. Why would a man do that? Why not pump twenty-five cents' worth of gas? Did he have plans for that dime? Or did he know the chain saw work he was doing required only fifteen cents' worth of gas? How would you know that?

I never came up with an answer that satisfied me, although right before I reached the motel, I wondered if maybe that man just felt better having something in his pocket, even if that something was a dime. Maybe that was a survival trick you learned from living in places like Birmingham, Maine.

Flanagan was sitting on the desk chair looking out the window when I walked back into the room. He wasn't as animated as I was expecting. Even took him a few seconds to turn away from the window and speak to me.

"A grand jury was impaneled in Portland yesterday to start working on the indictments. The district attorney sent them home an hour ago."

"Why?"

"I'm told his exact words were 'Come back when you know what the fuck is going on.'"

"What's happened?"

"We can't find Pearl Lafontaine."

THE SWEET GOODBYE

SHE STARED AT her cousin while he lit another Marlboro. Smoke ran through his long black hair as it rose to the ceiling, where it clustered and hovered like a false ceiling. Her cousin often had smoke swirling around him: from a cigarette, a campfire, a controlled burn in a stand of stunt cedar. Smoke and Beau Lafontaine went together.

"Why are you here, Pearl?"

"Why shouldn't I be here?"

"You were not invited," he said. He still used sulfur matches to light his cigarettes and there was an acidic flash of blue-and-yellow light, then a dark trail of black smoke mingling with the gray smoke of the Marlboro. Her cousin's office was designed to look like John D. Rockefeller's railcar. Beau had a photo of the railcar, a photo he had folded and refolded so many times the creases had resembled white fleece when he had handed it to her and asked whether she thought such a room would suit him.

There weren't many women around Paradise Lake and she assumed that's why he'd asked. She had no skills when it came to interior design. But after looking at the photo, she told Beau that old wood, yellow-brown liquor

192 | RON CORBETT

bottles and brocade fabric thick enough to be a shroud would probably suit him fine.

The photo was a strange affectation for a man who was honest to his nature in all other ways. He told her once that when he had meetings with bikers or crime family members in New York, on those rare occasions when he left the North Maine Woods, he hung his clothes over a campfire before donning them, smoked a large joint of marijuana inside his truck a few minutes before the meeting. Just so those boys would understand he wasn't from there.

He crushed the stub of the Marlboro in a crystal ashtray and reached for his pack. As he was leaning across the desk, he said, "This is about Travis Lee, right?"

"It is."

"I worry 'bout you, Pearl. You were always a . . . free spirit. That's a good thing. A Lafontaine thing. But now it seem maybe it be somethin' else."

"You think I'm crazy, Beau?"

"Are you? It crazy what you just do, coming all the way up the North Maine Woods to see me."

"Maybe you should have returned my messages."

He looked at her a second, his cheek twitching, but just when she thought he might yell, he opened his mouth and laughed. Then he started slamming his desk as though he might have been having a seizure. He took deep gulps of air for several seconds before he said, "That is fuckin' funny. You drive a hundred miles through the North Maine Woods because I didn't return your fuckin' text? Fuck, you really are a Lafontaine."

"So you know this matters to me."

"Why, Pearl? Why the fuck why? Does this guy have something on you?"

"Don't be stupid."

"I know. It not that. It some crazy love, some cuckoo fuckin' love you have for this piece of shit."

"We don't always get to choose who we love, Beau."

"You gonna sing me a country song?"

"Just telling you how I feel. Know anything about Amanda?"

"No. You?"

"All I know is, Travis is being framed for the murder of the banker. By Amanda and Tucker. You're helping them. Now Amanda is missing. I'm guessing she became a problem for you."

"Is that a question?"

"You don't need to do this, Beau. Let the banker stay an unsolved murder."

"Cops don't like unsolved, Pearl. Sooner the cops go away, the better it'll be for everyone. Better for you too, girl. You just don't see it."

"It's not fair, Beau."

He gave her an indifferent shrug of his shoulders. It was a weak argument. He was probably surprised she was using it. Coming through one hundred twenty miles of the North Maine Woods to tell him there was something in this world that wasn't fair? That didn't strike him as funny. That struck him as sad and stupid.

He smoked his cigarette, and as he looked at her, his eyes changed, narrowed into eyes she had not seen before. He's wondering if I'm a threat, she thought.

And there it was. Her path ahead. Her cousin had received fair warning, been told clear as clear ever got that this mattered to her. But he didn't care.

She was ready for that. "Maybe you're right, Beau," she said, giving her hair a small flip. "God knows that man has been nothing but trouble for me. He actually came to my house the other night, to say his wife was missing. Amanda's gone. Here I am."

"He don't treat you well. 'Bout time you see that."

"How is it going to go for him? He doesn't have to die, does he?"

"See, you are gettin' crazy. It gonna be good for you, Pearl, gettin' rid of this guy. Clear your head. Nobody wants Travis Lee dead. He got to stand trial for the banker."

"Aren't you worried he could flip on you?"

"He'll be dead if he do that. He'll know."

"You've already set everything up?"

"Yeah, it all set up."

"And Tucker is helping you?"

"Yeah. I still need someone to handle the money. I know this hasn't worked out the way you wanted, Pearl, but it's the hand we were dealt. You know that."

"I know that. But I must be thick or something, Beau. If you've already set everything up, why do you have Tucker still talking to the cops?"

He tried not to let it show. Her cousin had told her once that surprise was the expression you saw on a dead man's face. At least the dead men her cousin saw. So Beau tried never to show it. There was only a quick blink of his eyes. Nothing more than that. But she knew that was a lot for Beau Lafontaine. That was like landing a body blow.

When a few seconds had passed, and without taking his eyes off her, he said, "When was Tucker talkin' to the cops?"

SHE LEFT PARADISE Lake the same night, going out on a logging truck headed to a pulp mill in New Jersey. There wasn't enough wood on the bed of the truck to make a trip like that worthwhile, but there were cargo bins welded to the undercarriage, and the pills inside those bins would have bought that truck ten times over.

The driver was chatty and friendly the first twenty miles, giving off plenty of clues that he was open to being more than just chatty and friendly. It was going to be a long drive, he said a few times. She told him politely that she was tired, and would he mind if she got some sleep? He didn't say much after that, and he was never a problem. Her last name was Lafontaine. He'd have been crazy if he tried anything.

When he gave her a shove to wake her, it was early morning, the sun just starting to rise above the hills beyond the St. John River. Mist swirled around the headlights of the truck and she could hear grasshoppers in the high grass.

"This is Little Creek," he said. "Where's your car?"

"Just down the road."

"You got it marked?"

"Yeah. You can't miss it."

He drove till she saw the tree with the X notched in it. She told him to stop, giving him plenty of warning so he could gear down. "Wish we had more time," she said as she climbed down the stairs.

"Do you? I let you sleep there, but I got some time right—"

"I'm just being polite."

"Yeah . . . I know that. Sure."

"I'll let my cousin know you did a good job."

"Thanks. I appreciate that."

"Take care."

"You too."

———

SHE PARKED THE Honda on a side road half a mile south of the farm. She could see the dark sedan parked at the end of Dale Ferguson's driveway, under an elm that was almost big enough to hide it. The cops would have had no trouble convincing Ferguson to help them. Lafontaine was a name that opened some doors in Bustard County, closed just as many. The old bastard was probably bringing the cops coffee and asking if they needed lunch.

Mist was circling the cedar as she cut through the break, then across the fallow field behind her house. The field had once been rows of corn, the shorn stalks brushing against her jeans, the denim wet by the time she reached her back door. The house was silent and she took off her shoes as soon as she was inside. Walked upstairs quietly and found him asleep in her bed. She took off her clothes, got under the blankets and gave him a hug. He was smiling when he opened his eyes.

"Nice to see you. Everything go all right?"

"Yeah. I'd say so."

"Still not going to tell me where you've been?"

"You want me to?"

"What if I said yes?"

"I wouldn't tell you."

He laughed and rolled over, gave her a kiss. Before long, the kiss had turned into a caress, and then their limbs were tangled; her back was arching. You'd think the day would come when familiarity cooled the urge, dulled the senses, the tally of days finally too much for passion. But it never came. That had always surprised her. How it had never been anything different from what it had been at first.

He still looked the same to her too. Not in any symbolic way or figurative way, the way people who care for each other will sometimes lie to make the other person feel better, convince themselves it's true what they are saying. "You look no different, dear."

None of that clumsy nonsense. To her, he was what he had always been. Other people saw him different, had given up on him, laughed at him behind his back, but he looked no different to her from the way he had the night he'd said, "Out back, ten minutes."

She couldn't explain it. Just the way it was going to be for her.

———

SHE LAY BESIDE him for a few minutes and then threw off the bedsheet.

He was surprised to see her sit up. "What are you doing?"

"Sorry, hon. There're still a few things I gotta do today. Just wanted to see you. And kick you out. You can go home now."

"What about that cop parked next door?"

"You noticed him, huh?"

"There were quite a few cops there the morning you left. Yeah, I noticed him. Your neighbor seems quite obliging."

"Old man Ferguson didn't care for my dad. He'd probably let the cops move in if they asked him nice. That cop will probably follow you when you leave."

"Sounds ominous."

"Come on, you must be ready to go home. You not getting restless?"

"A little bit, sure, but . . . what is going on, Pearl? You can't tell me anything?"

"Won't do you any good, hon." She got out of bed and started to dress. Before leaving the room, she said, *"I need Tucker's number. For that cell phone he keeps off the books. You have that number, right?"*

"Course I do."

"Can you write it down for me?"

———

SHE KNEW WHAT *her cousin had done when she left Paradise Lake. Beau Lafontaine didn't allow doubts about his business partners. Tucker would need to be dealt with. She knew what that meant. Only thing she didn't know was the time and place.*

Her call was answered on the first ring.

"Tucker Lee."

"Tucker, it's Pearl."

He didn't say anything right away and she knew what he was doing. Sitting there running scenarios through his mind, trying to figure out why she was calling and what he could do about it. He could have asked her, but men like Tucker Lee never did that. They preferred to think and scheme.

"Beau wants me at your meeting," she continued. *"He said I could get the time and place from you."*

"What meeting."

"Fuck off, Tucker. I'm in a hurry."

There was silence for a few seconds. "If Beau wanted you at some sort of meeting, Pearl, why didn't he give you the location himself?"

"I don't fuckin' know, Tucker. Maybe he was worried about being overheard. Call him and ask if you want."

More silence. She figured Tucker Lee wanted to phone her cousin right then about as much as he wanted to throw himself into a wood chipper.

"Why would he want you at this supposed meeting?"

"Same answer, Tucker. Go ask him. All I know is he said it was important I be there and that I could get the place and time from you."

The silence wasn't as long this time. Tucker had finished his calcula-

tions. "The Northwoods Trail parking lot," he said in a voice he was probably hoping sounded jaunty yet authoritative, a CEO deciding to let a worker bee into the inner sanctum after denying for years there was an inner sanctum.

"Nine o'clock tonight. He phoned me last night to set it up. Do you know what in the heavens this is all about, Pearl?"

"No idea."

27

PEOPLE IN BIRMINGHAM remember the next morning as the day the seasons finally changed. Spring had come late, with heavy rains that turned the ground to a bog, an unpleasant marsh that sat beneath a sky as dank and gray as an old washcloth. Week after week of that. But that morning the sky was clear and the sun rose like a jewel. A light mist was on the river and a breeze came in not from the north that morning but from the Appalachians, a wind just strong enough to rustle the leaves on the birch, no stronger than that, a breeze heading off to the sea and carrying with it the scent of peat moss, pine gum and other ancient things just starting to come alive.

It was the sort of morning that could keep a person living in Northern Maine. Most of the reasons for staying there had disappeared a long time ago. Maine had one of the highest unemployment rates in the country, Bustard County the highest in the state. The jobs had gone, leaving behind abandoned rail lines and boarded-up factories, wood-shake homes turning yellow from age and deserted strip malls already crumbling.

Every reason to leave, but then you had a morning like this, which left you wanting more mornings like this, left you wishing the world would stop trying to drive you away. Call a time-out or something. Leave us alone.

Peter Webster felt that way about Northern Maine. He had been born and raised in Birmingham and he was up early that morning, noticing that the seasons had finally changed and marveling at what he was seeing. There were tree buds that had not been there the day before. Hard ground where yesterday there had been mud. A warm wind that yesterday was cold. He headed out before the sun had cleared the break of spruce behind his house.

Webster lived in the house with his father, who had worked thirty-five years at the Lee Forestry sawmill on Sleigh Bay. Pete Webster was on recall hours at the same mill, after being laid off two years ago. He'd had only seven years in when he was called into the human resources office and laid off. Not enough for even a "diddly-squat" pension, as his father put it.

His dad still left notes on the fridge for his son, scrawled names and phone numbers, the leads for potential mill jobs. Pete had phoned the numbers at first, but before long, he was talking to retired foremen who hadn't worked in years and barely remembered his father. He no longer called, although he didn't tell his father.

Mill jobs weren't coming back. Same way factory jobs weren't coming back. Someone told him a week ago that the city was still trying to sell the Davidson-Struthers Footwear factory, and that was the funniest thing he'd heard in months. The city had ended up owning the factory after the company went bankrupt. In high school a friend of his, a boy good in chemistry, told him six pipe bombs placed in the right locations would bring the factory down. You probably needed only four now.

He made his way to the parking lot for the Northwoods Trail, his Ford Bronco taking the switchback road in low gear. Trout season had opened that month, but because of the late spring and the heavy rains, a lot of the trails were still closed. Three miles down the Northwoods

Trail, where it crossed the St. Croix River, was a place where you could catch brook trout that was probably as good a place to catch brook trout as any other place in Maine, which was saying something. Webster was thinking of going in that Saturday and wanted to have a look at the trail. See how much mud was there.

It was a morning to feel good about living in Birmingham and feel good about the decisions you had made in order to stay living in Birmingham. Pete Webster had started a reclaimed-wood business with some friends. People in Boston were crazy for old barn wood and there was no shortage of that in Northern Maine, owing to the fact most of the homesteaders the government had lured to the state with land grants a century ago had moved on within five years. Hard to grow cash crops on top of granite and gneiss. Something the government might have mentioned to them.

Because of this deceit, abandoned barns and farmhouses were as common in Northern Maine as white pine and brook trout. Webster was going to take a look at one barn later that morning. Some of the old boys living in the original homesteading cabins would give you the barn for nothing, just so long as you hauled it away for them.

The Bronco pulled into the parking lot for the Northwoods Trail and Webster was surprised to see two vehicles already there. A Cadillac Escalade and some sort of expensive truck—a Ridgeline or an Avalanche, it looked like.

Both vehicles had their driver's side doors open. The Cadillac also had its headlights on, although the beam was low. Webster didn't actually have good sight lines on the Cadillac because of the way the truck was parked, square center in the parking lot with that one door open.

He put the Bronco into park and looked around. At the trail leading up the mountain. The empty road behind him. The two vehicles in front. There was no sound except the wind passing through the birch and the rustling of pine needles blowing in small eddies around his wheels.

Webster took the vehicle out of park and inched forward. Leaned over the steering wheel. Looked out his front and side windows. Drove past the Ridgeline and finally saw the rest of the parking lot.

It didn't register for about five seconds. Took Webster that long to put the images together, make sense of what he was seeing. After that, he slammed the Bronco into reverse and skidded out of the parking lot, taking the first turn down the switchback road so fast, he nearly slid into a creek.

Some mornings it's easy to believe your troubles are behind you, that only good days lie ahead. Those are dangerous days. The days when you forget that trouble rarely disappears. It normally just heads down the road a piece, sits down and waits for you.

28

THERE WAS NOT a cloud in the sky and the sun was sitting straight above the Davidson-Struthers Footwear factory. The chipped red brick of the abandoned building, when the sun hit it from that angle, made the brickwork look like a pool of old blood. The exact right color red. The same ragged edges. I was sitting in Flanagan's hotel room looking at it. We had been working, but then he got distracted, and now he was on a roll, giving me time to look out the window while I listened to him.

". . . I'm not kidding, Barrett. I never thought crime existed in the country. Always thought it was a big-city problem. Or if it *did* exist in the country, it was a long time ago and crime had hightailed it to the city, which would be the smart play, right? Tell you the truth, I didn't know how it happened. I just knew crime wasn't in the fuckin' country. You believe that?"

"No."

"You should. I *did* believe that. I blame bikers for what happened. They're the ones who fucked it all up. How many clubhouses you been in, Barrett?"

"Been in a few."

"Where did you find them? Out in the country, right? Down some fuckin' dead-end gravel road. Am I right? Bikers like the smell of pig shit or something."

I laughed. It was true. A lot of clubhouses were just like that. Living at the end of a gravel road was no different from falling off the edge of the planet.

"You're from Detroit. Did you ever think crime was a country thing? How could you? You had a monopoly on it for a little while, didn't you?"

Flanagan punched me on the arm. Whenever he retired, Jimmy Flanagan was going to be one of those law enforcement guys who sat on barstools and spun war stories, good ones, and as opinionated as he was now, it was probably just a prelude.

"So what do you think happened, Barrett? Did crime move from the city to the country or was it always there? I'd like to know, because I am getting sick and fuckin' tired of being dragged to shithole towns like this. I got bedbugs once. Did I ever tell you that?"

"No."

"I was staying at the best motel in town. If I'd stayed in the worst, I probably would have gotten crabs. So how did crime end up in the country?"

"You're serious? You're really asking me that question?"

"Yeah, I'm really asking you that question. I'm seven hundred miles from Boston, looking out over a future demolition site, and I'd like to know what the fuck happened. Why am I here, and who the fuck can I slap in the head for it? The fuckin' bikers, do you think?"

"You can't blame bikers. It's always been here. You just missed it."

"I don't miss anything. You're full of shit."

"It's always been worse in the country too. Big-city crime? That's for amateurs."

"Now you're making shit up. How do you figure?"

"Because places like Birmingham have always had the same problems as any big city—guns, drugs, poverty, addiction. You name it and they have it. Only difference is, in the country you get all that plus you get to throw in bad water, plaster-lath houses, no neighbors for two miles and shotguns."

Flanagan started slapping the table and hooting. "Fuck, that's a good line. That's fuckin' *great*. Are you Irish, Barrett? Who the fuck picked that name?"

I shrugged my shoulders.

"Ahh, tell me later." And Flanagan turned his attention back to the papers on the desk. "So how sure are you about the measurements for Lafontaine's house? They seem a bit wonky."

I looked back at the map Flanagan was drawing. He was doing it on top of a topographical map of Paradise Lake, the map enlarged and Flanagan drawing in the buildings and roads I had seen inside the camp.

"It *is* a wonky building, but I walked it. Eighty-seven paces. Should be accurate within a couple feet. It's two hundred feet long, that building. He came out the north end, by the lake."

"You do beautiful fuckin' work, pal. Distance from the back door to the lake?"

"Twenty-three feet."

"Twenty-three? Sure it's not twenty-four?"

"Twenty-three."

"You kill me. These side roads off the main logging road, did you get a chance to—"

And then his phone rang. Flanagan checked the number and took the call.

"What the fuck is it?" he roared. Then he didn't say anything for a long time. I saw his mood change during the call. He stopped fidgeting in the chair, stopped crossing and recrossing his legs. His chin dropped to his chest; then he started shaking his head, running his fingers through his hair. Eventually he said, "Fuck . . . where is this place?"

He pulled a steno pad from his jacket and wrote something down. Then he hung up the phone without saying another word. He stared at me a long minute. "The Birmingham cops have found two bodies on a hiking trail."

He stared at the map we had been working on and gave another shake of his head. Pushed the map away. "I'm going to have to go and check this out. You may as well come along."

"You sure?"

"Yeah, I'm fucking sure."

Out at a crime scene with the patrol officers and the I-dent team, the journalists and the gawkers. For an undercover agent, that was about as blown as blown ever gets. I didn't bother asking Flanagan who the cops had found.

=====

I SAT IN the passenger seat of Flanagan's sedan and watched him talking to Linton. Didn't look to be a friendly conversation. Flanagan was hopped up again, bouncing on his feet, talking to Linton, his face no more than six inches away. Linton kept his head down, as though hunkering his way through an artillery barrage.

I looked around the parking lot. There were two men in white hazmat jumpers looking inside a Cadillac Escalade parked at the far end of the lot. There was another vehicle, a Honda Ridgeline, parked in the center of the lot. Both vehicles had their driver's side doors open. There was yellow crime scene tape around the lot, and two patrol cars were parked at the entrance.

There were people on the other side of the tape, some with cameras, and there were vehicles as well, including a television news van from a station in Portland. When I saw the news van, I told Flanagan I'd stay in the car.

The two bodies were already covered with sheets. White humps with bloodstains showing through that looked like Rorschach cards. One body lay ten feet in front of the Ridgeline, one fifteen feet beside the Cadillac. There was a sawed-off shotgun not far from the white sheet beside the Cadillac. I looked between the bodies, judging the distance, the angle. I was still doing the math when Flanagan opened the driver's side door and got back in the car.

"That shotgun hasn't been fired, has it?" I said.

"You got it."

"Lafontaine would have brought it. He's the one beside the Cadillac?"

"Two for two, pal. Want to tell me who did it?"

"The other one is Tucker Lee?"

"Yeah."

"Thought you had eyes on him."

"Thought so too. I just reamed out Linton for it, but I can't hang him on it. The Birmingham police had Lee under surveillance. He went for dinner with his wife last night, some Thai place downtown. He went out a back door and left her there. Cop who was doing the surveillance knew he had a problem and didn't report it right away. He was hoping to track Tucker Lee down. Do you fuckin' believe that?"

"I wouldn't want to be that cop."

"No. That's a fuckin' career ender."

"What about Lafontaine?"

"*That* one's on Linton. The troll flew into the airport at Old Town last night. He didn't fly into Birmingham."

"Linton got notified anytime he flew into Birmingham?"

"That's right."

"But he didn't alert any other airports?"

"You got it. An airport a forty-five-fuckin'-minute drive from here, and they never got notified. I'm going to be holding Linton's heart in my hands before I leave this fuckin' shithole."

I didn't bother replying, looked out the window at the crowd on the other side of the crime scene tape. Another television news van with call numbers from Portland had arrived and a technician was raising a satellite tower. There was going to be a live stand-up soon by the man Barrett was looking at: middle-aged ex-jock, it looked like, with a bad comb-over and a white bib tucked into his shirt collar.

"Wish you could walk it out with me, Barrett, but looks like we lost our chance. So what do you think?"

"Shooter would have come up on them from the east. That big white pine over there would have been a good place to wait."

"Could hide a Mack truck behind that tree."

"Yeah, probably could. Find any shell casings?"

"Nothing. Do you figure the shooter would have been standing around there, right where that I-dent guy is walking?" And Flanagan pointed to one of the men in the white overalls.

"I'd say around there. Ground's still wet. You might be able to pick up some footprints."

Flanagan smiled and shook his head when I said that. He started slapping the steering wheel, a backhanded slap that wasn't forceful or angry, a dismissive slap of the hand, what maybe years ago you could have given a precocious child who was getting on your nerves.

"Dig this. The I-dent sergeant told me they looked for that right away, but they couldn't find any prints. They had Lafontaine's footprints beautifully, same for Tucker Lee, but nothing for a shooter. You're right about the ground by the way. It's perfect."

I thought about that a minute. "No other set? In this whole parking lot?"

"Didn't say that. There're plenty by the entrance and over by the trailhead, but where the shit went down, where we should *find* a third set of footprints, there's nothing."

"Could we be wrong about where the shooter was standing?"

"No. The spread pattern of the shotgun blast puts the shooter exactly where you figured."

"Somebody wiped it clean?"

"Better than that. Sergeant figured it out when he had a good look at Lee's footprints. Someone had walked inside them. Someone came right up behind that fat bastard, step for step, just to make sure they wouldn't leave behind any footprints. Who the fuck would think of doing something like that?"

"Someone pretty smart."

Flanagan snorted and almost laughed before saying, "Yeah. So that big white pine, you figure?"

"I figure."

"Think we'll find anything?"

"No."

"You're good at figuring, pal. I'm going to have a patrol cop drive you back to the motel. Keep your phone with you. I'll be in touch."

29

FLANAGAN STAYED ANOTHER ten minutes before racing back to Birmingham, telling one of the cops manning the crime scene tape to send out an alert; he didn't want to be stopped. When the patrol cop asked who he was, Flanagan said, "Just send out the alert, asshole."

He drove to the main detachment of the Birmingham police, a place he had never been, as he had been overseeing the investigation from his hotel room or the surveillance van or the rental car he was now redlining down a gravel road, enough dust coming up behind him to look like a mushroom cloud over Nevada. He fishtailed in and out of turns. Hit the asphalt at the bottom of the switchback road with enough force to send the car airborne.

There was nothing to gain from being quiet anymore. From staying under the radar or keeping cards close to the chest. This investigation was blown about as sky-high as it was possible to blow an investigation because of some local cop who didn't want a reprimand going into his file.

When Flanagan got to the detachment, he parked in front beneath a no-stopping sign. A uniformed cop walking down the steps looked like he was going to say something, but Flanagan gave him the finger as he ran past and the cop decided to keep walking. It was the end of his shift.

Inside, Flanagan went to a reception window where a man was talking to a woman sitting behind a sheet of Plexiglas. Two other men were lined up behind him. Flanagan yelled over their heads to the woman, "Where can I find your chief?"

"Sir, there are people ahead of you."

"Ain't no one ahead of me, darlin'." And Flanagan took out his wallet, flipped it open and showed her his FBI badge. "Where the fuck is Kowalski?"

"Sir, this is no way to conduct yourself. If you can wait a minute, I'll find him for you."

"Am I not speaking English? Is there some other language I should be using for you? Latin, French, some shit like that? Where the fuck is Kowalski's office?"

"I'm . . . I'm not sure if I should—"

"You don't fuckin' *know*?"

"Third floor. There's another receptionist there that can help you. The elevators are right down the . . ."

But Flanagan was gone, taking stairs two at a time as he raced up a staircase in the foyer. Who had time for elevators?

The third-floor receptionist looked at Flanagan like he had just escaped from the holding cells beneath the detachment. When Flanagan showed her his FBI badge, she looked only slightly less worried.

"Where's the chief?" he yelled.

"He's in a meeting right now. May I see your badge again, sir?"

"Which fuckin' room? This one here?"

"Sir, please!"

Flanagan banged on the door and opened it. No one inside. He headed to the next door.

"Sir, please, you need to settle down. If you can just—"

"Settle fuckin' down. You think that's what I should do? I've got a better idea, darlin'. Kowalski, where the fuck are you? What fuckin' meeting are you sitting in that is more fuckin' important than—"

A door at the end of the hallway opened. Kowalski stepped out, looking as angry as Flanagan. "Agent, what the hell are you doing! How dare you come into my detachment and—"

"How dare I? Are you fuckin' serious? How *dare* I?"

"I know you're upset."

"Don't tell me what you know, Chief. Don't dare fuckin' tell me what you know. What *I know* is that I should have been told Tucker Lee went missing at eight o' clock last night. Where's the motherfucker that screwed me? Where the *fuck* is he?"

Kowalski put his hands out and patted air, the gesture a parent would have given an unruly child when he wanted them to calm down. "You won't find him here. He's been suspended. I suspect he'd be getting drunk somewhere right about now."

"Suspended? He should be hanging from the windows of this fuckin' police station. His head should be on a fuckin' pike. Are you going to charge the motherfucker?"

"What would you recommend?"

"Impersonating a cop. How about first-degree fuckin' asshole."

"*Agent*, he has been suspended and he will be facing disciplinary charges. The process has started. I'm just as upset about this as you are."

"Don't think that will ever be possible. This investigation has just turned to rat shit. A year's work out the window because of your shit-can fuckin' cop."

Flanagan glared at him. The two men were standing no more than a foot apart. Kowalski held the stare. It went on for about thirty seconds before Flanagan finally let out a loud snort and ran his fingers through his hair. After that, he did a quick drumroll on the desk he was standing beside, using his fingers, a flick of his thumb on the desk lamp at the end for a cymbal effect.

That's all, folks.

"Feeling better?" asked Kowalski.

"Little bit. What the fuck was your cop thinking?"

"He wasn't thinking. That was the problem. I was just going to go looking for you. Probably didn't need that big entrance."

"And I don't need any dipshit apologies."

"That's not the reason I was coming to find you. Why don't we go into my office for a minute?"

For the first time Flanagan noticed the manila envelope Kowalski was holding.

"You have something?"

"I'd say so. Might even cheer you up."

=====

THEY WENT TO Kowalski's office. The chief motioned for Flanagan to sit but the FBI supervisor remained standing, looking around the office and waiting for Kowalski to open the manila envelope. There were bowling trophies on the shelves. Civic awards and citations on the walls. Flanagan looked around the office once, but there was nothing that brought him back for a closer inspection.

"There's a gas station on Highway Five, less than a mile from the turnoff to the Northwoods trailhead," said Kowalski, taking photos from the envelope and placing them on his desk. "Fellow who owns the station got fed up with people filling up and taking off on him, so a few years back he installed cameras."

"Where?"

"One on the pumps. One on the highway."

"He caught something."

"Yes, sir, he did. Not a lot of traffic on Highway Five this time of year. Last night only three vehicles passed that camera. There's Beau Lafontaine's Cadillac heading toward the Northwoods turnoff. Time of the photo is eight twelve p.m."

Kowalski pushed a photograph across the desk. Then he pushed another so it lined up beside the first. "That's Tucker Lee's Ridgeline.

Time stamp is eight fifty-two. Neither vehicle was photographed coming back, but you already know that."

Flanagan leaned across the desk to grab the last two photos.

"Photo on your left was taken at six fifty-five p.m.," said Kowalski. "Photo on the right was nine thirty-two p.m. So you have the vehicle going up and coming back."

Flanagan stared at the images. Not much of a vehicle compared to the other ones. Rust around the tire wheels. Some sort of discoloration on the hood.

"I can't make out the plates."

"Looks like they're covered. A cloth of some kind."

"It's a Honda, right?"

"It is."

30

PEARL LAFONTAINE WAS brought in for questioning at two p.m. the next day. She had shown up for her regular scheduled shift at the Red Bird that morning, even though there was an all-state bulletin for her detention and a police car parked in front of her home. No one had thought about the diner, where she drove her car into its normal parking spot at five forty-five a.m., went inside, put on her uniform and went to work. It was an off-duty cop who phoned Kowalski six hours later to ask if they were still looking for Pearl Lafontaine.

"Why, have you seen her?"

"Sure have. And I'll be seeing her again in about two minutes when she brings me my cheeseburger."

It was Kowalski who went to pick her up. It made sense for him to go. The FBI investigation was still on a need-to-know basis and Kowalski knew. He also knew Pearl Lafontaine. He took his hat off when he entered the diner. Walked to the cash register, where an elderly woman was standing.

"Afternoon, Gwen."

"Afternoon, Chief. Like a table?"

"No, thanks. Coffee to go, please. Large."

"Cream and sugar?"

"Just black."

"I'll have someone get it for you right away. Looks like you could use a little pick-me-up, Chief."

"Long day."

"God should have invented different ones."

"Yes, that would have been nice."

When she left, the chief looked around and saw Lafontaine in the middle of the restaurant, three plates stacked up her right arm. She was talking to Des Vachon, an old man who used to own a truck yard in Birmingham until he lost it in '08. Vachon still came to the Red Bird three or four times a week, dressed in dark green factory pants and long-sleeved canvas shirts as though on his way to the yard.

Kowalski managed to catch her attention when she was walking away from the table. She looked at him and he gave a slow, what he hoped was almost imperceptible nod of his head. Then he looked outside and back at her. She seemed to nod back and then went into the kitchen with the dirty dishes.

Kowalski wasn't sure if he had just done anything. Wouldn't make sense, really, if he had. What sort of message was that? Yet he was not surprised when it was Lafontaine who brought him his coffee. "Here you go, Chief. Mrs. Snyder said it was on the house."

"No, I should pay." And he took a wallet from his back pocket. Opened it and flipped through the bills in the folder, looking for a five. As he was doing that, he said, "You need to come with me, Pearl."

"Right now?"

"When is your shift finished?"

"Twenty minutes. Gotta cash out after that."

"I'm parked outside. You need to come see me when you're done."

"All right."

"I'm going to have to take you downtown, Pearl."

"You're arresting me?"

"No. But you have to come with me."

"All right." She was looking him straight in the face when she said it, didn't blush or tremble or do any of the things Kowalski feared she might. He had been expecting some reaction, but there was none. He headed to his car and waited.

—————

HE PUT HER in the backseat. Said she was being detained on a possible felony charge and left it at that. It seemed strange saying it, let alone thinking she might be the person responsible for the double homicide at the Northwoods trailhead. He wondered if he should have handcuffed her. Just saying, "You have the right to legal counsel," made Pearl Lafontaine seem dangerous in a way he hadn't been expecting.

On his way to the detachment, he opened his mouth a few times to say something that would make the drive more comfortable, but the right words never came. So they drove in silence, almost to the detachment before she said, "How's your wife doing these days, Chief?"

"She's doing well, Pearl. Thanks for asking."

"She beat it."

"The doctors don't like to say that. She's in remission."

"That's got to feel like a win though."

"Yeah, I guess it does."

"You deserve a break like that, Chief. You're a good man. I appreciate what you did for me back at the diner."

"Didn't do much, Pearl. I'm bringing you to the detachment."

"Yeah, but you did it in a kind way. Didn't embarrass me. There're different ways of doing just about everything in this world, don't you think?"

"I suppose there are."

"You're someone who likes to do things the right way. We're lucky to have you. You should have been the chief thirty years ago."

If Pearl Lafontaine was trying to make Kowalski feel comfortable, she was having the opposite effect. Was he supposed to thank her for the compliment? Someone who might be a multiple killer sitting in the backseat of his family car with no handcuffs, no wire-mesh partition between them and back doors that really did open from the inside.

The more breaches of protocol that occurred to him, the more Kowalski's stomach turned. He was relieved when he drove into the rear parking lot of the detachment, the chain gate rolling into locked position behind him when he tripped the signal. He looked over the seat when the car was parked and said, "Let me open the door, all right."

"It would look strange if I just jumped out?"

"Yeah, it would."

"I'll be a perfect lady, then. No movement from me until a gentleman opens the door."

"Thank you."

He brought her to the holding cells and left her with the staff sergeant. Then he took the elevator to his office, wondering if he had ever had a stranger car ride. Feeling sorry for a person one minute, fearing them the next. Twenty minutes in which his perception of Pearl Lafontaine must have changed a hundred times, like some house-of-mirrors reflection distorted in different ways each time he looked at it. Someone he thought he knew, but maybe he never had.

He took some files from a cabinet and put them on his desk. He would get caught up on some paperwork. Stay in the detachment until her interview was finished. He didn't think he could go home without knowing how it went.

31

THE INTERVIEW ROOM had a long, rectangular table, four metal chairs and a mirror on one wall as long as the table. At six twenty-three p.m. Flanagan walked into the room, carrying two file folders.

He sat in a chair opposite Lafontaine, leaned back and crossed his legs. He was wearing a dark mustard yellow suit and a green chino shirt, a brown-and-white tie unknotted to about the third button on his shirt. He tilted the chair back and smiled at her. "I'm Supervisory Special Agent Jim Flanagan with the Boston FBI. I understand no one has told you yet why you're here."

She looked at him a second before giving her hair a small flip. "You're a long way from home, Agent."

"I haven't just arrived, Ms. Lafontaine. Been here awhile."

"Have you, now? What do you think of the place?"

"I think it's a shithole. Thanks for asking. Are you curious to know why you're here?"

"I figure you're going to tell me soon enough. Am I wrong 'bout that? If I'm wrong, I'll ask."

Flanagan gave her a stare that must have lasted a good twenty seconds. "You have been brought in, Ms. Lafontaine, for questioning as part of an investigation into the double homicide that took place at the Northwoods trailhead two nights ago."

"I'm not under arrest?"

"At the moment, no. You are being detained for questioning."

"There's a difference between being arrested and being detained? It don't feel much different."

"You don't seem surprised to be told that you have been brought in for questioning as part of a double-homicide investigation. Why is that?"

"Why should I be surprised? My cousin was one of the men who got killed up there."

"Yes, Beau Lafontaine. How well did you know your cousin?"

"Pretty well."

"You were close?"

"Didn't say that. Said I knew him well."

"Would it surprise you to know that your cousin has become quite well-known to the Boston field office of the FBI?"

"Wouldn't surprise me to learn Beau was well-known anywhere."

"You're saying he was quite a character."

She laughed. "Did you ever meet my cousin? Beau Lafontaine was a lot of things, and he was called a lot of things, but I don't think anyone ever once called him 'a character.' If you're trying to find out whether I knew my cousin was a dangerous man, yes, I knew that."

"But you stayed in regular contact with him?"

"Family. You don't get to pick 'em, do you?"

"You have been a waitress at the Red Bird Diner for how many years, Ms. Lafontaine?"

"Part-time for four years, full-time for twenty-seven."

"That's a long time."

"I'm trying to get a plaque."

"It's a good job?"

"Money's not bad. I have regulars. The best shifts, on account of how long I've been there. Yeah, it's all right."

"Your cousin was a rich man. Did you know that?"

"I heard that."

"And you're a diner waitress." Flanagan reached for one of the file folders. Opened a corner of it as though peering at a hole card. "Interesting family."

"Is that a question?"

"Did you know your cousin was in Birmingham the night he was killed?"

"I did not."

"Even though you were close to him?"

"Never said I was close. Said I knew him well."

"Right, that's what you said."

Flanagan opened the file folder and took out two photos. Slid them across the desk so she could see them.

"A security camera at a gas station two miles from the turnoff to the Northwoods Trail took these photos the night of the murders. That's your car, Ms. Lafontaine, heading up to the trailhead and heading back."

She looked at the photos. Pulled them closer to her. Leaned forward in her chair and examined them for several seconds before saying, "That can't be my car. I wasn't at the Northwoods trailhead that night."

"It's a 2011 Honda Civic. The same car you own."

"A rusted-out Honda, yeah, I see that. My neighbor's got two of 'em. You sure about the year?"

She looked right at him when she said it. Flanagan held her stare and wondered if it was a coincidence. They weren't sure about the year.

"It would help me a lot if I could make out the plates," she continued. "Does it have plates? I'm looking at these photos but I can't see any plates. If there're no plates, it's definitely not my car. I drive a registered, fully insured vehicle."

He left the file folder open on the table, leaned back again in his chair. He tipped it this time so he could rock back and forth. "You knew Tucker Lee as well."

"I did."

"And you know his brother."

"I surely do."

"How would you describe your relationship with Travis Lee?"

"Good friend."

"Good friend?"

"Am I going to need to say everything twice for you?"

"A lot of people in Birmingham would call your relationship with Travis Lee a bit more than good friends, Ms. Lafontaine."

"Would they, now? Well, that's funny, 'cause I would call it *exactly* that."

"His wife is missing. Did you know that?"

"I did know that."

"Any idea what happened to her?"

"Amanda Lee disappearing? How would I know anything about that? She and I don't talk much."

"You don't seem overly concerned by her disappearance."

"I have not spent one second of my life being concerned about Amanda Lee. Can I leave if I pretend to be?" She crossed her arms and gave him a pout.

It was a strange pout, thought Flanagan, not annoyed, not even what you'd call petulant—a pout that maybe wasn't even a pout.

"I'm not sure what game you're playing here," he said, "but you're in serious trouble, Ms. Lafontaine, and maybe it's time you treated it that way. I'm not talking out of school when I tell you that your boyfriend is in serious trouble as well."

"Well, thank you for the telling. Is that why I'm here, so you can tell me stuff? 'Cause if that's all this is, I've worked all day, I'm tired and maybe you can tell me the rest tomorrow."

She crossed her arms again. Gave Flanagan the pout that maybe wasn't a pout. Forty-nine years old? He never would have guessed that.

"I have a theory on what happened at that trailhead. Want to hear it?" he said.

"Do I have a choice?"

"I think Tucker Lee and your cousin didn't have your Travis Lee's best interests at heart. Matter of fact, I think they were trying to frame him for the murder of Robert Powell. How do you like my theory so far?"

"I like stories. Go ahead."

"You'll love where we go from here, then. I think these two fuckin' trolls— I'm sorry to say that. I know one of those trolls was your cousin, but a troll is a troll and I'm not going to call 'em anything else. I think those trolls were up at that trailhead *conspiring* against Mr. Lee. You hear what I'm saying?"

"Uh-huh."

"Now, let's say a good friend of Mr. Lee's found out about this meeting and went up there to try to talk these trolls out of committing this *criminal act*. Let's say that was her *original intent*. But things got out of hand and those trolls *threatened* this good friend of Mr. Lee. Or this good friend *felt threatened*. Are you catching these words, or do you want me to write them out for you?"

"I'm catching them."

"Good. Now, let's say this good friend of Mr. Lee's was a diner waitress who'd worked at the same joint for thirty years, a good-looking woman who'd never had so much as a fuckin' parking ticket. And the dead guys, well, they're fuckin' trolls. Ms. Lafontaine, it would not surprise me to see lawyers lined up outside this good friend's house, begging to represent her. Some pretty damn good ones too. Just fuckin' begging to represent this good friend."

She looked at Flanagan but didn't uncross her arms. The pout stayed on her face. She had not once seemed nervous, it occurred to him, never once seemed unsure about what to say. A diner waitress who had just been told she was a suspect in a double homicide.

"Do you understand what I've just told you, Ms. Lafontaine?"

"I surely do."

"Jurors would have a lot of sympathy for a good friend like that. *I* would have a lot of sympathy for a good friend like that. But right now this is a fork in the road for this good friend. I'm going to feel one way or another about her when I leave this room and that won't ever be changing. Do you understand?"

She nodded. Then she uncrossed her arms, leaned forward in her seat and looked again at the two photos. After a few seconds, she looked up at Flanagan and said, "Are these the *best* photos you got?"

32

I HEARD FROM Flanagan three days later. When the phone call came, he told me to come to the Alexander, and as soon as I walked into his room, I knew the investigation was finished.

The last two times I'd been in that hotel room, there were file folders and bankers boxes spread everywhere, stacks of paper on the bed and the windowsills, the top of the minibar. All of that was gone.

"We're shutting her down," Flanagan said, handing me a beer. "We're going to arrest Travis Lee later today and charge him with racketeering, money laundering, tax evasion, maybe an alien abduction or two. A meeting I was at yesterday had the number of federal and state charges he'll be facing at twenty-one. Probably be more by the time everyone gets finished piling on."

I sipped my beer and looked at him. He was wearing wide pants, Charlie Chaplin sort of pants, and a button-down shirt with a two-tone collar. He looked like he could be singing in a barbershop quartet. If the barbershop was a front for something else. And in the wrong part of town.

"We'll seize the assets of Lee Forestry and start forfeiture proceedings," he continued. "The mills will close by the end of the week, I'm sure. Don't know how long Lee will want to drag this out, so I don't know when they'll reopen. Lee Forestry was one of the biggest forestry companies in Maine at one time and people are about to find out the company has been little more than a money-laundering arm for Beau Lafontaine's troll fuckin' army for years. There'll be a huge stink. Could be a national story."

Flanagan took a sip of his beer. He didn't seem all that happy that it could be a national story. "You did great work, Barrett, but we're not going to need your testimony. It's going to be all accountants and lawyers, come tomorrow."

"What about Paradise Lake?"

"Can't go up there right now. All the court filings started with Beau Lafontaine. With him dead? What can I tell you? There are legal problems."

"That place is hell on earth."

"I know."

"And the murders? No one's getting charged with any of the murders?"

"Seems to be the way it's going to play out."

"What about the Northwoods trailhead? She gets a walk on that? A double homicide?"

"Not my call. Yesterday I was given a legal opinion that we have no reasonable prospect of obtaining a conviction against Pearl Lafontaine. All we have against her are those photos of the car."

"You don't think you can build a case against her?"

"I don't. She's a smart woman, Barrett. I'm sure we'll never find the murder weapon. I'm sure there will never be a witness. And I can't see her ever panicking or feeling bad about what she did. I might not either. She did the planet a favor by taking her cousin off it."

I didn't say anything. Just drank my beer and looked at him.

"You're disappointed?" he said. "You've worked enough cases to know that's how it goes sometimes. We're not going to get perfect justice here. When those indictments come down, we're going to leave those murders unsolved, walk away from this rat fuck and tell the world we did a grin-ass-wonderful job of shutting down Lee fuckin' Forestry. Maybe we can get an official commendation for our fine work. Do you want one of those? I can put in a request. Can't use your testimony, but maybe I can get you a Cracker Jack prize."

I kept staring at Flanagan, then took another look around the room. Bitterness like that didn't normally come right at the end of an investigation. A little while after that, sure, when you had taken in just how bust everything went, how futile and doomed it all seemed in hindsight. But not right away. Flanagan was frustrated. I could see now that although the room was neater than I'd seen it before, there were toiletries in the bathroom and a bag of laundry waiting to be picked up by the door. The room was neater, but not about to be vacated. Judging by his suits, Flanagan was probably a neat man by nature. The mess had been the aberration. A man obsessed.

"So you won't be needing my testimony?" I said.

"No."

"This is a long exit interview."

Flanagan snorted and drained his beer. "Yeah, a pretty long exit interview. You're a smart cowboy. Why do you think that is?"

"Because you have one play left."

"You see it?"

"I think so."

"What do you think of it?"

"It might work. Won't shut down Paradise Lake."

"I know that."

"So why do it? Nobody is ever going to miss those guys. You said it yourself."

"Dead trolls make up the bulk of my business, Barrett. And maybe

I don't like wasting my time. Ever think of that? If I don't make this play, I'll be left with three unsolved murders and an unsolved disappearance. How is that *ever* supposed to sit well with me?"

It was personal. If I didn't know that already, I'd just been told.

"When would you do it?"

"Later today."

"Hold him overnight?"

"What I was thinking. I'd do the initial interview tomorrow morning, six a.m."

"I should be here for that."

"You should."

33

TRAVIS LEE WAS arrested while walking into the Starlight Club a few minutes before happy hour began. Which meant it took no more than an hour before he was sober enough for the detective to turn on the video camera and take an initial statement.

Lee was told once again that he was under arrest for the murder of Robert Powell. He had the right to remain silent. If he couldn't afford a lawyer, the court would appoint one for him. He had the right to an attorney right now, if he so chose.

After Lee waived his rights, the detective went through the evidence against him. That was all the detective needed to do—make sure Lee knew he could go down on a murder charge. Because the case was never going to be credited to the local police, the detective doing the interview did the bare minimum. Thirty minutes and he was done.

Lee was told his car had been seen in the vicinity of the crime scene five minutes before Robert Powell was shot. Two .260-caliber hunting rifles, same as the murder weapon, were registered in his name.

Lee had a motive for the killing. The detective laughed when he said that. "Plenty of motive," he repeated, and Lee could see the stack of Lee Forestry banking statements in the file folder the detective had put on the table. The detective asked Lee where he was when Robert Powell was killed. Lee said he'd had a blackout that day and couldn't remember. The detective snorted before saying, "No alibi either." After that, Lee was taken to the holding cells.

The cops in the holding cells made sure he got a bad night's sleep, booking a couple of drunks in the cell next to him just before midnight. He didn't seem to mind. Was singing along with them until four in the morning. At five forty-five a.m., the night duty sergeant came and brought him back to the interview room.

———

LEE LAUGHED WHEN Flanagan walked into the room and introduced himself.

"The FBI. I was wondering when you boys might show up."

"Been here quite a while, Mr. Lee."

"I was beginning to suspect that. Bad form not introducing yourself earlier. We could have had drinks. I certainly would have arranged better surroundings than what you've managed."

"I wouldn't be making jokes right now, Mr. Lee."

"Do you think I'm joking?"

"You're under arrest for murder, Mr. Lee. The case against you is a strong one. It's a beaut really. The penalty in this state for first-degree murder is life in prison, no chance of parole for twenty-five years. How old are you, Mr. Lee?"

"Not the foggiest. I go with a state-of-mind age. How old are you?"

Flanagan stared at him. The next part couldn't start until Lee was scared of the first part. I moved a little closer to the two-way mirror in the other room and stared at him.

"You don't care about yourself, Mr. Lee. That's fine with me," Flanagan continued, "but I'm here to offer you something you don't deserve in my humble fuckin' opinion. But people smarter than me say I have to offer it to you. It's important you understand what I'm offering you before I leave this room. So may I have your fuckin' attention, Mr. Lee?"

A look of curiosity passed across Lee's face. "Now that you've asked nicely, yes, by all means tell me why you have brought me here," he said.

"The FBI has been investigating Lee Forestry for more than a year. We'll be laying racketeering charges against you later today, Mr. Lee, at the same time as we charge you with first-degree murder. We will seize all assets and banking accounts associated with Lee Forestry. I've been given a legal opinion that you'll probably serve more time on the racketeering charges than you'll serve on the murder charge. Life is fuckin' funny some days, don't you think, Mr. Lee?"

It was a good line for Lee to pounce on. But he said nothing.

"All that starts the minute I walk out of this room. Your mills will close. Your money will be seized. Lee Forestry will be in Chapter Eleven within days. We're going to make sure that happens, Mr. Lee, because there are people out there who are pretty fuckin' pissed about what's been happening in Birmingham. Makes the whole state look like *The Gong Show*. These people would like nothing more than to see you and your company disappear for all time."

Lee didn't have a quip or a witty retort for that either. Although he didn't look worried. He was letting Flanagan talk.

"As I've told you, I'm here to offer you a deal, Mr. Lee. Here, let me show you something."

With that, Flanagan opened the file folder he had brought into the room and took out two black-and-white photos. He slid them across the table for Lee to see.

"Look familiar? I believe you've ridden in it often enough."

"Are you sure? Doesn't look like the sort of vehicle I would ride around in."

"That car was caught on closed-circuit camera heading to and coming back from the Northwoods trailhead last Tuesday evening."

"To drive off a cliff, I would think."

Flanagan stared at him a few seconds before shaking his head.

"You're a hard man to offer a break to, Mr. Lee. You know whose car that is. You know who's driving it. And you know what the fuck happened at the Northwoods trailhead that night."

"That last part is true. I *do* know. I read all the details in the newspaper. Did you think I didn't? Honestly, this is looking less and less like a good reason to pull me out of happy hour."

"Are you sick in the head?"

Lee looked startled. His body jumped and he sat straighter in his chair. I had gone drinking with Travis Lee for three nights, but I had never seen that expression on his face. Flanagan had hurt him.

"I didn't realize we were at the insult stage. You could have warned me. Is it my turn?"

"Mr. Lee, my job is to ensure you know what your situation is and that you understand the deal I'm about to offer you. We can insult each other all fuckin' day after that if you want. Now let's cut the shit. Your girlfriend is the one who murdered Beau Lafontaine and your brother. We're going to arrest Pearl Lafontaine, we're going to prosecute her and we stand a very fuckin' good chance of convicting her.

"But there are some holes in our case. We don't have a witness. We don't have a murder weapon. And there are people out there who have a better motive than your girlfriend for killing those men. Defense lawyers can have a lot of fun with a case like that. We'd like to close those holes. That, Mr. Lee, is your lucky break."

"You want me to betray Pearl?"

"Let me finish. If you cooperate with us in building a case against Ms. Lafontaine, the state is prepared to drop the murder charge and cut a deal on the racketeering charges. The racketeering deal can be structured in such a way as to leave Lee Forestry a solvent company. You'll never run it again, never run anything again, but it is possible you could be left with shares. In addition to this, whatever criminal sentences you receive will run concurrently. You will stand a reasonable chance, Mr. Lee, of walking out of jail in ten years if you accept this deal. You might be able to do it in less."

"Ten years?"

"That's right. Are you figuring your age out now, Mr. Lee?"

———

I STOOD BESIDE Flanagan, both of us with our hands clasped behind our backs. We looked at Travis Lee on the other side of the two-way mirror. He was whistling.

"What song is that?" asked Flanagan.

"No idea."

"It's not 'Oklahoma,' is it?"

"Wouldn't know."

"Whistling a show tune like some fuckin' frat boy. This guy kills me. So what do you think?"

"I think he's considering it. Ten years versus life. That's a good deal you just offered him. Twisted but good."

"What's twisted about it?"

"He didn't murder the banker. He was being framed for it, and that's the evidence you're using to squeeze him. It's fake evidence. You'd have to drop the charge."

"There's nothing illegal about threatening a suspect with a criminal proceeding that has no reasonable chance of succeeding. You know this."

"Sure, but normally the guy you're squeezing did it, and you just can't prove it. Everything about this case is twisted, right down to the evidence we're using against the guy."

"What the fuck's going on with you? Do you like this guy or something?"

"I don't hate him."

"He's a fuckin' money launderer. That cat's out there helping the fuckin' trolls, Barrett. Thought we were on the same team here."

"Money launderer? You can say the same thing about most political action committees."

"Not in public you can't. Are you having some crisis of fuckin' faith

here? You've done some outstanding undercover work. How can you do
that without lying to people?"

"You can't. But this is an odd case. There doesn't seem to be a
straight line anywhere."

"You like it when the world is running straight and true. When
everything is fuckin' *plumb*?"

"I do."

"So do I. Never seen that fuckin' world. Do you want to back out?
Now's the time to tell me."

"No. I'm here for the duration. I already told you that."

Flanagan nodded and turned back to the mirror. When a few seconds had passed, and without looking back at me, he said, "Anytime
you're ready."

34

WHEN I WALKED into the room, Lee looked at me with eyes so sad and lost, they reminded me of eyes from a clouded daguerreotype, eyes from some forgotten tragedy. Betrayal, the genuine thing, is about as cruel and primeval as it gets.

"I take my FBI joke back," said Lee. "Looks like we *have* been introduced. What's your name, pal?"

"Danny Barrett."

"That your real name?"

"Real for now."

"Real for now. That's good. If the situation were a little different, I might think that line was worthy of a drink."

"I don't think much is worthy of a drink right now. Do you, Mr. Lee?"

He glared at me but didn't speak. I waited a few seconds before starting the pitch. "I asked to speak to you, Mr. Lee, because I wanted to tell you it's a good deal you just got offered. Pearl should pay for what she did, no matter her reasons for doing it. She put herself in this situation. It wasn't you. You're being offered a way out. That's all that's happening here. You have the right to protect yourself, Mr. Lee."

"That's quite rich, my friend. I should betray the woman who was trying to protect me in order to protect myself. Wherever will the circle end?"

"It's not a circle, Mr. Lee. It's a dead end or an open door."

"Who the fuck do you work for? Are you FBI?"

"No. I've been seconded to their task force."

"Do you really come from Detroit or was that bullshit?"

"It wasn't bullshit. I come from Detroit."

"The Ben E. King story?"

"Complete bullshit."

Lee looked shocked. He took a deep breath and held it, and then he started laughing. Before he was finished, I was chuckling along with him.

"I thought you'd like a story like that, Mr. Lee. And I like Ben E. King. I wasn't lying about that."

"But you never saw him?"

"No. I saw Weezer at the Copper Penny once before they got big."

"Who are they?"

"That's why I didn't tell you that story, Mr. Lee."

He laughed some more. Took a sip of water from the glass in front of him. "I had you pegged for one of the good guys. It was a refreshing break, drinking with someone like you. The good ones all seem to have fallen by the wayside somewhere. Must say I'm disappointed."

"I enjoyed it too, Mr. Lee. I'm sorry you're in this situation."

"Are you? This is rather your job, isn't it?"

"It is. But I still think you've been on a run of bad luck. I can still feel sorry for you, Mr. Lee. I'm allowed to do that."

"You're not going to become my friend now, are you? Double-dipping? Fuck, you are good."

"I'm not going to insult you, Mr. Lee. But I am hoping you'll let me give you some advice. From someone who's sat in a lot of these rooms, having a lot of conversations with people just like you."

"I'll bite. What's the advice?"

"I think it's time you thought about yourself, Mr. Lee. I know you're not good at doing that, but I wish you would. Think about yourself, think about your company, think about the people you got working for you. Do you think this town can take one more hit?"

"That's unfair, don't you think? You can't pin the welfare of this city on me. I tried that once. Didn't work."

"I know you did. But that doesn't change things. Your great-great-granddaddy was a lumber baron, Mr. Lee. You are who you are and there's no escaping it. You've tried hard enough. Whatever you do, it's going to ripple out a long way. Don't deceive yourself about that."

"Is that what you think I do, deceive myself?"

I had spent enough time with Travis Lee to know I wasn't being asked a petulant question. Or a throwaway question. There was curiosity in his voice. I had touched upon something Lee must have considered before. Maybe many times before.

"Yes, I do, Mr. Lee. I think you deceive yourself. But I think a lot of people do that, and I think it's happening more and more. Nostalgia, that's a form of deception, isn't it? The past always seems better than what it was. Like those fishing boats you remember on the St. John River? You remember these brightly colored sailing boats—like kites, you said. Those fishing boats are gone, Mr. Lee, because no one can work them anymore and make a living at it. The last few years on those boats, for the men working them, it would have been just about as far removed from flying kites as a thing can be."

"There seems to be a message in there for me. What else am I mistaken about?"

"Your options."

Lee looked at me as though I had switched to another language.

Confusion mixed with vertigo mixed with disbelief. I'd seen the look before. People sitting in rooms like this, on the other side of tables like this, they often end up with that look.

"Mr. Lee," I continued, "the deal you just got offered is a good deal and it never gets offered to people who don't know the other person. It's always family, or friends, who get offered these deals. Most people take the deal. It's a difficult decision, yes, but make no mistake about the decision you're being asked to make. Do I survive? Yes or no. That's what you're deciding, Mr. Lee."

"You should find someone else to do this."

"There is no one else."

"It's not right."

"Never said it was. Just the best you have today."

This answer also seemed to startle Lee. His eyes darted around the room and I knew his mind was darting as well. I wondered how long it had been since he'd had a drink.

That was unfair. No one in Lee's situation was ever looking or acting their best. It wasn't natural, what we were asking Lee to do, despite that old ATF agent saying betrayal was the second thing humans ever did. There was more to that story, but I never bothered getting into it with him.

Most people don't like betrayal. It happens. There are reasons for it happening. You convince yourself they're good reasons, that it needs to be done. But waking up in the morning and thinking that's what I want to do today—betray someone—most people don't do that. It's not a natural human aspiration.

Many times a field commander has given me what they thought was a compliment, telling me I was a "natural" undercover agent. I never seemed uncomfortable or worried about what I was doing.

I'm still not sure how to feel about being told this. Doesn't seem like a compliment, being told deceit and betrayal come natural to me. Doesn't seem wrong either. That's the part I wonder about most.

I leaned back in my chair and waited. It takes time to justify an act of betrayal, so I kept my head down and avoided eye contact. I figured Travis Lee would be at the outer limits of the time needed.

I was right. We didn't say anything for almost twenty minutes. The silence finally ended when Lee said, "Do you have some sort of a plan?"

35

LEE WAS BROUGHT upstairs to a conference room on the third floor.
The duty sergeant asked if he wanted coffee and Lee said that he did.
We sat in the room and waited for the coffee to arrive, along with Lee's
personal effects from the holding cells.

Linton was in the conference room when we arrived. We kept our
eyes off Lee, but Linton never stopped staring at him. Eventually he
said, "I'm Special Agent Paul Linton, Mr. Lee. I started this investigation."

"Congratulations. Initiative is a wonderful thing."

"I've been watching you for a long time. Has anyone told you how
long we've been watching you?"

"More than a year."

"That's right. I've been monitoring your company, watching your
money, watching you and your wife. I've seen you throw up in front of
the Starlight. I've seen you fuck in the backseat of your Mercedes."

Lee looked at him with a sad smile. "Well, the Starlight hardly seems like an accomplishment. As for getting caught fucking in the backseat of my car, let me think. . . . Seventeen? Yes, I would have been seventeen the first time that happened. It was a deputy with this very police department who caught me. Doubt he's still around."

"Right, the football hero. I forgot. I love bringing down people like you, Mr. Lee."

"You must love diner waitresses too."

It was so quick, so cutting, it stopped Linton from saying the next thing he was going to say. Left him with his mouth open, getting ready to say it, but Lee stopped him, left whatever it might have been irrelevant and off point.

So Linton responded the way clumsy people with authority often respond in situations like that. He got angry.

"You're a fuckin' piece of work, aren't you? Your girlfriend kills two men and you're sitting here making jokes. Yeah, I'm going to like bringing down Delta fuckin' Dawn. Just wish we didn't have to deal with shits like you to do it."

"Paul, shut the fuck up, please," said Flanagan, giving Linton a tired look. "Mr. Lee has got himself into a fine mess. We're all grown men and we can all see that. No need to pile on. Mr. Lee, it looks like your coffee is here."

A civilian dispatcher was at the doorway to the office holding a plastic cafeteria tray with four coffee cups, a pitcher of milk and a bowl of sugar. The duty sergeant came in while the dispatcher was unloading the tray. The sergeant had Lee's coat, wallet, Rolex and the keys to his Mercedes. Lee made himself a coffee and listened to Flanagan explain next steps.

"This won't have to take long, Mr. Lee. Like I said, we're not building a case against Ms. Lafontaine. We're simply adding to what we already have. We don't need to know what happened at that trailhead. Just need her to confirm she killed those men."

"Wouldn't it be *nice* to know what happened up there?"

"I'm sure that will come out at trial. I'm saying you can keep this short. We don't need a lot of details right now. Just confirmation. I'm hoping that will make it easier for you."

"'Easy' doesn't seem the right word."

"It probably isn't. I apologize."

Linton snorted so loudly, it could have probably been heard in the hallway. Flanagan flashed him a look not as tired as the one he had given him a moment ago. The tired-to-angry ratio was shifting.

"My choice of the word 'confirmation' is deliberate," Flanagan continued. "We don't need a blow-by-blow account of what happened, and we don't need a fuckin' Perry Mason confession. You remember Perry Mason? Great fuckin' show. But we don't need that. May I give you some examples of how confirmation works?"

"Examples?"

"Yes, I find it useful. I know you're a lawyer, and I don't want to insult you, but I find it useful. Do you mind?"

Lee looked at Flanagan with sudden interest. "Well, it's been a few years, and it was corporate law. But yes, please, give me some examples."

"All right, let's say you were talking to Ms. Lafontaine, talking about what happened at that trailhead, and you said something to the effect of 'It must have been hard, killing your cousin,' and Ms. Lafontaine replied, 'Yes, probably the hardest thing I've ever had to do.' That statement would be clear confirmation for the killing of Beau Lafontaine."

"That's leading the witness. And an absurd conversation."

"No such objection to a confirmation, Mr. Lee. And I strongly recommend absurd. You need to be specific. Your brother and Beau Lafontaine were murdered. That's what you need to be talking about. No hidden meanings. No fuckin' metaphors. It would be great if you could use the word 'murder,' but we don't need it. Just don't be shy."

"Don't be shy."

"That's right."

"Well explained. You could have been a law professor."

"Already got a government job. Now, given how recent these murders are, and given your special relationship with Ms. Lafontaine . . ."

It was too much for Linton. He gave another loud snort and this time Flanagan's knuckles came down hard on the wooden desk, hard enough to make a bang, lift the telephone in the air an inch. Linton's head snapped back. Flanagan didn't bother looking at him. He kept on talking.

"Given that special relationship, I don't think you'll have any trouble bringing up the topic of the Northwoods trailhead. Sometimes I write a little script for people to help them out, but I don't think you're a person who needs a script. Do you have any questions about what you need Ms. Lafontaine to say?"

"No."

"Good. I know this is a lot to take in all at once, but in my experience, dragging these things out only makes it harder on everyone, you most of all, Mr. Lee. How are you feeling?"

"Never better."

"Seriously, how are you feeling? We have all the authorizations we need for this. The equipment is here. We can get this done today."

"Today? How would you do it?"

"Go meet Ms. Lafontaine when her shift finishes. She's off at four. We've already checked. We can be set up at the St. John Motel. There's not much involved in getting you ready."

"Take her to the St. John?"

"Yes. I'm not spinning you a line here, Mr. Lee. It's best to finish these things quickly."

Lee rubbed his chin and thought about that. He looked at Barrett, and a sleepy smile came to his face. Finally he said, "I'm tired."

"Pardon?"

"You asked how I was feeling. I'm tired. I didn't get much sleep last night, and what time is it now?" Lee picked up his Rolex from the desk. "Nearly noon. Yes, I'm tired."

Lee looked each of us full in the face before adding, "Let's do this tomorrow, boys. One last mañana for the road."

36

LEE WAS TOLD he was still under arrest and would be under police surveillance until he was brought back to the Alexander the next day. Flanagan told him not to leave his house, touch his computer, make any calls or send any texts. I could tell he was annoyed when he gave Lee the instructions. Flanagan had his bags packed and would be taking the first flight out of Birmingham once Pearl Lafontaine was arrested.

"If you're this tired, Mr. Lee, I'd go to bed and stay there for the night. I would stay away from the fuckin' Scotch. Tomorrow is not a day you want to be hungover."

"That is making assumptions about how I regard hangovers."

Flanagan looked at him a few seconds, then laughed and shook his head. "You're a grown man, Mr. Lee. Just remember your ass is grass if you fuck up tomorrow."

Then Lee was escorted to the lobby, where a cab was waiting to take him home.

I HAD AN afternoon to kill and I walked back to the Three Pines. It took me three hours. I could have done it in less but I meandered, walking down streets I hadn't walked yet, into corner stores that had been converted to vape shops or computer-repair joints, looking at the moldings and the windows, the columns and the floors, getting a sense of what the businesses would have looked like in the heyday of this lumber town, when there probably would have been sawdust on the floor and an icebox in back, kids sitting on the cement stoop all day long.

The sidewalks were chipped and caved between the joints of the cement slabs. They didn't make sidewalks like that anymore. The sidewalks looked better on the arterial street that led to the highway, which would have been the quickest way to get to the Three Pines, but the arterial was crowded with muffler shops and fast-food restaurants and I stayed on the older streets.

I bought a six-pack of Pabst and some bread and deli meat at a grocery not far from the motel. Went to my room and made sandwiches, turned on the television. The old Clint Eastwood movie *Escape from Alcatraz* was on and I started watching it. I had seen the movie before and remembered wondering afterward if Frank Morris could have escaped, like the movie hinted, or had he drowned in San Francisco Bay, his body never found? I was curious enough at the time to do a Google search, figuring the movie probably lied about a number of things, but it turned out to be pretty accurate. And nobody knew if Morris made it.

I did another search that night and saw there were now dozens of Google pages for "Frank Lee Morris, American Criminal." There was reference after reference to television shows and documentaries, magazine articles and blog sites. The latest assessment of the June 11, 1962, escape attempt from Alcatraz by Frank Morris and brothers John and Clarence Anglin? Nobody knows what happened.

I sat in my motel room, eating a mock-chicken sandwich, wondering how much time and effort gets expended every day, across the world, by people trying to get a different answer from the one they already got.

My phone vibrated. I looked at the number and saw it was Flanagan.

"Barrett."

"About tomorrow," Flanagan said, as if we were already having a conversation. "I want you to go fetch Lee. He should be driving one of his cars to come here to the hotel. It'll look odd if he isn't driving. You'll need to take a cab to his place. Leave the rental car at the motel."

"Does Lee know that's the plan?"

"He knows he has to be ready for nine a.m. You'll be his knock on the door."

"All right." I could hear a basketball game in the background. The tinkling of ice cubes. "What are you doing?"

"Not much. Having a cocktail. Watching a ball game. Remember when the Knicks had a good team? Whatever happened to that?"

"The millennium changed. Anything bothering you? Anything I need to be concerned about?"

"Concerned? Other than running point on an undercover sting that I figure, at best, has a fifty-fifty chance of not blowing up in our faces? No, I don't see why you have anything to be concerned about."

"You don't think Lee is going to go through with it?"

"He's a weak man. You know that. He could freeze. Or he could fall on his sword and tell Lafontaine what we're doing. I also think he might go through with it. No one ever feels good about doing this sort of thing. He may take the path of least resistance and get it over with. I can see him doing that."

"It's a good deal."

"It is."

Flanagan said that two more times, his voice sounding like a fading echo. There was silence for a few seconds before he said, "I wanted to be a priest once. Believe that? I was dead serious about it too. Not some fuckin' whim. I was on my way to seminary school. Know what went wrong?"

"You got lost?"

"Ahh, good answer. No, I got laid."

"You're not worried about Lee screwing up, are you?"

"You don't think?"

"No, I don't think. You're more worried he'll go through with it. Then you'll have to send someone you half admire off to prison for life."

"I've done that before, Barrett. Paddy Busby was the most interesting guy I've ever met. He's in the pen, and I'm still standing. I don't like wasting time. Already told you that."

"You did. But this case feels different, doesn't it? There's something about the hills around here or the mist or the old brick buildings— something about this city that makes you seem cut off, like you've lost the reference points."

Flanagan snorted and then he yelled, the noise in the background letting me know someone had scored a basket. "Yeah, you're a smart cowboy," he said next. "I *am* looking for reference points. Might be having what an old parish priest of mine would have called a crisis of faith. Sitting here asking myself questions I thought I'd asked and answered a long time ago. Can a criminal go unpunished yet justice be served? Should people suffer in the pursuit of justice? Yeah, a lot of old questions."

"What answers are you getting?"

"Same ones I would be getting from that parish priest if he were in the room to hear my confession. 'Justice is not a fixed mark, Jimmy. It is a goal. It is sufficient in the eyes of God to have good intentions and a good heart in the pursuit of justice. God protects the innocent.'"

"There you go."

"Yeah, there you go. Only one little problem with Father Robert's answer."

"What's that?"

"When did God ever give the innocent a pass?"

━━━━

THE BIRMINGHAM POLICE reported the lights were out in Lee's house at nine forty-seven p.m., his bedroom window being the last one to go dark. The bedroom lights came back on at seven fifteen a.m., after that the lights in the en suite bathroom, and then in the kitchen. At seven forty-one a.m., the front door of the house opened, and Travis Lee stooped to pick up a copy of that day's *Boston Globe*. He was dressed in flannel pajamas and a terry-cloth robe.

At eight fifteen the police saw him watering a rock garden beside his house, using an old tin watering can. He was still dressed in his terry-cloth robe. He picked a few sprigs from some herbs, weeded around a few others, then went back inside the house. A moment later he came back outside with a cup of coffee and sat on a cement bench in the middle of the rock garden. He drank his coffee and watched the sun rising behind his house. Then he went back inside.

At eight fifty a.m., I arrived at Lee's house in a Shamrock cab. I rang the bell and he answered without using the intercom. He was dressed in dark khaki pants and a white shirt under a gray sweater. He was clean-shaven and carried a windbreaker under his arm. He didn't look hungover.

"Right on time," he said. "I've never known a tree marker to be anything but punctual. We did our research well when we hired you, didn't we, Mr. Barrett?"

"No comment. You're looking good this morning, Mr. Lee."

"Didn't want to get into trouble with your boss. We're off to see him, I gather?"

"We are. He says we should take your car so it doesn't look suspicious when we get to the hotel."

"I'll be driving?"

"Yes."

"Well, I shall enjoy that. I wasn't sure how we would be doing this. I have Sirius in the car. Anything you care to hear? Sports? You probably like sports, right?"

"If it's sports and not a couple of frat boys with stupid nicknames *talking* about sports."

"We shouldn't have any problems finding a station. Come inside and I'll get my keys."

37

I WAS DRESSED in the work clothes of a tree marker: Kevlar-lined canvas pants, thick-soled work boots with a natural toe, a plaid jacket and a watchman's cap. Travis Lee with a forestry worker. That's how we looked when we cut through the lobby of the Alexander. Lee got some stares—his brother's murder was still on the front page of the newspaper—but no one took a second look at me. No one questioned why I was there.

We made the ride to the sixth floor in silence. It was Linton who answered the door when I knocked.

"Shooowtime," he said, and then he laughed, thinking that was funny.

I guided Lee into the room, where Flanagan was sitting behind the desk, reading a *Boston Globe*. On the bed were the small recorder and omnidirectional microphone that Lee would be wearing.

"Here, let me show you how this works," I said.

"That's it?"

"That's it. You were expecting duct tape and black boxes like in *The French Connection*?"

"I was."

"Not that exotic anymore. Sorry to disappoint you, Mr. Lee. This is all you're going to need. You can put it right in your coat pocket. We're going to be two doors down, in room fourteen. This is the button that—"

"I've been thinking about that."

I stopped talking, surprised by the interruption. Travis Lee had been as docile as an old dog on painkillers since he'd been turned. Which wasn't a worry to anyone. It was even welcome. Docile was the perfect personality trait for a confidential informant.

Now Lee seemed agitated and had cut me off midsentence. Something was bothering him.

"Thinking about what, Trav?" asked Linton.

"The motel room. Do we have to do this in a motel room?"

"Why? Forgotten the way?"

"Fuck, Paul, shut up," said Flanagan. "What is the problem with the motel room, Mr. Lee?"

"What do you think the problem is?" answered Lee. "I'm about to betray a woman who has been nothing but kind to me, a woman I've known since high school, and you're asking me to betray her in a motel room in the middle of the afternoon? Would that be the dictionary definition of 'adding insult to injury'? Or would that be more a salt-in-the-wound thing?"

"Mr. Lee, we're all set at the motel. The surveillance equipment, the recording equipment—it's all there. I've been married four times. Did you know that? Maybe I know women. Maybe I know shit, but I've never known the woman who would give a fuck about the location once we're done. Trust me, Mr. Lee, she won't care."

"But *I will*. I don't want to do this in a motel room."

"What are you suggesting?"

"Change the location."

"To where?"

"Maybe someplace outside? Can we do that?"

We looked at him. It wasn't uncommon to make last-minute adjustments to an operation like this. The informant becomes nervous and you need to do something to calm them down, or the suspect doesn't show or shows at the wrong location. All sorts of tweaks, and when you're in this far, that's what you do. You tweak. Do whatever it takes to keep everyone calm and moving in the right direction. You never need much more than a ten-minute performance from an informant. Just need to get them up on stage.

"We'd need to have a surveillance van in position, Mr. Lee. Any ideas on where we could do this?"

Lee thought about it a moment. "What about Champlain Lookout? There's a big parking lot there for your van. Some picnic tables. I could take her there."

"A fuckin' picnic? Is this what I'm hearin'?" yelled Linton. "Trav wants to take Delta Dawn on a fuckin' picnic?"

"Shut up, Paul. I think we can accommodate Mr. Lee. Does anyone know this place?"

"I do," I said.

"Would it work?"

"It would."

"All right, that's where we're going. Timeline remains the same. I'll get the equipment moved out of the motel room."

Linton looked at Lee with a loathing so palpable, it seemed to fill the room. I shrugged and continued explaining how the recorder worked.

———

LEE WARMED TO the picnic idea. I remember that. While Flanagan and Linton made final preparations with the surveillance van, I took him grocery shopping.

We went to Saslove's Deli first for meat and pumpernickel bread so thick and dark, it looked like Christmas cake. Lee said there used to be

~~a deli not far from his dorm room at Harvard that sold the same bread,~~ and years ago he'd asked Paul Saslove to stock it. Amanda never cared for the bread and Lee would often bring loaves home only to find them in the garbage the next day. He kept buying them, as he felt obligated. Paul Saslove died years ago. The boy behind the counter didn't remember him.

After Saslove's we went to House of Cheese on William Street, where Lee bought bricks of Havarti and Emmentaler; after that, a bakery near the St. John River to buy four different kinds of fruit tarts. He bought a blanket and a thermos at a Ferguson's department store, and coffee at a Starbucks, putting creamers and sweeteners into a paper bag.

Flanagan had told him he couldn't buy wine or beer. Said he was willing to play along—fuck Linton. Go have a picnic—but there couldn't be any alcohol. A smart defense lawyer could have a field day with something like that.

Shortly before noon we drove to Champlain Lookout to meet Flanagan. He wanted to have a look at the place. It was two-thirds of the way up Mount Peck, a ridge of granite so large and wide, it was identified on some maps as an escarpment. It had some of the best views of the St. John Valley in all of Northern Maine, and in autumn, when the hardwood leaves had turned, there were as many cars heading to Champlain Lookout on a Sunday afternoon as there were cars driving around Birmingham.

When we were standing in the parking lot, looking at the picnic tables, the four-foot-high fence that ran along the edge of the escarpment, the loop trail to the east of the parking lot that went to a small waterfall a mile away, Lee asked Flanagan what sort of range the microphone had.

"Why do you want to know that?"

"Just thinking out loud, but there's not a lot of privacy at those picnic tables, is there? I think this situation calls for some privacy. Also, now that I'm here, I'm realizing Pearl would be suspicious if I took her to one of these tables."

"Why?"

"Well, we *know* this place. It's why I thought about it when you asked me where we could go. Pearl and I have come here quite often, and if we were to have a picnic, we wouldn't sit at one of these tables. There's a spot just down the trail where we'd go."

"You're just thinking about this now?"

"I'm sorry, but yes."

Flanagan looked to where Lee was pointing. "You're worried she'll think something is up? Most people in your situation don't worry about a thing like that. Why do you care?"

Lee looked away, over the St. John Valley and the river that meandered through it. There were whitecaps in the middle channel, the last remnants of the spring runoff. They wouldn't be there in a week.

Without looking at Flanagan, Lee said, "I think I *do* want to survive. I've been thinking about it all night, and I can do ten years. I *think* I can do ten years. What I can't do—and I *know this*—is betray Pearl Lafontaine twice. This is rather a one-shot deal for me."

Flanagan thought about that a few seconds, then shrugged his shoulders and said, "Come show me this place."

38

LEE HAD ONE more request. He seemed to have figured out he could make requests, and they would be granted. He told Flanagan he wanted to go to the Starlight before picking up Pearl Lafontaine.

"No alcohol, Mr. Lee. I've already told you that."

"I won't drink. Ginger ale. That's all I'll have. I just want to see the place. I'm assuming this will be my last chance for quite a while. Am I wrong about that?"

He wasn't wrong about that. Flanagan said he had one hour. I had to go with him. Flanagan would meet us at the Starlight at three p.m.

I had never been in the Starlight in the afternoon and it had the midafternoon feel of a good bar. There is something special about a good bar in the middle of the afternoon, the quiet time of day when bartenders stop to have their cigarettes and restock the coolers, when the lunch crowd is gone and the sun is coming through the windows at just the right angle to light up the liquor bottles, turn them into earth-tone diamonds. If you had the right windows and the right liquor bottles, that's what happened. A good bar would have those.

We sat on barstools, and when Lee ordered ginger ale, the bartender hammed it up. He held his chest as if he were having a heart attack. Wobbled on his feet before correcting himself.

"It's early in the day, George," said Lee. "I'll be back this evening and have a proper drink with you."

"Early in the day? Did I just hear Travis Lee say that?"

"You did. Now quit looking like I've grown a second head and get me a ginger ale. If you're not too busy?"

The bartender snapped a towel in Lee's direction. I told him I'd have the same and he went to get our drinks. Hammed it up again when he placed them in front of us, getting paper doilies out to place them upon, serving the drinks with cherries and orange slices, like a kid's drink. Lee chuckled and waved him away.

"Sorry I can't let you have a drink, Mr. Lee. But Flanagan is right. You need to be stone sober for this."

"Ahh, it doesn't matter that much. It was nice of him to let me come. I'm beginning to feel like a condemned man. Will any wish be granted?"

"No. Although you can probably milk it some more."

"What do you suggest I ask for?"

"Is Ben E. King still alive?"

"Now? You tell me this *now*?"

Lee laughed and clinked his rocks glass against mine. The bartender was having a hard time not looking at us. Travis Lee sitting at a bar not having a drink? The man was curious. After glancing over at him a few times, I saw with surprise that it was more than curiosity. There was concern there as well. Most hard-core barflies, the bartenders don't care if they live or die. Just remember to tip.

"You're going to miss this place, aren't you, Mr. Lee?"

"Very much."

"Flanagan wasn't lying to you. If this goes the way it should, if you do your time well, you can be out in ten years, maybe less. Don't screw up in there, Mr. Lee. Don't let anyone provoke you. Ask for segregation if you need it and you'll be back here in ten years."

"Do you think the Starlight will still be here?"

I looked down at my drink and didn't answer. Fair question.

"It won't be," said Lee. "You know that. I honestly don't know how it has survived as long as it has. It already feels like a museum to me. Do you know this bar is a continuous piece of oak? There's not a joint or nail in it. White oak. We milled it for them in 1946. You'll never see a bar like this again. Who can afford it? Who wants it?"

"It's a lovely bar. It's worn down like the neck of a good acoustic guitar, a Martin or a Gibson. Something smooth and worn down and loved."

"God, that's good. What a pity I can't buy you a drink."

"Another time, maybe. I'll look you up in ten years."

"Would you really do that?"

I thought about it a minute. "I've never done it before, but yes, I'd do that. Would you like me to do that?"

"That's an interesting question. Let me think about it."

We had two more ginger ales, the bartender serving the next ones straight, no cherries and no commentary, but Lee never came back to the question. He asked me about Detroit and the Upper Peninsula. How many board feet my uncle had milled in the best year for his company, whether that was a mix of softwood and hardwood and what they had there in the way of hardwood, anyway. Rock elm? He'd heard they still had elm.

A few minutes before Flanagan was to arrive, a man came up to Lee and asked if the ball had been on the Harvard side of the field or the Navy side when he threw that pass. The man had a bet going with some men at his table. Lee looked at him a second before saying, "You know, I honestly can't recall. Sorry I can't be more help in settling your wager."

The man looked shocked. The bartender more so. Bartenders are not stupid people, not the good ones, anyway, and that bartender was probably wondering who I was, what was going on and when he would see Travis Lee again when he walked out of the Starlight in a few minutes.

"Not like you to turn down that story," I said after the man had left.

"Do you think we have time for it?"

"He just wanted the field position. It was the Harvard forty-eight, right?"

"You know, Mr. Barrett, or whatever your name might be, I think it's time I retired that story. Never cared for it as much as other people. Tell me—if I get ten, what do you think Pearl will get?"

"Hard to say, Mr. Lee. But like Flanagan said, she has a good defense. Her state of mind when she was up at that trailhead, that's going to be important to a jury. If she has a good lawyer—there's a lot she can work with."

"I don't know if Pearl has money for a good lawyer. I take it I will be unable to help her financially after we are done today?"

"I'd say you were right about that."

"Then she'll be trying to defend herself on a waitress's salary."

"She could get a good lawyer, or a firm, just on the facts of the case. It will be a high-profile case. A lot of good lawyers would jump at it. I wish Flanagan had been able to convince her to go that route. We wouldn't be sitting here today."

"That was never going to happen. Pearl has no faith in the criminal justice system. So how many years?"

I thought about returning one more time to the good-defense argument, then realized how fake that would sound to Lee. "If she's convicted, she won't be as lucky as you, Mr. Lee. Homicide gets you life in prison in a non-capital-punishment state like Maine. Parole eligibility is mandatory with a sentence like that. It's usually twenty-five years."

"Twenty-five years?"

"Yes."

"She'll be in her seventies."

"If that's how the math works."

Lee didn't speak for a minute. I sat there wondering if I could have found a way to make twenty-five years sound like something different from twenty-five years. Just then the phone in my pocket vibrated. I didn't bother looking at it.

"Flanagan's outside."

"Well, then, we must settle our tab. George, how much do I owe you?"

"Not a thing, Mr. Lee," said the bartender, walking over to them. "Four ginger ales? I think I can cover you for that."

"Well, I must give you some money. It's rather bad form, I think, to leave without giving you money, George. That's why you're here, isn't it?"

"One of the reasons, Mr. Lee. Yes, it certainly is."

"Well, then, money you must have. If I can't pay for these delightful ales, then I will settle my other tab with you."

"Your bar tab?"

"Yes."

"It's not the end of the month, Mr. Lee."

"I know that. But I want to give you some money, George, and my bar tab is all I have to fall back upon. How much do I owe you?"

The bartender didn't move. He looked to be in his early sixties, with a neatly trimmed gray mustache and slicked-back hair that probably still got slicked back with Brylcreem. He had a slight build and good posture for a bartender. Looked like some British army officer you'd see strutting around with a baton tucked under his arm. The man didn't move and didn't speak, and then with a gesture so deliberate and slow it looked like pantomime, he put his right hand atop Lee's.

"I won't take your money today, Mr. Lee. I'll take it at the end of the month, like we always do. I'll be here waiting for you. Don't you skip out on me, hear?"

Lee was speechless. Only time I ever saw it. He opened his mouth a few times and closed it immediately, and he never did find the words he wanted to say. Eventually he put his other hand atop the bartender's and gave a small nod. Then the men unclasped and Lee hurried outside. I followed, staring at the bartender the whole time.

The people who stay with you, who go on to share your dreams and memories, who live with you as surely as the people lying next to you in bed—no way of ever knowing who those people will be. Some will be the ones you expect. Many won't. I didn't even know his last name. The wisest man I ever met? The most clairvoyant? I've been living with that bartender a long time.

———————

AT THREE FORTY-FIVE p.m., Travis Lee drove his Mercedes into the parking lot of the Red Bird Diner, tilted the seat back and closed his eyes. We had a camera in the car and a live feed in the surveillance van. He turned on the radio. Flicked back and forth between stations. He listened to a Turtles song, and when it was finished, he went back to flipping channels. Stayed on an all-sports channel for a minute, then back to the oldies.

"Stand by Me." Lee laughed when he heard the song. Turned up the volume. He caught the song near the beginning, so he heard all three verses, got three chances to sing the chorus. By the way he was singing, you could tell he thought he was nailing it. There was probably a time when everyone thought that.

———————

FLANAGAN SAT IN the surveillance van, watching the video feed from the loop trail. They had put a camera in an oak, after Lee had shown him where the blanket would be spread, and they had it framed perfectly. Audio was good.

The unmarked police car that was following Lee from Birmingham to the Champlain Lookout was wired to pick up Lee's microphone on the dispatch radio. When he pulled into the parking lot, the feed would be switched to the surveillance van. The van was parked so it had good sight lines on the start of the trail. They were going to need only the one camera in the oak.

"Is Lee going to lay his jacket down beside her when it's showtime?" asked Linton.

"Yes."

"And he knows where she should be sitting so she's facing the camera?"

"I marked the spot for him."

"Where are they now?"

"He just picked her up at the diner."

"All right, this is going to be fun."

<hr>

JUST AS "STAND by Me" was ending, Pearl Lafontaine walked out the door of the Red Bird. She saw the Mercedes right away and came walking toward it, swinging her hips, sashaying a bit. She was doing that for him, trying to put a smile on his face, no doubt, although Lee sat in the SUV with his eyes closed. When he heard a clicking sound, he opened them and turned to her.

"Go for a ride, girl?"

"Just got in, didn't I?"

THE SWEET GOODBYE

THEY DROVE OUT of Birmingham and down the shoreline of the St. John River. Spring had come late but now it was early summer and the bad spring had been forgotten. The forest was filled with hardwood trees showing their early-summer leaves, a bright Kelly green, the dead brown leaves of winter blown away. The river had slowed from the spring runoff and sat quiet and cool, a blue line cutting through green hills. Green and blue—that's the way the world looked that afternoon.

Five miles south of Farrelton, he took the turnoff to Champlain Lookout and they started climbing a switchback road. They drove beside the Blackton River, a tributary of the St. John that came from headwaters hundreds of miles north, way past the Canadian border. During a dry summer in Birmingham, it was little more than a muddy creek come August, but that afternoon the Blackton was running down the bluff like an ornamental waterfall. He lowered the windows so they could hear the rushing water. She stuck her hand out and let it flutter in the wind.

"How have you been?" she asked.

"Been OK."

"You look good. How did it go with the cops?"

"Lots of questions about Tucker. Kept telling them I didn't know much. They interviewed you as well, right?"

"Yeah. They didn't hold me as long as they held you. How come so long for you?"

"Like I said, Tucker."

She nodded but didn't say anything. It was too late to be disappointed, she told herself. And people have to do what people have to do. That morning she realized it was thirty-four years since he had picked her up at the Red Bird and asked if she wanted to take a road trip to Boston. What if that grift had worked? What if they had checked into the Four Seasons with the money they had stolen from that nightclub, gotten hammered, lived on room service and come back to Birmingham two days later just like they'd planned?

She had begun to think you spend half your life wondering what's heading your way, the other half wondering what you missed.

"So just a lot of questions about Tucker?" she asked, her hand still out the window fluttering in the wind like a bird's wing.

"Yeah, just a lot of questions. Thought we'd have a picnic. What do you say?"

"Sounds lovely."

═══

SHE NEVER HEARD, in any AA meeting or rehab group session, the reason that Travis Lee drank. Never heard anything that had the ring of truth to it. Closest she ever came was a magazine article. And it wasn't about addiction. It was about the Beatles. Not even the Beatles. Pattie Boyd.

People said Pearl looked like the ex-wife of George Harrison, during Boyd's red-hair phase, but that wasn't why she remembered the article. It was Boyd's description of the Beatles and how each regarded fame.

Boyd said John thought he deserved fame; Paul thought he'd earned it; Ringo was glad to have it; and George—he never understood it. Never understood why he had been chosen to become one of the most famous people on the planet.

The Lees were like that—Tucker thought he deserved the family fortune; the old man thought he'd earned it; Amanda was just glad to have it; and Travis—he never understood it. Why he had been chosen to be rich when most everyone else in Birmingham had been chosen to be poor.

George Harrison eased his guilty and questing mind with Hare Krishna chants and trips to India. Travis eased his with McCallum's and trips to the Starlight. Only real difference she ever saw.

═══

HE PARKED NEXT to a white van with the name of a plumbing company on the side panel, one she had never heard of before, with an Old Town address and phone number. There were only two other cars in the lot. At one of the picnic tables, a young couple sat holding hands. At the other, a family was having a picnic, two small boys running around a soccer ball, a father barbecuing, a mother sitting in a foldout canvas chair, reading a magazine.

He took the groceries and a blanket from the back of the Mercedes and they started walking. The sun was casting filigreed patterns on the ground. In a few weeks, the hardwood leaves would be full grown, and the ground would lie in shadows. They walked hand in hand through the dappled light. "Let's stop a minute," he said.

He put down his bag and started picking wildflowers. She looked at him and laughed. Then she looked around and saw that there were columbines and lilies, asters and early-season violets everywhere. It seemed as though they were standing in a greenhouse nursery with diffused sunlight coming through a tautly stretched panel of plastic. He slipped a columbine behind her ear and gave her a kiss.

She put down her bag and began picking flowers beside him. They worked for several minutes, comparing the bouquets they were assembling, working their way toward a large boulder around which wildflowers were growing in profusion. He took off his jacket and laid it beside the boulder.

Wiped his brow. She looked at him sadly when he did that. The high school quarterback now winded by picking wildflowers. Alcohol took its toll after a while. No sane person could deny it.

They worked their way around the boulder, and when they had collected enough flowers for decent-sized bouquets, they bowed and presented them to each other. After that, they picked up their bags and continued walking.

=====

SHE HAD STOPPED thinking about him. Stopped getting pricks of sadness when she saw his car on the streets of Birmingham, seven years since Boston and she was over it, had started dating a building contractor who was already talking about the house he would build when they got married. Seven years and then one night she got off shift and there he was.

When he saw her, he must have stepped out of his car because he was standing beside it, stumbling and crying when she approached. When he tried to hug her, she pushed him away, but she pushed so hard he fell and so she had to help him back up, which wasn't easy, he was so drunk. Then she had trouble getting him into his car. He was talking the whole time, what sounded like gibberish at first, but eventually she made it out.

He was asking her a question. Wanted to know if she'd ever wanted to go back in time and make a different decision, go in a different direction, wanted to do that so badly it became just about the only thing she ever thought about night or day. Had she ever felt that way?

Life is full of mysteries, but what are you supposed to do when a man describes to you the only way you've felt since you were sixteen? Just what exactly are you supposed to do?

She fell in love.

=====

HE SPREAD THE blanket on a granite rock covered in fern moss. It was a large, flat rock that ran to the edge of the escarpment, ringed by spruce and maples and a giant white oak that was so tall, boats on the St. John

River could see it from five miles away. The tree was often used as a naviga-
tion marker in the autumn.

She put down her bag and walked to the edge of the escarpment. The
forest beneath her spread as far as she could see, green hills that resembled
a furled blanket thrown upon the ground. In the mid-seventies, two teenage
boys high on acid jumped off this cliff, thinking they could fly or thinking
they could lie down on the green bed beneath them. Who knew exactly what
they had been thinking?

Although they were expecting the opposite of what they got, that much
seemed certain. When she turned away, she saw that he had started to
empty the grocery bags, spread the food on the blanket. "You remember the
first time we ever came here, hon?"

"Sure do. I think we did it three times right over there." And he pointed
at the white oak.

"It was two. And I thought we were going to roll off the cliff the second
time. Remember that?"

"We laughed the whole way back to Birmingham, imagining how the
obituaries would have read. Sure, I remember. When was that? Ten
years ago?"

"More like fifteen. Gosh, think of that. I've always loved this place. One
of the best views of the St. John anywhere in the city. With the sun sinking,
the city can look real pretty over there."

She stared at the skyline of Birmingham on the other side of the river:
the aqua green water tower, the turrets of the Alexander Hotel, the roofline
of the Davidson-Struthers Footwear factory. A sinking sun did seem to
soften it all. Sweeten it somehow.

He made sandwiches with the pumpernickel bread and sliced ham, the
Polish pickles and Havarti cheese. Laid out the fruit tarts for after the meal.
They ate their sandwiches without talking, and when they finished, he
poured coffee from his thermos into a plastic cup. She drank ginger ale from
a can.

They drank their coffee and pop, looking out over the Kelly green world *beneath them. Then he put away his cup and lay down, resting his head upon her lap. He lay there a minute before saying:* "Those cops aren't going away."

"I know, hon. That banker was helping them, wasn't he?"

"I'm not sure. Maybe. I've been running it through my mind, and I'm not sure where it went wrong. What do you think?"

"Not sure either, hon. You're probably wasting good time asking yourself a question like that."

"You're right. Stuff we know. That's what we need right now. Did you know the only good dreams I've had since I was twenty-two have had you in them?"

"Is that true?"

"I think so. The dreams that didn't have me falling or being chased, the good ones with color and horizons in them, you were in those dreams."

"That's sweet," *she said, and she kept staring at the skyline of Birming-ham. That's all it was ever going to be, she thought. Something like that. Maybe something less.*

The wind had picked up and she shivered, wrapped her arms tighter around him. Although it had been a pleasant early summer, the air had cooled and it would not surprise her to see snow that night. It had snowed every month of the year in Birmingham in one year or another. It seemed like the kind of day they could have snow late at night.

"The toughest days are always ahead," *he said sleepily.* "Do you remember saying that to me?"

"Said it more than once."

"Yeah, you did. It always reminded me of a story. The Lady with the Dog. Could have been about us. Ever read it?"

"No."

"It's Chekhov. Story ends with a guy saying the difficult part was just beginning. Toughest days ahead. That's the same thing, right?"

"I suppose. Why'd the story make you think of us?"

"It's about a couple. Toughest days ahead. It's Chekhov."

"It's Bustard County too, hon. Lot of people say that."

He laughed. "I read once that Chekhov was asked, flat out asked, if he believed the most difficult days were always ahead. Good question. Know what he said?"

"Travis Lee, I'm betting you know that I don't."

"He said, 'Yes, the toughest days are always ahead. Until they aren't.'"

Neither of them said anything for a long time. The sun started to slide behind the Davidson-Struthers Footwear factory. The shadows lengthened and reached out to them from across the river. "That's a funny answer," she finally said.

"Yeah, it was all a little funny. Here's another one. Did you know I have only one regret in life? Most people would never believe that, but it's true."

She ran her fingers through his hair. She wished—with a desire that seemed a physical thing right then, that pushed down upon her until it hurt—that she could say, "Just got in, didn't I?" one more time.

Instead she looked at him and said, "Are you going to tell me what it is, hon?"

He smiled and closed his eyes. "I never should have murdered Tucker and Beau. Never should have gone up to the Northwoods trailhead and done that."

Right after he said that she heard a popping sound, a hollow sort of sound that reminded her later of a distant clap of thunder; or an exhale of breath after someone had been holding it a very long time.

39

THE SILENCE THAT followed was the strangest I've ever heard. Five men in a surveillance van wanting to say something, wanting to say something about as desperately as a man could ever want to say something, but no one speaking because no one wanted to miss the next sound. An anticipation that became material after a few seconds, that pushed down upon us like a weight. Linton ended it at just under ninety seconds.

"What the *fuck* did he just say?"

No one answered. I kept staring at the video screen that showed Lee lying on the blanket, his head resting on Lafontaine's lap, her arms cradled around him. He hadn't moved since he'd spoken last.

"Have we lost the transmission?" screamed Linton. "We're not hearing anything. Has he done something to that fuckin' recorder?"

"Shut up," said Flanagan, not bothering to look at him. He came to stand beside me. "You'd better go down there and take a look, pal."

SHE SAW ME as soon as I rounded the bend in the trail. Then she gasped and threw her arms tighter around Lee. I could tell—by the way she was holding him, by the way Lee's body was bent—what had happened. I waved at the camera in the white oak, letting Flanagan and Linton know they could come down.

"I'm going to need to have a look at Mr. Lee," I said when I reached the edge of the blanket. "Can you put him down for me, Ms. Lafontaine?"

"You're a bastard."

"I need to look at Mr. Lee."

"You can look at him fine where he is. Walk on over. I don't bite."

I walked on over. Lee's eyes had fallen back into his head, so I didn't bother with CPR. I placed two fingers atop the carotid artery and watched a minute pass on my watch. I sat close to Lafontaine like you would on a crowded bus. She smelled of lilac and baby powder.

When I was done, I unzipped his coat. The handgun was right there, a snub-nosed .22. I pulled the sleeve of my shirt over my hand, pulled the gun out, stood and took a step back. When Flanagan and Linton arrived, I showed them the gun.

"Jesus fucking Christ. It's the size of a toy," Flanagan said.

"Yeah. He had it pushed right up against his heart."

"Serial numbers are filed down?"

"Yeah."

Linton had been listening to the conversation and he started screaming, "Are you serious? Did Lee just fuckin' off himself?"

"Paul," said Flanagan, but Linton kept yelling.

"And Delta fuckin' Dawn was here the whole fucking time? Did that fuckin' bitch—"

"Enough!"

Flanagan's shout sounded like a blast from a skeet gun. "Enough!" he roared again. "I can't take any more of you. Not another fuckin' minute. Go away, Paul. Go sit in a fuckin' corner somewhere. Go buy a stupid hat and do whatever it is that stupid people do. Just get the fuck away from me!"

Linton stared at Flanagan in such shock and hurt, I almost felt sorry for him. His mouth opened and shut a few times, but no sound came out. He turned to leave, and when I couldn't see him anymore, I stopped feeling that way.

Flanagan waited a good minute after Linton had left before speaking to Lafontaine. "This is a sad way to meet again," he said.

"A sad and mournful day."

"Yes, it is." And then he hesitated before saying, "Where's that from?"

"Bunch of songs. Travis sang 'Will the Circle Be Unbroken' that way. Old country song."

"Old country song. Course it is. Ms. Lafontaine, the paramedics will be here soon. They'll need to examine Mr. Lee. You'll need to put him down on the blanket when they get here. Is that going to be a problem?"

"No, sir," she said. A second later she realized what she had been offered and then she started nodding her head so fiercely, her hair was flying. "No, sir, there won't be a problem. Not at all."

It took nearly ten minutes for them to get there. It wasn't as awkward as you might have thought. No one tried to speak. No one looked up at the sky and pretended Lee wasn't there. No one faked it.

I looked over a couple times and thought Lee looked peaceful, knowing it makes no sense saying a dead man looks any way at all, but that's what I thought and I've never thought any different. Travis Lee was at peace with how things ended for him.

Flanagan kept staring out at the St. John River and I could take a guess at what he was thinking. This was the case that was going to retire him. After a formal hearing. Some sort of reprimand or censure added to his file. In two years, Paul Linton might end up exactly where he was hoping to be when this investigation started—working out of the Boston field office with clear sight lines to Flanagan's former office. Linton was about to get the wonderful career gift of screwing up at the exact same time as another man imploded and made a bigger boom.

I wondered if Linton was smart enough to see it. Flanagan would be leaving Birmingham with three unsolved murders and two dead informants. You don't recover from something like that. Maybe it's right that you don't. Flanagan must have lost a step or two somewhere along the line. He probably didn't think he had, but maybe losing a step or two is the sort of thing that needs to be pointed out to a person.

A Birmingham patrol car arrived at the same time as the ambulance and Lafontaine did as she'd promised. She laid Lee down on the blanket, then backed up a few feet and watched the paramedics work on him. There was a purple foam around his mouth now and his eyes had rolled back farther in his head. It wasn't more than five minutes before the paramedics were rolling him onto a gurney.

Five minutes more and they were making a three-point turn to get back to the parking lot. I watched the ambulance until I lost sight of it on the switchback road. Flanagan, who had also been watching the ambulance drive away, turned when we lost sight of the vehicle and said, "We'll need to hold you for a few hours, Ms. Lafontaine, to confirm it was Mr. Lee's fingerprints on that gun. The patrol officer will take you to the station."

"All right."

"That's what we'll find, right? His fingerprints?"

"Yes."

"It won't take long, then."

He walked away after saying that but stopped after taking just a few steps. He stood there awhile, his back turned to us, considering something or trying to remember something it looked like. Eventually he turned and said, "I'm sorry for your loss, Ms. Lafontaine. I know how much Mr. Lee meant to you."

When I heard that, I knew I would never be seeing Jim Flanagan again.

40

PEARL LAFONTAINE WAS released later that night. My next assignment came three weeks later and I spent the time in Birmingham, after checking out of the Three Pines and moving into the Alexander. I thought it was time for a better room.

My time between cases, it's always different: how long it is, what I do with it. I've headed south. Gone back to Detroit to see family. Although that happened last year for the first time and I'm not sure it will happen again anytime soon. I have problems back in Detroit. Another reason I like to move around.

When I checked into the Alexander, I told myself you don't always get to go trout fishing in country as beautiful as Northern Maine. But even then I knew I was fooling myself. I didn't do any fishing in those three weeks, didn't do much more than sit in my hotel room and go for long walks through Birmingham.

One night I walked all the way downtown to the Starlight and sat on a barstool drinking Pabst beer, not talking to anyone. It was Motown

Night and I knew every song. Before leaving, I ordered a McCallum's neat and left it sitting on the bar.

When I wasn't walking around, I was remembering what had happened at Champlain Lookout. I kept asking myself how I could have missed the gun. Every once in a while, I asked myself if I was still missing something. Had she known he was going to do that? If she had, when had she known?

I tried to remember how long they'd been out of sight behind that boulder when they were picking flowers. Long enough for Linton to ask, "What the fuck is he doing?" and a few seconds more before they reappeared. Thirty seconds? That seemed too long. When you're living every second, as we were in that surveillance van, thirty seconds is a long time. Twenty maybe?

Enough time to have told her what he was doing. Enough time for her to get ready and play along. Maybe not for most people, but for those two, quick on their feet the way they were, creative the way they were, it was enough time.

What would you do for love? That was the question I was left with after all that walking and wondering.

And then my next assignment arrived. I was to report to the FBI office in Seattle, Washington, in three days. I looked at the mug shots I had been sent, suspects in a bank heist that went way south, leaving two security guards dead on the pavement. I had never been to Seattle.

I reread the e-mail, shut down the computer and got a beer from the minibar. I sat on the bed, looking out my hotel window at the roofline of the Davidson-Struthers Footwear factory. I finished the beer and had another, and then I left the hotel and began walking to the Red Bird Diner.

41

I SAW HER as soon as I entered the diner. She was holding a pot of coffee, counting out change, doing two things at once. Most waitresses would have put the coffeepot down, but she didn't need to do that. She was talking to two men, an animated conversation that had them laughing. She would have been one of the older waitresses in the Red Bird, but she was still attractive. More than that. She had the height and stature of a model, ringlets of red hair falling over the collar of her yellow uniform. There were no empty tables in her section.

I was seated two sections over and had already ordered my dinner before she noticed me. A good waitress keeps eyes on her section, doesn't notice the other ones so much. When she saw me, her head gave a little snap. You wouldn't have noticed it unless you were looking for it, and even then it could have been mistaken for tossing her hair back. But I saw it. She stared at me a second, then turned and went to the kitchen.

I ate my club sandwich and made no effort to make eye contact with her. I read the *Birmingham Sun*, a weekly newspaper you could pick up at the cash register. Twelve pages. Sad. I was starting to read the newspaper a third time when I heard, "Is there a reason why you're here?"

She was standing beside my table with three dirty plates stacked in the crook of her arm.

"I was hoping we could talk."

"Why would I want to do something like that?"

"Because I'm hoping you can help settle some things that have been on my mind. Before I leave Birmingham. I'm leaving tomorrow."

She looked at me and it was hard to tell if she was annoyed. A dispassionate look that seemed more passionate than that. "Settle some things on your mind. That's a strange thing to say."

"That's all I'm doing. There's no investigation anymore. I'm sure you know that. I just want to talk."

"Sounds like you're describing a big waste of time, this little chat of yours."

"Wouldn't be that way for me."

"Why not?"

"Because I liked Travis Lee. Before leaving Birmingham, I would like to know what happened to him."

———

WE AGREED TO meet when her shift finished at a coffee shop on Water Street. The shop was crowded, and I ordered our coffees to go. We walked until we reached a boardwalk running beside the St. John River and then we walked down that. It was well past time for the city to have done post-winter repairs, yet many planks were missing, and we had to walk carefully. It looked like a recent thing, the city not doing the repairs.

We found a bench near Pig's Island and sat down. Some sailboats were circling the island. The river was slow there, and Pig's Island was a popular place for children to learn how to sail. It looked like a class of some sort.

"So what is it you want to know, Mr. Barrett? I'm guessing that's not your real name, is it?"

"No."

"What is it?"

"Danny Barrett. That's the name I have right now. That makes it real enough, don't you think?"

"Not sure that it does. I'm a Lafontaine. Call me anything else you want, I'm still going to be a Lafontaine from Bustard County."

"That matters around here, doesn't it?"

"It surely does." She took a sip of her coffee and turned to look at me. "I find it funny, you saying you liked Travis. You're an undercover cop. You betrayed him."

"No, I didn't. Travis Lee was in trouble long before I got to Birmingham. I had drinks with him. Saved him from getting mugged once. Nothing he told me was ever going to be used against him in a courtroom. I did nothing more than spend a few nights with him at the Starlight, and yes, I liked him."

"What did you like about him?"

"His honor. I thought he was an honorable man."

A sad look came to her eyes when I said that. She turned away. "That's a strange answer. Not many people saw him that way."

"I did. In this day and age, finding an honorable man, a kind man, it's like finding a precious gift."

She turned back to face me, the first signs of curiosity on her face. "You have a funny way of speaking, Mr. Barrett. A precious gift? Beau used to say Travis was one of my baubles, a bright shiny thing I went out and collected one day. Did you know I like shiny things?"

"No."

"Oh, I get teased about it all the time. People give me birthday cards and they're always covered in glitter. I got a cell phone case so bright, you can use it as a side lamp." She ran a hand through her hair. The other hand held the take-out coffee cup. "My precious gift. That might have been a good way to describe Travis. Did you know I had sex with him long before he ever slept with his wife? That's how long we were together. On our second date, we robbed a nightclub."

She was looking right at me when she said it, and I must have given her the look she wanted because she laughed.

"Oh, I was bold back then, Mr. Barrett. We both were. There was a time when Travis and I thought people would be writing folk songs about us forever."

"You never wanted to marry him?"

"No."

"Why?"

"Never would have worked. And it never mattered that much. I suspect you knew Travis better than most people, even though you didn't know him that long. Do you think it would have mattered to him?"

"I suspect not."

"You suspect right. I'll never meet another man like Travis Lee. Every day I have that thought, and every day when I have it, it's like he dies all over again."

I could see her eyes were starting to mist. It was turning from late afternoon to early evening and shadows were falling across the river, the boats starting to head to the marina on the far shore. Kid training boats are small, and there were a fair number of them heading to the marina.

"Did you know what he was going to do?" I asked.

"What do you think?"

"I think you did. I just can't decide when you knew it."

"Why does that matter?"

"I'm wondering why you didn't try to stop him."

I reached into my pocket for a cigarette. I had started smoking again. Ten days. I had vowed not to take a pack with me to Taos.

"Do you think Travis wanted it to end a different way?" she asked.

"No. I think he was at peace with how it ended. I just need to know *how* it happened. Seems like the sort of thing I should know. Maybe the sort of thing he'd *like* me to know. To settle my mind."

"There you go again. That is *so* like something Trav would have said. You think about stuff all the time, don't you?"

"I do. Can't stop it really."

"Trav was the same way. Maybe the problem you're having is that you think too much and too much like a cop. How did Travis die? Who knew about it? When did they know? Those are cop questions. But people die all the time and you never get much of an explanation for it. Same way a town can die for reasons that never seem clear to you."

She stared out at the river and finished her coffee.

"You seem like a kind man, Mr. Barrett. I wish you luck."

She stood and walked away. I stayed on the bench a few more minutes, looking at the sailboats. All the boats were clustered around the break wall of the marina now. A bright splash of color bobbing out on the St. John River.

<hr />

I PHONED LINTON the next morning before leaving Birmingham. It was considered good form to do that, although I had no need and little interest in talking to him. He was in a good mood, so I knew right away that Jim Flanagan was in trouble.

"It's an almost unprecedented rat fuck," he said happily. "The lawyers tell me a dying man's confession is the gold standard for courtroom testimony. Only DNA evidence is better. And in this case, the confession is on a police *wiretap* and Flanagan *arrested* him two days earlier. One lawyer told me Lee's confession might be *better* than DNA. Can you fuckin' believe that?"

I told him it was hard to believe and wished him well in Boston, where he said he was being transferred later that month. I flew out of Birmingham under an early-summer sky that was neither blue nor gray, an indifferent sky you couldn't have any sort of opinion about, no promise to it, no threat to it. I was in the air almost an hour before I put it all together.

Travis Lee had made Pearl Lafontaine bulletproof. Last thing he ever did.

THE SWEET GOODBYE

THAT SUMMER WAS a good one in Birmingham. The days were warm but rarely humid, the sky normally light blue with only high cumulus clouds. It rained early in the morning, or late at night, when thunder rolled in off the Appalachians and sheet lightning appeared in the sky, but never for long and just enough rain to keep the forests a lush Erin green through to August.

Pearl Lafontaine didn't know how she would cope with what she had done, for how could you ever know about such a thing? But as the summer wore on, she began to believe she would be all right. Beau had been the hardest, but she knew that when she drove up to the Northwoods trailhead. Family. A person she owed. She had problems with Beau.

The banker never bothered her. When Beau phoned her, told her what the banker was doing, she saw the logic in helping him. The banker had earned his fate.

Tucker was almost easy. Tucker wanted to make a deal and that was still unbelievable to her. Tucker Lee never once knew where he was standing, not one day in his whole life. Always got it wrong. Like the way Amanda

Lee strung him on for years, Tucker thinking he actually had a shot, blinders on that boy thicker than what you'd put on your dumbest plow horse.

If Tucker had pleaded, cried, acted remorseful in some way, it would have been harder for her. She wouldn't have believed him, and it wouldn't have changed anything, but she would have felt different about what she'd needed to do. Felt sad and determined about it, the way people sometimes feel when they have to do something cruel and they've convinced themselves the best way to do that is to be quick about it. Lay someone off. End a marriage. Tell someone the test results weren't what we had hoped.

But Tucker had tried to make a deal with her, for money, and when she shot him, she wasn't sad, just determined. She pulled the trigger and he flew back thirty feet, maybe more, so far back he landed past the arc of Beau's headlights, only his feet showing by the time he stopped rolling, the rest of him left in darkness.

The shotgun blast had two echoes and it was ten seconds before silence came back. And it was complete silence for a little while. No animal sounds. No wind. Then came the sound of water coursing, a small creek she had missed somewhere. A few seconds later, she realized it wasn't a creek but Tucker's body lying on an incline, blood pumping from his chest and rolling downhill.

Beau turned his head when the shotgun went off, but kept his hands in the air, the way she had told him. He looked at Tucker Lee, at the blood pooling around his feet, the rest of him lost in the darkness beyond the Halcyon lights of his Cadillac, and he said:

"Well played, ma fille. A better trap, I do not know if I've ever seen one."

"Not going to thank you, Beau."

"Bien, no. What a pig he was, eh? What he offered you to spare his life? A pig would have more shame. Was there anything he could have said?"

"No."

"Ahh, how did he live so long? Mysteries surround us, eh, ma fille? Is it all right if I have a cigarette?"

She nodded. "I wish it hadn't come to this, Beau. I tried to find another way. You know I did."

"Fair warning. That how you see it?"

"I do."

"Your cousin?"

"Your uncle? Family only goes so far, Beau."

"Yes, of course. I'm still surprised. Travis Lee—that man means this much to you?"

"I'd say it was pretty obvious he does. Wouldn't you?"

He didn't say anything to that. Lit his cigarette and took a deep drag. Then he stood there smoking, as casual as you please, like there wasn't a dead man lying next to him, like there wasn't a shotgun pointed at his chest. He took deep hauls from his cigarette. Blew a few smoke circles. The longer she waited, the more convinced she became that Beau had only one thing left to say but wanted to finish his cigarette before saying it.

He finally threw the cigarette on the ground and stepped on it with the heel of his Tony Lama boots. When he looked up, he said, *"It really is love, ain't it, girl?"*

She took it the way Beau intended it, no doubt in her mind about that. Her cousin had just told her what no one else ever had and never would again: the love she had for Travis Lee was undeniable. Beau had given his blessing. Her own family.

"It really is," she answered. Last thing she ever said to her cousin.

———

THE GOOD SUMMER in Birmingham was followed by a good autumn. The leaves turned color early and stayed on the trees a long time, no night being cold enough to kill them, no wind strong enough to rip them from their branches. For most of that season, the forest was a quilt of bright oranges and reds, royal purples and butter yellows. Only very late in the season did the cold wind come, and after that, there were only brown and yellow leaves.

The bankruptcy sale for Lee Forestry was held at the end of October. The company was sold to a Swedish pension fund that kept every mill open and never canceled a shift. Within a few weeks of the sale, people in Birmingham were calling it the Christmas Miracle.

Travis Lee was buried in St. Leonard's Cemetery on the north shore of the St. John River. Amanda was to have been buried there as well, but when her body was found the following spring, her father objected and so she was buried in a cemetery in Old Town.

Amanda not being there made it easier for Pearl, but she would have come, anyway. Travis's grave was on the north end of the Lee family plot and it was private, with a large beech tree and a fine view overlooking the St. John River. She brought flowers every week. Changed out the old flowers. Would sit down and stare at the city across the river.

If a building crane appeared on the skyline of Birmingham, she would see it from where she sat. If traffic was heavy on Highway 7, she would notice. If they ever got around to tearing down the Davidson-Struthers Footwear factory, she could have watched.

"We'll just sit here and see what happens to that old city," she'd say some days. "Tree with roots, hon. You know me. I ain't going nowhere."

She came for many years until dying of a heart attack in her kitchen one winter morning. Pearl Lafontaine would have turned fifty-nine the following week.